2nd Anthology of Horror

Trees and other Dystopias

2nd Anthology of Horror

Trees and other Dystopias

Fruitjack

Published by Xinoeph

ISBN: 978-0-9960419-2-8

Published by Xinoeph
xinoeph@hotmail.com

Table of Contents

Preface

By the summer of 2012, after a year' s worth of post-doc'ing at Colorado's NREL, I realized my days writing fanfic were over. I didn't mean to create an anthology of horror, though, that was an accident. Seriously.... OK, you got me! Aye, all along, wasn't it my aim to recreate – in spirit if not in flesh & blood – the joy I felt as a kid when I'd get my hands on the latest booklets The Watermill Press sold to us as fairs? With the added mature / adult bent, of course. But I enjoyed the experience that produced my 1st. And I plotted to write my 2nd 'soon'.

Well if that wasn't five years ago.

☹

Eerily, my delay wasn't due to writer's block. Quite the contrary – I produced drafts of twenty stories – drafts that I whittled into the 9 that 'made the cut'. Wilakers! The 'leftovers' are enough to fill my 3rd. Eventually. (I don't make promises to humans; only vaguely worded threats & such.)

The culprit of my trouble? RL! My progress was up-ended by sequences of events beyond my control. Briefly, I survived: injuries, moves, struggles to find a job, moves, struggles to keep that job, and, ultimately, promotion into my current & cushy academic position. Oh, there were breakups and reunions as well as other, intimate epiphanies. Enough of that! The grit stays out of the spotlight. I require anonymity to function amidst society.

Billed as horror, the tales that comprise this anthology cover a broad range of subjects from humor to sci-fi / fantasy. Settings are unified by geography every so often. Themes are revisited and contrasted. You'll find Easter Eggs in the forms of call-backs or shout-outs to my muses and even to my 1st anthology of horror (relax; you don't need to read it). The NAZIs resume their role of lurking, creeping malevolence. Wendigos / Skinwalkers may or may not make cameos. As do ghosts, aliens, cults, and evil of 'everyday' pedigree.

Equally as varied are my inspirations! Mad props go to Poe, Lovecraft, Blackwood, and Alvin Schwartz – short story writers whose work I devour. I extend credit, too, to those whose names are not known. I refer to folklorists and their immortal, blood-soaked yarns, passed from campfire to campfire, that kept me awake so many nights.

The collection opens with "Trees", a retelling of a story I heard as a Boy Scout. Over the years I revisited and revised it, changing the characters and the settings, altering everything but the conceit, the trope at its heart. It's about kids / teens hiking through a wilderness. But they upset the forces that control the land. And the land fights back.

We switch from South to North American wildernesses with "Dog Walks Ahead". It, too, is a retelling of folklore – that classic tale of the dog leading the hiker into something awful. The twist is the contrast of the ghastly dog and the very real and very ordinary evil of man.

Isn't it just too much? So it's the job of "Follow The Traffic" to let us breathe. It's a dark comedy of errors followed by the longest and craziest trip through the guts of New Jersey that you'll likely ever read. It may be the only such travelogue you'll ever read. So take it for what it is.

And then we reach that point, that point from where we cannot return. Resist? Fools! Gasp as we sink into the absurdity of "Blue Beelzebub", a tale that doesn't give a hoot what y'all think of it. The narrative takes the shape of a magazine article vs. a detective story. The objective is to unravel the mystery of a game created by cultists that contains the unspeakable and the unnamable. What is that video game about? Why would anybody make it? Why would anybody play it? **Although not a single of act of violence is depicted, it is implied as it toys with the idea of snuff so it may be triggery – beware!**

Look, every anthology I've ever read gets saddled by a weepy romantic epic – tragic, doomed, whatever. "Please Come Back" is haunted not by ghosts or by cults but by prejudice. It's an intimate portrait of loss, and gain, and acceptance – whose backdrop is the apocalyptic West. Just imagine if the last two years became the next twenty years - or longer. As civilization retreats, and the world itself regresses & decays, all of the progress that we attained simply vanishes.

"The Jeffreys" came to me as a dream. Sort of. Yeah the dream gave me the plot but not the story. I struggled to understand how to tell its tale. The theme is that technological advancement is not identical to sociological advancement. The execution is that of a story-within-a-story. The frame let me wax poetic about the Colorado countryside; it follows a geologist as they hike into a ghost town where they spend the night at the saloon. There they find a journal with a secret to say about that ghost town – if only it weren't missing every other word!

"Ogden's Domain" may be the most oblique certainly the most esoteric of the tales. It wasn't always so cryptic. It's juvenilia that I wrote between my junior and senior years at high school then expanded for this collection. Originally, the kids seek the hideout of the monster responsible for their town's decline. The monster is / was a crude sort of shape-shifter who steals faces. I didn't know squat about wendigos or skinwalkers when I penned it way back when. For the upgrade I opted to make as much of it ambiguous. Even the monster may not necessarily be a monster. Y'all need to unread what you read.

"The Girl in The Window" is also about an entity that fools & lures people into madness. Except that it's 100% malevolent, 0% benevolent. No ambiguity! It's also a love-letter to my favorite ghost-hunting show. Cthutlu forgive me for I sin! I live vicariously through the antics of the Ghost Adventures crew. Let me add that it's equally inspired by Ancient Aliens. Yeah, the cult is at it again.... Damn those guys are creeps! **Trigger – again – for suicide.**

The collection closes with "Exiles". We're so obsessed by terrestrial and / or man-made cataclysms that we forget the universe is vast and violent, easily capable of swatting us out of existence. After the Sun is struck by a giant planet-like object, its composition changes and its age accelerates. Humanity has only a thousand or so years to get off of the Earth before it's burnt to ash. Naturally, it's the rich & powerful countries that will be rocketed to safety. Won't be room enough for everyone, if you know what I mean.

- FJ

Trees

Cousins, Tom and Jack, shared a raft that (always) lagged. Ahead: brothers, Mark and Luke, competed to match each other's pace. Beyond: the guide, Gabriel, paddled with wide, deep strokes while the runt, Zachary, 'navigated'. All were into their 5ifth day at **the Chaco**.

"Can we do it?" Tom gasped for a lung's worth of air. He brought the oar onto his lap, his fingers curling, his hands shaking. "No. No.... No." With his sleeves he wiped the sweat by his eyes – the left eye, then, the right eye. "What, do you think **the Chaco** was a mistake?"

"If it is? Too late to retreat." Jack did not want to speak of it. It was easier to paddle than to revisit **the argument**. They wanted that journey, despite alarms raised by the outpost, despite costs incurred by the mission. It was a chance to explore Paraguay and its mythical, exotic geography. Candidly, they ought to have factored their strengths and their weaknesses **as a unit**.

The domain of **the Chaco** was unlike any they experienced. Its air's texture thickened as it oozed out of the wild. Its water's mood swung by turns as either stretches of calm or flashes of storm. Sunlight, purified by trees, attained a palette to color that world as if it were a dream, more imagined, less real. Then, adding anxiety to uncertainty, they encountered **silence** – past the interplay of leaves, past the thatchwork of branches, where a universe of life should have echoed there lamented a void.

As that river approached a sink, it spread then it thinned, exploding into turbulence. The water roared everywhere. It whipped. It lashed. It threatened their doom.

They withdrew onto the coast.

Gabriel leapt from the raft, to the stream.

Zachary stood – and suppressed a fear that, if he slipped, he would be thrust into the sink. As a unit their ambition overwhelmed their experience, yet, watching the guide, he wanted to be worthy more than he wanted to be afraid. He stood less and less hesitantly; at last, **defiantly**, he jumped off the vessel.

They caught up and the two, man and boy alike, towed their craft ashore.

Mark and Luke came later to repeat the procedure the guide taught them at the trailhead. It was the coast not the river that endangered them if the procedure was not adhered to. They were careful. One minded the hazard at the front. One dragged the raft at the back. They knew to organize their labor efficiently. Only the perceptive might have discerned a pattern of division that emerged.

Everyone waited for Tom and Jack.

"Aye, go to," Gabriel's English resonated with a unique mixture of accents. Speech was fragmented, declarative. **"Andale!"**

"You heard the boss," Zachary added; the boy often served as the man's (impromptu) translator **and enforcer**.

Tom attempted a jump but completed a tumble. Jack vaulted then struggled against the flow. They arrived drenched from head to toe. Their vessel was dry by comparison.

"How do we reach **Bahia Negra** like this?" the guide whispered through a strain of **Ache**. He wished to advance as he did not approve of wandering those (seasonal) rivers of **the Chaco**. Nevertheless, he felt **obligated** to come. Perhaps, if his skill offset their ignorance, it ought to mitigate the offense of the intrusion.

Objections had been raised but the managers overruled the workers. Their outpost lived and died by tourism not by superstition. The journey was not **forbidden**. Simply – the journey was not **practical**. As the majority of adventurers preferred **the Paraguay** to **the Chaco**, few guides and explorers were adept to the trip's **peculiarities**.

Who may have known its cause? Stories were told, from time, to time. Partially, it was due to war. Mostly, it was due to myth. Time and (un)familiarity obliterated distinctions between fact and fiction. For such or such a reason people avoided it. For aeons upon aeons it was 'taboo' to enter. 'Til man became a stranger.

That. so far, was a kernel of truth as the trip would be dangerous entirely due to isolation.

Gabriel explained (via Zachary) that their next dip into a river would be after an hour's walk. Jack, Mark, and Gabriel folded then stuffed their rafts into their packs. Tom, Luke, and Zachary toted their supplies.

"Let's go," Mark said to Luke as the unit assembled by the coast.

Portage was required where streams became innavigable. Since they embarked at the trailhead, obstacles were plentiful. Hazards, chiseled by erosion, conspired to hinder their progress and to astound their imagination.

It was absurd to believe nations battled throughout that geography. The evidence could not be denied, however, as they unearthed relics of conflicts at odd intervals. The smallest were bullets. The largest were tanks. Either Mark or Luke thought they spotted a jet; Gabriel would not let them approach it. All of it lay as if it were asleep, overgrown by the advance of Nature – especially – by the slaughter of trees.

Trees just appeared to burst out of the wreckage as if they had been the weapon that killed the enemy.

The party of five missionaries and one native traversed a stretch of dirt encompassed by creeks. The creeks had to be avoided as they were intermittent – some wet, some dry. They were part of **the Chaco's** drainage – a network through which the rainy season's harvest collected from the mountains and funneled to the oceans. The creeks formed the periphery of the network where they conveyed debris chewed off the Andes.

The jungle soared in front of them. Its entanglement was a cloak of green beyond which their eyes could not penetrate. Every so often that cover thinned enough to reveal azure skies with wispy, thin clouds. Or sun. Or moon. Or vistas of other, altogether melancholic colors. Colors whose power of association they could not comprehend.

At a rise they caught a glimpse of **the Chaco** as it merged into the horizon, dropping then curving onto **the Paraguay**, visible as a river of sparkle amid that splendor.

The trail took them into a field that encompassed a curiosity. Its mystery was so subtle, it was not until they stood at its midst that they realized just how out of kilter it appeared. At the center it was a circle of such extent and of such perfection it demanded a creator. At the periphery it was a width of soil maintained equally as artificially. At the boundary between that circle and that width of soil grew shoots.

If not by form, then by function, it served as a nursery for those glassy, fragile trees-to-be.

There, where they stood at the center of the field, they found a stump.

Although it had been a tree, it was not entombed into the earth. Rather, it was free. Free to move if it were not so heavy. Its roots, too, were not fixed and they curled upward, inward.

"Maybe somebody set it here?" Mark said of the stump, whose four roots were aligned with the mountains and the oceans.

Zachary hovered at the stump with his knees and his elbows latched onto its rim. The stump itself was pallid outside and wizened inside. And it was not rotted as it ought to be, given its exposure. But the wood was not familiar.

Where were the rings? he wondered.

The wood was decorated by rays instead of rings – and by an embedded ax.

The runt dared to nudge the ax but its bite was too deep to dislodge, swallowed, as it were, by the stump.

"Careful," Luke warned, "remember your skeleton?"

Zachary sighed; he (almost) forgot that tank he climbed into then could not escape. "It's a stump not a skeleton."

"Na, it **is** a skeleton," Luke teased. "Anyhow, Mark might be right, **it might be a memorial**."

Jack took a photograph of Zachary toying with the ax.

"**A memorial?**" Tom wondered. "**Who's** memorial?" The ax had been weathered a century. As were the relics planted by war. Was **that** the age of the field? Younger? Older? Who might be coming to the field year after year to maintain it? "Somebody cares for it," he concluded. "What if they're nearby?"

"Aye, go to," Gabriel grasped the runt by the shoulder as he implored them to withdraw. The site inspired a sense of dread. He, too, imagined it might be a 'holy' site, worshipped by somebody. And he did not want their invasion of it to be construed as disrespect. **And** it was imperative to make progress by noontime.

Soon the jungle enveloped them but the puzzle of the field was a matter of gossip. It rekindled their curiosity. For a while, at least, the goal of **Bahia Negra** was forgotten. Thoughts of their families at the capital were displaced by the fascination that brought them into **the Chaco**.

"Look!" Tom shouted. "At the trunk of the tree."

Everyone paused to gawk at the site the teenager indicated.

Its trunk **glinted**; the texture smoother, the color lighter than a tree with bark should have been capable of. Its shaft was thinner and shorter than the average: from its base to its divergence it spanned at most six feet of height and three feet of width. Above its divergence, its trunk split into two, diametric limbs, like a 'T'. Below its divergence, its limbs supported networks of thin, long leaves. Its weepy, droopy canopy sparkled through a dew that seemed to be drawn free from the air.

The tree was unique – its fruit, however, invited attention.

Anchored at the divergence – where they developed as a clump of four – where they grew into flattened sides and sharpened peaks – the fruit was a bounty that waited to be picked. Their skins were vibrant shades of reds disrupted by rays of deep, deep onyxes. Their vessels throbbed, they wished, **they hoped**, with a taste of nectar.

Yet to Gabriel the throb did not suggest juice, the color did not suggest edible, the hide – the hide with its spikes and its ridges – the hide did not suggest fruit.

"OK, fruits, we see fruits, lots and lots of fruits," the guide said to rouse the unit away.

They continued – **quietly** – and the jungle reflected the restraint. They found the dearth not the wealth of life. It felt as if not a creature stirred. Especially by the **'T'-trees** that dominated the landscape.

They did not probe the situation. How would they? How could they? It was not expected – so what were they to do about it? **The Chaco** as a whole was uncorrupted by man's encroachment. His comings and goings were transitory. War had been an episode – the exception not the rule. What the silence might or might not be, it was **how** the jungle operated. It was **Nature**. It was **pure**.

The clock tolled noon when they stepped out of the ravine and into the river.

The stream flashed a reflective, placid complexion whilst the current roared. They encroached into lower and lower territory and their rafts responded as if they skimmed the surface of the river. They were dragged by such a power that they paddled to decrease not increase their speed.

To Gabriel's relief they progressed.

So the river conveyed the party and they relaxed. As a unit they wallowed through the luxury of a daydream amid that solitude. Magic enriched the landscape. Gloom, too, slowly but certainly tainted the experience. It was the reality that the trek would be complete soon. That they would be, again, among their kind. As they advanced, **the Chaco** retreated and retreated and retreated, until it would be confined to memory. They always counted the steps to **Bahia Negra**, then with eagerness, now with sorrow.

Forgotten was the argument between Mark and Luke that they were not prepared to venture so far.

The journey they elected was not (often) attempted or granted – as it blazed through zones of **the Chaco** that had not been mapped for a century. War – and the tales of **the Ache** – and the stories of other, Amazon natives – everyone and everything conspired with geography to keep that realm unspoiled for aeons. They asked why it was taboo. They did not expect the answer. Or – perhaps – they should have. **There was no answer.** Few alive understood what tantalized the legends into existence.

They would not be the first. They would not be the last. Certainly, they were among the scant who dared. For at least a week they would be as distant from man as earth allowed.

Their families hesitated then relented – and the mission, flush with more inflow than outflow, secured the arrangements.

At a jump their siesta shattered – and, as their rafts drifted, they faced the coasts where sounds echoed.

By the edge of the river an orchard of 'T'-trees appeared to sprout out of that water. They stood at intervals and at angles as if they were fingers of submerged and monstrous hands. They displayed similarity to a degree that felt improbable. Details Nature left to chance were too, too finely duplicated. Trunks. Branches. Leaves. Canopies and their weeping, droopy veils. All were identical from tree to tree. Only **a** specimen diverged and its variance came from age – also, **it was notched by an ax**. The rest had to be copies of it and their uniformity was an artifact of reproduction.

Mark and Luke shrugged at the perfection of the symmetry.

That sound – a mixture of rattling leaves and creaking wood – it burst through the orchard – it erupted from a 'T'-tree. Its canopy surged out of the water. Its trunk swayed as it came to rest. While it shook it sprayed a kind of rain at the rafts.

"What? What was that?" asked Luke. "What **was** that?"

"What else could it be?" Mark muttered. "Something pushed it into the water, then held it, then released it."

"It swung like a catapult. Alright, then, so what's that **something** of yours?"

Nobody yearned to contemplate the answer to the question – then – Nature **intervened.**

It was yet another disturbance connected to that particular, 'catapulted' 'T'-tree. A few of its leaves shook. As they gawked, something **struggled**. Something **alive** must have been trapped by, **caught by**, its canopy. Then, the shaking eased.

A fish dangled out of the canopy where it rattled. First, the head, gasping. Last, the body, flopping. After its gills the fish had been reduced to its skeleton. As it slipped that leafy, green net, it caught onto a notch and it fragmented into a rain of flesh and bone.

"Weird," Zachary shrugged.

"Ah, that's it, it's hiding under the canopy," Mark conjectured. "It's a predator that learned how to use trees."

The idea's implication induced a fear of that 'T'-tree. If it were ... a predator ... a monster? If it were ... hiding under the canopy? What would it be? What could it be? If it were strong enough to use a tree like a weapon and go **unnoticed**? What was it?

Distracted by their confusion, they were surprised by motion at the edge of the orchard. It was a 'T'-tree. They caught a glimpse of its trunk surging, its canopy rising. It appeared as if it too had been catapulted out of the river.

Its sway launched a dew that did not feel entirely like water.

"Wait, wasn't that the tree with the scar?" Tom said to Jack. "It was upright, I swear it. Did any of you see it move?"

Nobody noticed. Not how the trees levered in or out of the river. Not how the agent they constructed pinned then catapulted the trees. They saw just the aftermath – the effect not the cause.

After the midday hour, and a sequence of rafting and hiking, Gabriel insisted that they stop to eat a bite of food. Rations were meager given the size of the hunger. A 'full' meal was the promise of that night's encampment. Supplies were limited and required to endure until they reached **Bahia Negra**.

"Has ... ventu ... **venturado** aqui?" Zachary struggled with the Spanish. The runt noted how the native's attitude toward the wilderness was altered by the episode with the fish.

"No," he shook, "estos lugares, **entiende**, estos lugares **no era para nosotros**."

"Wait – I thought you **Ache** guys...."

Again, he shook, "estos lugares," he replied, waving at the jungle that engulfed them, "we avoid it ... no good, no good. Si, no good."

"Great," Mark exhaled – and recalled the ruckus at the outpost among the company – it came (and went) when they agreed as a unit they wanted **the Chaco**.

When they selected that journey, it spurred a 'discussion' among the natives. That 'discussion', as it were, appeared to do with who to send as their guide. There were many, many aspects of its danger that they kept from the outpost.

Such was the extent of the concern relayed in front of the Mormons.

At the end they were told the trip would be strenuous as **the Chaco's** rivers were more seasonal than permanent. But the jungle was an obstacle. And surpassing that obstacle was the point of adventure.

Americanos!

"Still, you understand this area, where to go, what to do?"

"Yes."

"Good, then, let's go!"

They were (vaguely) aware of the extent into which they encroached **the Chaco**.

Mark was troubled and – by way of expression – transmitted that unease to Luke – all would be well as long as Gabriel was not lost and they kept toward **Bahia Negra**. If the worst came to be, they needed to follow the 'flow'. Eventually the drainage merged into **the Paraguay**. Despite the precautions (fears?) the remainder would be a rather straightforward excursion.

They hiked a trail that undulated by a stream too rough to raft. Gabriel led. Luke and Tom toted the vessels. Mark and Jack packed the supplies. Only Zachary's duties did not change.

They advanced.

Then Mark and Jack broke off to follow a path parallel to that trail which ambled through a grove, a stretch enshadowed by those 'T'-trees.

"Guys, look," Mark called. "I see it, again, that fruit. There's a tree with that fruit right in front of me. Let me reach it!" He jumped at the tree, reaching almost grabbing the fruit. "Time for a juicy treat," he laughed, eager to forget his worries.

Everybody halted – they, too, were relieved by the promise of the fruit.

Activity centered at a 'T'-tree whose trunk was shorter and thinner than the rest of its kind. That stature allowed the unit to examine its fruit. It was by-the-by identical in shape and in color to the fruit they already noted. Aspects of its skin differed, though. It grew a coat of fuzz – tactile yet imperceptible. It displayed weird networks of veins. It shriveled as though dehydrated.

Was it ripe? they wondered as the prospect of eating it passed from adventurer to adventurer.

"Why don't we go?" Zachary asked. A look at those veins impelled revulsion. Those **weird** veins throughout the hide of the black and red fruit played with his imagination. As did the fear of predators, monsters. What if **they** wanted the fruit for **their** food? The orchard just felt as if it shut in on him. "Come on, guys, what if there's ... something ... wrong with this?"

Gabriel patted Zachary's shoulder.

"Don't trees make fruit to be eaten? Part of their **cycle**? Isn't it?" Mark looked at Luke but the expression was neither for nor against the pilfering. "It's just fruit, it can't kill us, I'm sure, it can't kill us."

"Leave it alone, anyhow," Luke said of it when he gauged Gabriel's and Zachary's posture. "It doesn't look good enough to eat. And what if it gets mad?"

Mark simply laughed.

Striking with his shoulder, Mark fought the grip the tree asserted onto the fruit. He hit and that area oozed a white, thick sap where its bark cracked. He hit – again and again – and a sample of fruit was freed. It tumbled onto the dirt. It spun, spraying debris left and right. It came to rest at the center of the party. When it stopped they noted it demonstrated a wide, deep rip.

Tom and Jack kicked it and that rip expanded. Veins, that had been severed by the rip, oozed the paste mirrored by the bark. Inside, what could be seen of the black and red flesh, glistened with juice. Mark and Luke aimed to reach it. Gabriel kicked it away.

Curiosity came to its end as did their daydream of a bite. Entombed by the flesh and its vivid hues, they caught sight of what might have been a shoot at that 'memorial' they trod through earlier. Except – **it squirmed**. Like a worm. A worm with stumps for heads and tendrils for tails. Two stumps. Four tendrils. Curling. Uncurling. Sweeping at the air as if ready to jump at them.

Zachary screamed. The teens kicked at the fruit, passing it from foot to foot, dropping it at the river where the flow washed it away.

Then – trees swayed – branches, leaves, **everything** rustled.

A roar formed out of that fury and echoed from the orchard, to the wilderness.

They stood, dwarfed by the immensity the jungle revealed of itself.

Tom shook. Jack paled. They drew together to wonder what could be agitating the trees. They wanted to blame the wind while there was not a breeze to be felt.

"Aye, go to," Gabriel ordered.

They fled; as fast as they wished to be, though, they could not escape what encompassed them. Running simply witnessed its power and validated its conjecture. Their fear **came** true with a veracity reality was incapable of. It could be anything. Any shape. Any form. Anything to come out of the shadow and darkness was part of the predator, the monster.

When they stumbled onto a calm stretch of river, they shoved into its water and paddled until the jungle silenced itself. As with their legs then, now with their arms, they raced as though chased. Gabriel and Zachary led. The brothers followed. The cousins did not lag.

At least for a while....

"Faster," Tom implored.

"I try."

The raft at the rear tired. Tom and Jack languished and the separation extended. Then the rest of the unit could not be seen past the entanglements of trees that invaded the coasts.

They could not narrow the gap.

"They won't abandon us," Tom stated aloud to assure himself. "It's just one stream. It's just one current. It's just one direction. If we keep going, we'll reach **Bahia Negra**. We won't get lost."

Jack nodded.

Around them, at the coasts of the river, the 'T'-trees started a new and different performance. The previous tree swayed then stopped. The next tree swayed then stopped. Thus, from neighbor to neighbor, a pattern traveled like a wave.

"Tom," Jack whispered as he held the oar like a rudder. "Tom – the current changed."

As revealed by the wake stabbed by the oar, their south–eastern flow was replaced by a north–western trickle. A shiver worked through their spines. They fought against the water as it dragged them to where 'T'-trees rattled like torrents.

The four ahead stopped when they felt the absence. They turned then paddled – and as they retreated they could not refute their confusion. Confusion at the shift of the current. Confusion at the coasts – **thin** where they had been **thick** with trees. Then, as they approached Tom and Jack, they gasped, they froze, while Tom and Jack struggled against a frenzy that flouted comprehension.

It was the trees by the coasts that shook as though caught by a whirlwind.

'T'-trees, from top to bottom, **bobbed** – falling in and rising out of the water – broadcasting waves through the current that altered the flow. Trunks thrust like weaponry. Assaults struck not randomly but precisely. The predator(s) understood exactly what it wanted and how to accomplish its task. The effect of it, repeated again and again, dragged the prey to the trap.

Tactics shifted as the boys almost rammed ashore. The trees **pivoted** like limbs. The canopies hurled like nets. They spread then retreated to snag the rafts.

As everything happened it felt as if a cloak veiled the agency of the operation. A swirl of sounds and sights, **inspired by fear**, distorted the periphery. Or was it, perhaps, not a reflexive but a conscious reinvention of what they could not accept into a palpable if vague cause?

Maybe Gabriel caught a glimpse of that truth when he yelled.

"Jump!" Zachary shouted as though to echo the guide.

Tom and Jack plunged into the river then grasped the rope and towed the raft. A tree slammed the water and struck exactly where the vessel would have been if the cousins had not acted. Its bark scratched their faces.

Everyone screamed then Gabriel signaled them to be quiet.

Immediately, the shift of the current ceased.

As the stream resettled, they drew away from the coast.

The tree that left a kiss of blood remained embedded into the river. Its shape had not been affected by the forces that wielded it. It had been uprooted and projected without damage. Yet – the aftermath of the attack was strangest of all. It was the silence that rapt the jungle. What may or may not have impelled the violence simply melted into the wilderness out of which it sprung.

"We go slow and we stay together," Gabriel commanded through the runt, "we keep away from the trees."

"It's crazy," Mark stated, "What did we do?"

Luke and Tom switched rafts. With everyone matched, they surged. The river was swift and they followed its route easily. Individually, they were vulnerable. Together, they were formidable. At least by their size if not by their might. They came to accept that avoiding the 'predator' and its 'territory' was paramount. Forward, through the margins of the coasts, it was the only way to reach **Bahia Negra**. Deviation would have delayed their arrival and exhausted their supply.

How was it possible? Trees, **uprooted**? Trees, **projected**? Trees, wielded like weapons? Those **'T'-trees**....

Was it shyness that prevented a full reveal (attack)? Or was it the fear of man – more for his strangeness than his threat – that forced it to act so **indirectly**? Or was it not aware of them?

The clock advanced.

At the west the sun grazed the toothy, ragged grin of the Andes. The sky displayed a warm, dusky color. The land replied with cool mixtures of scents. Together, above and below, **the Chaco** cast a disposition that added a primal, gloomy quality to the jungle. It could have been a trillion years ago and what would have changed? Alarmed, as it were, they realized how blindly **if not recklessly** they tread through a realm that was not ruled by man.

Evening....

The river widened into a lake. An island appeared off its center. At its left it was framed by a thin, rocky channel. At its right it was dominated by a crest. As they gauged it, it became less like an island and more like debris amassed through aeons.

Gabriel directed the rafts to the island.

"No es grande," he explained, "pero es seguro."

"We'll be safe at the island," Zachary summarized.

They repeated the task of portage except their roles were not rigid. Everybody shared their load, gathering supplies, dragging rafts. As they scaled the crest they found that it was not a very large island. But it was in the water not in the earth. And it was as distant from the wilderness as they could be.

When they stood at the interior of the refuge they wondered if they would be safe **anywhere**.

While natives avoided the area, there had been others, plenty of others to be certain, who ignored experience and ventured where they did not belong. A few returned with tales to tantalize the morbid. Many were never to be known of again. Atop the island endured a remnant of adventure – a camp – whose fate they could not judge by its appearance.

A relic of war? they assumed. Until, as they explored, they discovered that the camp was not congruent to the style of the military.

The tents were not tinted to match a jungle but a desert. They would have been spotted by an enemy if they had been at war. Then – no sign of battle – no weapons, no munitions. Except an ax that had been used to mark a trail.

Tom wanted to run. Jack was too guarded to be so irrational. Meanwhile, faced by the alternative, Mark and Luke considered the island to be less and less foreboding. Elsewhere, Zachary and Gabriel wasted daylight as they surveyed the island.

The tents contained items that spanned a typical, early 20th century expedition. Tins, dated from 1932 to 1936, could have been food. The rest of it was the spoil of science: vials, slides, optics.

Then, at another tent, at another safe, they unearthed notebooks and photographs. Of the images – the majority were fuzzy, either badly exposed or developed. They were images of trees. 'T'-trees, to be exact. Of the writings, they were tables, figures, observations. They could not be read but there was disagreement if it was the language or the deterioration that kept the work unintelligible.

They discovered the envelope and the letter.

As it unfolded they gasped.

How could it be that it survived **as if not a day passed**?

Germany was a major contributor to the culture of the region.

Life was not easy for missionaries of their particular brand of Christianity. So it was best not to poke at a nation's wounds. As their families were oft to say, the 'unfortunate' history of Paraguay was not to be discussed.

"Alright, who or what they were, they dropped everything in the middle of **the Chaco**," Jack summarized.

"They were driven away."

Everyone glared at Luke.

"Let's go back. Obviously, that river's got to be **the Paraguay** or part of **the Paraguay**. We just keep going. We just let the flow take us to **Bahia Negra**."

"Tom, you're panicking," Jack stated.

"We will be safe," Gabriel insisted.

Mark flipped through a stack of photographs. He stopped at the image of a man ready to chop a 'T'-tree. The ax – *was it not like the ax they found at the memorial?* Then he shuddered as he connected the ax to the tree with the scar – the eldest of the orchard. That wizened tree contradicted what the image depicted then he recalled the decades that passed since the photograph that captured their imagination had been taken.

Gabriel strung his largest stretch of English: "or we stay here or we stay there – **with the trees.**"

That was the end of it – the island's mystery might have been vexing but its turf offered security.

Tents were pitched. Rafts were packed. Supplies were counted and spread.

In the wake of moonlight, they ate.

After a round to gawk at photographs and wonder why **NAZIs** penetrated **the Chaco**, it was curfew. Gabriel and Zachary went to collect water. The rest watched them vanish into the haze past where the fire's glow reached. They conversed; plans were raised, argued, settled. It was assured they were a day from **Bahia Negra**. They needed to avoid what harassed them. The coasts. The 'T'-trees. Staying clear of that seemed to be the way to continue.

Then a scream pierced that island.

Gabriel struggled into the camp crying 'Zachary'. His clothes were torn, the skin of his arms and his legs were shredded as if he crawled through sandpaper. His words were a slurred craze of language they could not comprehend.

The boys were stunned as a familiar disturbance returned – a roar that formed itself out of the jungle.

They fought against fear to approach the edge of the island.

At the river they caught a glimpse of Zachary netted by a 'T'-tree. At once the whole, entire visage of Zachary and 'T'-tree smashed into the current. Thrashing. Splashing. **Shrieking.** Then – everything stopped. When the sight reemerged just a hand latched to a branch could be seen. What remained of a skeleton rained onto the water.

Paralyzed by the fear of it, before they screamed, before they ran, they stared at a sight they knew was true though they could not believe it. Maybe they always understood yet rejected it? For there were no predators, no monsters, only trees.

★

Dog Walks Ahead

Trinidad Lake wasn't famous (anymore); a quiet if solemn treasure, its perimeter enveloped a canyon nuzzled somewhere south of Jeffersonville, north of Raton. The park didn't get the notice of those wild, majestic vistas Colorado was famous for. It only drew its fill of Naturalists far and wide at the fall – that most fragile yet romantic of Earth's seasons. Locals just kept away **far** away from that torment its past stirred.

To high school seniors, Peter and Cody, **Trinidad Lake** topped their lists of haunts. As others fled **east**, they aimed **west**, steering their **jeep** from the ruckus of the RVs at the park's gates to the solitude that waited the brave a further ten or so miles across **Route 12**. That trek of theirs brought them into the junction of **Reilly Canyon**'s road, where they braked and waved to caravans passing by. Then, after the intersection emptied, their drive resumed onto a course that slacked between hills and valleys – features unique to the park's **far** side.

Reilly Canyon itself stalked the adventurers **inches** off their tire's treads. Ages ago a stream ripped that trench out of the ground and gnawed at it year by year. 'Til the county altered the dam at the lake. Its currents thinned into trickles, patchy by-the-by. Its chasm remained, exposed – a ghastly visage of what it used to be. Wizened, as it was, that canyon's cliffs fired their awe where ever they caught too keen a glimpse of it.

Reilly Canyon's road stopped at the trailhead's lot. Given the lot's position relative to the road's layout, from the trailhead they could have lapped five odd miles to reach the reserve they scouted earlier. They would have hiked its length – but tonight their endeavors were more astronomical, less pastoral – and it didn't feel right to lug their equipment over such a distance. Rather, they opted to extend their drive toward the lot's end. Their weeks of explorations revealed how it converged into yet another road, that wasn't documented by the map, which garnered them a shortcut to their camp-to-be.

The trail they blazed wasn't forgiving. It forced the boys to blitz by the dynamo that straddled the canyon (which itself continued, unbroken if diminished, straight into the park). Of the structure: its upper portions – mere facades of north facing, south leaning posts – threatened to topple while its lower portions **yawned**. As the route climbed the canyon, its view of that relic revealed mazes of intricacies – cryptic chambers and remnants of 19th century industry – whipping suggestions of a maw full of grinding, chewing teeth.

The trail meandered, swerving in to and out of the daylight then it expanded into a level stretch of turf.

Their drive stopped where the route melted into the topography. At their front spread a broad jagged hillside. Around, left and right, undulations like dunes arced west to east. Behind, snaked the canyon – that became more and more like a ditch – and further, further behind **everything**, loomed the slopes at the park's southern rim. The park's lake and dam were confined by distance to their imagination. The park's gates – and its trains of RVs, zippering then dashing into destinations beyond – struggled to reach their eyes through the wilderness that smothered the view.

Crisp wintry breezes burst by their faces as Peter and Cody gazed out of their windows. Whirlwinds stirred the forest – and they stared afar as if to discern a scent that air transmitted. The whole, entire vision – with its vivid, autumnal color – stood in gloomy opposition to the air's flowery spray and so fueled their appetite for the mystery of it all.

"**Tee**," Cody said of it, "that's the strangest whiff. Like perfumes girls wear."

"Great, the stuff you think of, Co."

"Like you're innocent!" Cody let his left hand rise then fall to rest as a fist at Peter's right shoulder. "So we're seeing stars tonight? That so?"

"**Sirrus**? It should be overhead by midnight, more or less."

"More. 'r less. Man, we could be **anywhere**. You and your crazy ideas."

The driver arched an eyebrow: "Me **and you**."

Cody flashed his wicked grin as he drew aside curtains of braids the breeze wove of his hair.

The truth was that there weren't a lot of options. As seniors, they were old enough to drive without supervision – a fact they took advantage of to visit their spots. It was, rather, the dearth of money that conspired to curb their adventures into weekends or, as was the case, into breaks like **Thanksgiving**. Perhaps next summer they'd strike at their vow to see the rest of Colorado? Or, **if they saved**, they'd get that spring break at Breckonridge.

The sun's dying drama set the expanse ablaze – it wasn't quite 2 PM yet – four or so hours of daylight were left to burn.

At their **jeep**'s tailgate, they sorted then divided their equipment. Cody took the tripod and the larger (not the smaller) sleeping-bag. Peter took the scope and the tent (folded like a parachute by their mothers). Other packs contained their camp's odds and ends – ample provisions for a day's rations – and those, too, were distributed by weight.

As they shut their vehicle, their activity echoed at the canyon they stood aloft of. When that reverb settled, the crackle of the stream trembled into their ears. The trench it washed through had to be a hundred yards to the south. Amid that waning, setting daylight, they caught a glint of its current where its force gouged into the chasm. Further to the south of that stream – softened by amorphisms of evergreens and slanted into a lofty, azure horizon – the valley called. It was then, **then**, then as they gazed, that they heard **the yelp**.

"Junior said **what** 'bout dogs?" Cody asked of an exchange that Monday at the locker-room.

Peter scanned the landscape – his eyes roved left to right but couldn't find the yelper.

"Maybe a dog's lost. Must've been the storm from Halloween. There's houses **that** side of the canyon, Co," he said of the park's southern rim. "Doesn't this park get a break?"

Ever since their families relocated to Jeffersonville, Peter and Cody were told to be leery of **Trinidad Lake**. Locals whispered stories about children. Children, especially, who'd wander toward the water never to be seen or heard again.

It used to be that the dam was lower and the lake was higher. The excess funneled into streams that powered dynamos. Even after the county's **alteration**, nobody attempted to raze the dynamos, as they were already abandoned and dismantled. Under the ground, though, they retained their works – deathtraps – that continued to lurk and validate otherwise flimsy, airy legends.

Neither Cody nor Peter lived at Jeffersonville when its scars were fresh – they arrived just as they reached eight years of age, past the paranoia's climax. Earlier **that** year the disappearance of seven children sparked the townfolks' ire. Schools brought officers to educate families about **cults** – the scare du jour – yet that inflamed the fear simmering tragedy after tragedy. Citizens, pushed to their wit's end, turned **militant**. The mayor, increasingly embattled and isolated, deputized searchers as a last ditch effort to pacify the community.

That ordeal bloomed into a calamity after **60 Minutes** featured Jeffersonville's plight and broadcasted its woes for the country to witness. Its portrait of a stumbling, bumbling jurisdiction, too inept to act, sparked fallout of its own. Authorities failed to explain why their children were targeted. The mayor escaped disgrace, as if by intervention, for – as summer waxed into winter – the disappearances stopped **and didn't resume**.

"Let's get," Cody said to Peter.

The advantage they uncovered deep into the park was a shortcut. A shortcut that connected them from the vehicle to the trail at exactly where their hike would have settled onto a ledge. Albeit a steep, narrow ditch, its impromptu climb shaved three and a half miles off their travel.

At a turn, they meandered into groves of junipers. Afterward, they followed that trail as it traced the rim of the gorge. At yet another turn – a sharp, left tilt – they encountered a bench. The park sported a bench every so often. Its seat offered rest but the boys abstained. Still – they paused to gawk aback. Aback at orchards whose shapes rustled tunes inspired by breezes.

Wasn't that the yelp? Weren't those movements? Movements by the trees? No – it couldn't be – how could it be? They were alone....

"It's nobody," Peter said of it, "dogs, maybe, they're smart enough to know this park isn't theirs."

"Not dogs I worry 'bout."

The past wasn't coherent at its periphery. The evidence documented by the state attested the fact that children started to vanish at **Trinidad Lake** circa 1975. Reporters from Denver suspected the onset dated to '73 or to '72. Neither dates nor incidents prior to 1975 withstood scrutiny or were, at best, **at best**, suspect. What the investigators could be certain of was that in '75 a girl wandered away from the park's gates. Then – a trickle of boys and girls followed at a pace of two per year. Given the era, and its sleepy sloppy bookkeeping, that rate evaded inquiry.

Then, in 1977, the mayor's five–year–old daughter and puppy were added to the list. A witness at the park's RV lot stated that the girl chased the dog into the woods by the lake. The pup, a Lab / Shepherd mix, would be fished out of the stream past the dynamo where it had **almost** drowned. Police assumed the girl was lost to the innards of the works. Divers refused to probe it further due to safety. The theory of currents dragging kids to their deaths wasn't tested simply presumed as the likeliest cause for Jeffersonville's many, **empty** graves.

After **that** the county reconfigured Jeffersonville's water usage policy. The dam got higher. The lake got lower. The combination of factors effectively curtailed the water's ability to drag their children to their doom – funerals **paused** for a year.

'Til, from 1979 to 1984, events accelerated to a point where the state concluded the cause wasn't **accidental**. An average of five kids per year were taken – usually at the summer – usually at the park. Word spread throughout Colorado – then – throughout the country. The community developed a skewered reputation that exacerbated issues already faced as coal fled to sites elsewhere. Tourism took a hit – yet, **perplexingly**, it was people from far, from away, (and out of state), people ignorant of the lore budding at the park, it was **they** who'd come and go seemingly untouched by tragedy.

Authorities compiled a dossier and fit details into models only then supported by technology. Any and all doubt that existed ceased to be. **How had it been denied?** It **was** Jeffersonville's children who were **targeted**.

That breakthrough proved to be a pyrrhic, moral victory. In spite of their effort, their hunt for the perpetrator was stymied by the fact that a suspect defied identification. The victims shaped a pool too random to establish a motive.

As summer transitioned into winter, at Old Hallows Eve – or so it was said – the mayor's dog escaped after a freak, autumn storm. Reports that the animal had been spotted at the park's south west quadrant wormed into print. It was by all accounts a large, black breed of dog that stalked those woods – a sight tough to forget. Like the children, the dog, too, vanished without a trace.

With its life returned to the ledger of the lost, its sacrifice accepted and appeased, Jeffersonville's plight ceased.

Nobody from that community had been taken after 1984.

At a hilltop, at a reserve carved out of that canyon's north west rim, they discovered a forgotten oasis amongst a forgotten sea. It wasn't easy to reach its seclusion from any of the park's lots or trailheads. Few of the transient Naturalists dared to venture so far as to find it. So it went for days if not for months without a footprint save their own. It was the perfect spot to launch their adventures.

The pair started as if everything had been arranged. Who could have said how the turns were tallied? There were subtle even subconscious structures to their rituals. It was never always either the one or the other tasked to complete a particular role.

The tent was unfolded then erected. Its corners were secured by rocks cultivated off the reserve. The tripod was extended then aligned. Its sights were aimed at coordinates of interest.

Peter and Cody ambled into the center of that reserve where its trees were too sparse to cloak the sky. There they stopped and stood to gauge its lay. There they **listened**. Every so often a breeze rattled a tree. Or a twig snapped. Or a dog yelped.

The same dog.

The same yelp.

The yelp was faint, distant – and by degrees so gossamer the whistle of the air that carried it obliterated it.

The sky glowed into twilight and that climate inspired a gray, detached melancholy. Yet – it wasn't the clouds that passed – it wasn't the cool that settled – it was, rather, a strange **alteration** or, perhaps, **revelation** about the woods that engulfed them which stirred the rut. It was as if the trees were growing and they were shrinking else becoming imperceptible. That sense of the world's inversion struck at them whenever face to face with the vastness of a truly wild kingdom – not the manicured if boondocked trails of **Trinidad Lake**.

To avoid detection, they opted not to build a fire. It was safest to stay by the tent anyway. They kept together – Cody on the log, Peter on the turf.

The yelp – it played like a record, **a copy** – could it be – **might it be?** – getting closer?

"Ever suppose the park's haunted, **Tee**?"

"Tough to say. It's not like we've looked for it. We've never spent the night – eh – **here** not **there**," he drew a thumb to the east.

"Yeah but there's got to be something 'bout the stories – **they happened**."

"They happened – **then** – stopped. Hauntings and stuff like that don't."

"**Real** hauntings, well, maybe this, this whatever this is, sleeps? Or waits. Don't think it's monsters like they say."

"No?"

"Hard to keep hate going. **Real** hauntings 'r' love not hate."

"**That so**?" Peter gazed up at Cody – who picked at the scruff of his chin's stubble with his blade's tip. His eyes thinned into slits as he added: "Yeah, I'd haunt you."

"Eh, not if I'm first."

For a while they stared at the skies. They had been painted the vivid, bright reds of dusk. Now they were streaks of deep, azure swaths, spread from east to west and layered by frail white tendrils.

"It's **New Jersey**, you know," Peter said at last as evening flourished. "Dad takes us to a park. It's always **that** park. We'd walk around its awful **fake** lake. The sis and I find this area by the lake. We'd never saw it or noticed it before. It's a wooded area. It's New Jersey. Not anything like **this**. Not anything like wilderness. Just an oasis. But that area, hm, it was like a piece of a forest. Maybe it was bigger and I remember it wrong? I donno. The sis and I follow Dad into it. Ahead there's a lot with cars. We see it through the trees. We walk and I donno how but the sis trips. I get a hold of her shoulder. I remember **this** clear. There was this, this guy, who kind of reached to yank her 'til I grabbed her. And we run to Dad."

"Why didn't you scream?" Cody asked.

Peter grimaced: "I donno, maybe, maybe 'cause I got her away."

"Eh, **should have screamed.** Before we moved to **Jay Vee** we lived pretty remote – wasn't a village – just – a road. Everything that mattered kept outdoors anyhow. We'd hunt like a family. Grandma, she'd tell us these stories to keep us good – you know – those '**behave 'r else**' stories. We **had** to be good when we helped mom and dad hunt. Her favorites were stories 'bout this monster – its name – she'd say its name – we weren't supposed to say it's name. **At all**," he exhaled. "Sometimes, I tell you, that made **her** scarier. It's a spirit, a **forest** spirit, takes people. **Takes children. I had** a sister."

"**Cody.**"

"Yeah – older – **older** sister. Don't know what we were doing that day just that mom and dad didn't want us at the house. **So** we went to the river where we fished. We were at the water's edge, playing by logs. We heard a voice – **grandma's** – she's yelling at us – that we didn't behave – she's telling us to get. **She called us by name.** We were bad, see. I remember the sis turned to me, shaking like crazy, whispering to stay by the logs and to keep out of sight. Then the sis told me she'd never ever call for me – she'd come for me **not** call for me. **Peter** ... what if she knew? ... she went into the bush. Everything got – **not quiet** – it felt like I wasn't part of the world anymore. Like I died and didn't know it. I hid **hours**, crying. When mom and dad shouted for us, I didn't move – you know – I didn't move. When they found me ... it's not that they didn't believe me, they didn't **want** to. Grandma, she got helicoptered to Fairbanks and died that afternoon. When you're a kid, what do you know? I should have screamed."

November sky dazzled overhead.

That night's target, **Sirrus**, surged out of the horizon earlier than they anticipated. They almost missed it as its transit across their view lasted a brisk thirty or so minutes. Other sights by–the–by left mixed impressions. Clusters failed to focus. Stars alternated to their eyes as either sharp or fuzzy smudges. Not to be deterred, though, they shifted to a steadier, easier program – a hunt for planets that yielded peculiar views of Mars and, later, of Saturn.

After a while they stopped to eat and drink – and – to enjoy their solitude.

The boys noted a watery odor to the air – **the ghost of the Great Halloween Storm**? they joked. Mixed – or, masked – into it was a sizzle of meat, rancid and gamey. They wondered if a deer had been caught and butchered nearby. Yet their explications failed to connect as evidence mounted against their ideas. They simply couldn't fathom from where or from what came that spark to startle their senses.

All the while the yelp didn't cease – it only wandered in or out of their awareness.

Peter and Cody spent their yawning hour readying for a retreat to start that dawn – then – they withdrew into their tent. They unzipped and laid the sleeping–bag at the floor where they slipped under its cover. At their feet were remnants of their night's adventures, sorted not packed (yet). At their heads were their tent's flaps unclasped. Outside, gusts jumbled trees. Inside, they rattled.

"Didn't we get here at the same time?"

"Aye, **at the same date** – feels like, like forever ago, don't it, **Tee**?" Cody's sly grin lit that pocket of warmth they shared. "Was fall, too. Dads took us here that week we met. That **first** week we met. Can't forget it. Dogs never bothered me. **Still don't.**"

"Is it 'cause they're getting closer?"

"Don't think it's dogs. Didn't we camp fancy and keep by the RVs? ... never ever strayed so far **here**. Haven't we survived worse? Why 'r' we afraid of **this**?"

"Nobody said anything about dogs. **Kids** got taken. They'd wander away from the RVs. Not lured – **wandered**. They got into trails they shouldn't have. They got into places they shouldn't have. **Cody**, it's a tiny blip of a park, really, but – **remember** – the hike to find this camp? We got lost at a ravine. And we **had** the map. Besides, everything stopped that fall."

"That fall **of eighty-four**. Wait! There **was** a dog," Cody declared, turning up from Peter to the crack of the night spread at the tent's flaps. "Twice, too. When the mayor's **girl** vanished. When the mayor's **dog** vanished."

"Yeah – that dog escaped, didn't it, and **that** was the end."

"Last victim. **Tee**, what if it **knew**? What if it knew **everything**? ... knew and **believed** ... if only it were stronger, it might have saved the girl. So it escaped and returned. That's the thing about animals, their hearts 'r' too pure."

Peter joined Cody at the front of the tent where its flaps flailed.

A rumble accompanied that yelp – as did the echoes of sticks rubbing, of stones grinding. Something was treading into their camp. Something was coming closer and closer. Something that wasn't a dog yet **suggested** a dog.

The adventurers kept low to the ground. On their knees and elbows they lurched forward. They aimed to leap only to stumble out of their tent. So they spilled to the ground facing their respective sides and gradually, achingly turned toward that gap ahead where the trail would have lead to their vehicle and to the rest beyond. The squabble of rocks crunching rocks pounded out of that opposite end of the reserve. If it had been a moon lit night, the interloper might have been spotted. Such as it was, they struggled to understand what verged into their oasis.

At first they laughed.

It couldn't have been a dozen yards away from them. Low to the earth, like a blot not like a fog, its **shape** clutched at the gap parted by the trail through the forest. Not until the stars overhead shattered that whirly, inky cloak which smothered their camp was it bright enough for the shape to confess its textures – then – its details.

They noted what their weak grasp yielded of the interloper. There – was its head. There – was its body. There – were its legs. All of it ruffled, pelted by a fur that failed to mask the flagrancy of its skeleton. The catalog of what that beast could have been felt endless. Then its head, **its face**, shifted from back to front – it hadn't even looked at the teens. Now.... Now – when it eyed them they realized **it was a dog**! A dog that stood with its muzzle wide. Yet its teeth weren't flared. It wasn't that sort of display. That posture gave the impression of a mood more quizzical, less aggressive. As they gawked, the dog trotted into the trail almost out of their sight. **Almost**, not quite, **not quite** – for it idled – it circled and punctuated its revolutions with **the yelp**.

"I can't see a collar," Peter said to Cody.

They followed and a mile later the forest receded and exposed the gorge. The chase endured – the dog at the front gaining – the boys at the rear losing – until the gulf surged. They lost sight of it. They heard its call and so they persisted, past the bench, past the junipers. They stopped to sweep the canyon with their flashlights. Their beams dropped colors where ever they touched none of which hinted at blood, or, at prints – save their own from when they arrived.

Then – to their gasp – at the root of the hillside in front of their shortcut – the dog waited by their **jeep**.

That beast **waited** – pacing and stopping and pacing – regurgitating **the yelp** throughout.

Single-file they crept the length of the shortcut and as they neared their vehicle the dog lurched toward the trench. They paused somewhere midway between the highs and the lows of that slope. The dog, though, continued unabated as if confident of its command over the boy's attention.

Peter and Cody, frozen where they stood, shrieked at the sight of the dog by the chasm's edge. Wasn't it aware of them? Or, could it be, **might it be**, that inadvertently it lent them a glimpse of truth they oughtn't be privy to? The beast angled its face so that its eyes stabbed their eyes and against its silence its eloquence so issued would have been a ghastly **human** expression if it weren't constrained to a dog's profile.

Its legs were especially if uncommonly emotive just by the way they clenched tightly to its body. It attested the idea that the dog reflected not emitted fear. That, perhaps, it replayed events – events that required a witness for whatever the reason.

What was it showing them? – they wondered.

They gasped when it jumped in to the trench. For a while it kept out of sight. They stifled, uncertain if to move or if to speak, then, it soared freed of the chasm.

That beast darted about the woods at the park's southern rim.

"Couldn't be hurt, not the way it moved, hey, **Tee**, that you?"

Was it always there?

Had they seen it a dozen times already? Or, if not seen it, felt it, a nagging anxiety that something of the universe came awry.

How many times did they simply walk by it?

Maybe it wanted a night like that night to be noticed?

*Was it **always** there?*

Ahead – directly – and enmeshed by the evergreens carpeting the slopes at the park's southern rim – a light flickered through that wilderness. A single throb of light. It wasn't a fire – it was too wide, too unsteady. Rooted at its source, whatever that was, it neither advanced nor retreated. Its glow **quivered** as if it were ready to burst.

"People gotta live there, don't they?"

"Feel how quiet it got?"

"What if we go back? It's gone – **home** – right? It's someone's dog, anyhow." Peter itched a retreat and that itself spurred **the yelp**. From across the chasm they heard it – only it wasn't the call they came to expect. **That** yelp gained a visceral glut of pain not altogether a dog's. "So that settles it."

The stream was alive that night – its surface reflected the stars and sparkled where it glided by obstructions like their boots.

What if the dog wasn't their business? Again, as they voiced any doubt, any doubt **whatsoever**, that beast replied, **aware**, in spite of its distance. **It couldn't be a mistake**, they reasoned, the dog – what it was or wasn't – it beckoned. Unreal as ever, it required their intervention for its cause.

Fronting the mysteries at the park's southern rim, the glow of which lured them away from their oasis, they struggled to gauge exactly **how** to reach its climax. There weren't trodden, forthright paths blatant to their eyes and the topography itself was too chaotic to attack directly.

Rather, it was easiest for them to climb a bit, zag and zig, then, repeat. They always stumbled onto **just** the right footing. So they realized that a path had been worked into that craze. It had been pounded step-by-step, etched year-by-year, camouflaged to ravel betwixt trees.

As they advanced through the forest, they completed the span of the rise and discovered a field like a garden. Its oval perimeter gave respite to their smarting, listing strides. It was as if they wandered into a secret, offshot world that they weren't entitled to trespass. Something like a dream world only fragments of which were true enough to be real.

The adventurers joked about how they were going to explain their late **late** return tomorrow.

"**If** we return," Cody teased Peter.

They spotted the dog at the distance. It didn't acknowledge their encroachment as it kept by a formation like a staircase. It waited, perhaps, too reticent to act – then – its body twisted its head **and scowled**. They stopped. **Cold**. Nobody breathed. Not until the beast mounted the summit of that cyclopean structure.

"Yeah, it ain't gonna end well, is it?"

They followed – their boots drummed their steps.

Autumn's litter crackled at their feet.

The wilderness broke into a road that arched upward to the left and downward to the right. Its extremes curved away from their sights. They aimed their flashlights at the bluff beyond the road as they visored their eyes. The target – it was there, **there** transformed from abstract to real. The light – it gurgled out of a window heretofore enshrouded.

"A house?" they declared of angular upright frames that came into view.

The road stopped at a roundabout in front of that house.

A **jeep** from the 70s idled under the carport. Its red wasn't as dimmed as their model's, a fact that unsettled the boys. By the looks of it – very, very recently – a tree from the yard collapsed over the carport. The debris pinned that vehicle where it had been parked. Spiked, so to speak, it wasn't apt to run or to salvage.

That tree performed yet another miracle – it breached the house and the rent it sliced gaped wide enough to let them eke through unscathed.

Peter and Cody were struck by how out of time and space the abode appeared. Like the vehicle, the house stayed pegged, more or less, to the 70s. Aside from the storm's damage **outside, inside** windows and doors had been insulated so completely that its shelter wasn't (yet) invaded by animals. Fixtures tantalized them and it wasn't easy to avert the urge to touch **everything**. That there weren't pawprints or bootprints or prints of any sort didn't faze them as they hadn't spotted tracks throughout their journey.

The light that drew them came out of the den. The culprit was a TV, a **Zenith**. Everybody owned a copy of it. The set had been left tuned to a station that, at their hour, reran the evening's newscast. Its audio was muffled. Its video wasn't snow just gray with glimpses of movements. Peter fumbled its switch. Cody pulled its cord. Its circuits issued a sort of wail as it welcomed electric demise.

Save for their flashlights, the house surrendered to midnight.

It was then, then **from below** that they heard the yelp.

"Did we do it wrong?" Peter asked.

"Look!" Cody exclaimed.

The floor had been disturbed as if it sprouted a mound. Peeling the rug revealed that planks had been bent or forced upward. The orifice they framed beamed a jagged toothy grin. The slit was wide yet narrow; either a kid or a pet could have skimmed through it but not a grown-up.

"**Somebody** tried to escape, Co."

Edging into the slit, their eyes floated over abysses their flashlights refused to penetrate. Aiming wasn't steady. Mostly what they found were scraps, debris – more or less – chewed by the violence that formed the slit. That clutter had been left to rain onto tarps. **Blue** tarps. It stung the eye to witness sky bright color juxtapose twilight. But that wasn't all of it. And as they braved the depths they realized something, something they couldn't ascertain from where or from what, struggled to gain their heed. It swayed, rocked as it jumbled – a spark of metal that twinkled like starburst.

They worried. That situation the dog pulled them into was a queer matter to explain, if pressed by authority. Just how far was too far for a couple of teenagers? It wasn't like somebody stopped them. Even as they scrambled for stairs, frenzied from chamber to chamber whilst they searched, nobody – **dead or alive** – stopped them.

The basement packed assortments of chambers into a footprint that exceeded the plot's dimensions. Signs everywhere pointed to an enlargement that wasn't finished per say. Rooms were sprawling, rambling areas, ill–defined in spite of their development. They sported **crates** from floors to ceilings. It wasn't litter – though – its details revealed its purposes. Labeled – and arranged by design – its contents suggested that an establishment had been transported there for storage.

Awareness, spurred at a depth independent of their will, drew their eyes, then, their feet to the rear of the basement.

A curious tangled path sprawled where it had been carved into the placements of the crates. There, at the end of the trail, a wall's appearance suggested a door's existence. The whole of it, wall and door alike, had been paneled to match thus to camouflage themselves. The way it stood – **shut** – crevices melted out of view except at cracks. Cracks – that signaled where the door split from the wall – that failed to gather dust as air whistled through them.

They couldn't spot hardware; neither joints nor knobs were part of its puzzle. Its riddle confounded them until they figured it was a door that **slid** not **swung**. It yielded to their push then coasted **freely** left and right. While there wasn't even a latch that might have, could have jammed it, to be safe, they blocked the door's way with a crate.

Past the door, their flashlights exhumed a chamber fit like a study. Under dust it remained a shade shy of tidy. A freezer capped the farthest wall: to its right was a draft desk and to its left was a cork board. Cabinets, stretching the study's height and width, dominated its construction. Medical texts and journals crammed the shelves – as did the relics of that craft.

Peter and Cody stopped in front of a cabinet to explore its folders. Its files were stuffed to the brim with sketches and photographs – **polaroids** – documenting autopsies of children. The teens simply weren't able to put aside its stack as if they were compelled by forces beyond their command to sift its contents bit by bit. Something, whatever it was, wanted, no, **needed** them to see the evidence. The children – there were so many, **so many** – there was something about their faces, their expressions, which had to be frozen by death, which strangely if defiantly weren't entirely identical from shot to shot. There was something about their postures, too, that – again and again – displayed a variety of action. Flipping the photographs, like frames of films, it didn't escape their notice how the world dashed into silence.

Notebooks – stacked heap atop heap – ranted at their readers past the edges of their pages. Words **everywhere** bled, carved into existence by a meticulous if fragile script. Its author felt compelled to document **everything**. Everything that transpired, be it real or imagined.

Their contents aged awkwardly but it was their script's mania **not** fade which made the tomes indecipherable. Only by–the–by were phrases coherent enough to read – like islands of clarity amidst expanses of absurdity. Fits of madness were what materialized into the margins and left the boys confused as ever. Lost ventures were lamented. Lost reputations were agonized. Screeds, against politicians and 'rabble rousers from Colorado Springs' 'stirring the pot' remained to echo for the ages to make sense of.

A notebook spread to its last **written** sheet waited atop the draft table. Cody lit it while Peter read it:

"'Caught **THE DOG**. Idiot prowled the house a couple of days ago, yelping and yelping, and digging my walls. Why won't it shut? Last thing I need is busybodies hearing it. Can't be too careful with snoops–what's–their–names. Mind your own business for once lady. Can't speak of regrets. Not with a chance to fix a mistake. Yeah, he kept your kiddies safe, didn't he, **JEFFERSONVILLE**? Couldn't even keep his dog a–'"

"So it just stops," Cody shuddered.

A cutout of newsprint dominated the cork board. That article, headlined '**Elvin Clinic Shut By Order Of The JVPD**', dated to '73. Its story told of the mayor's caving to pressure from activists who demanded moral and civic purity. The mayor's picture had been scratched straight into the wall. Clippings twisting out of the '73 profile chronicled a who's who of disappearances that followed. The mayor's daughter consumed a lot of area. The record expanded then stopped at a headline that shouted '**Not Missie Too! Beloved Town Mascot, Only Known Abduction Survivor, Missing!**'. **That** article dated to '84 and there wasn't anything posted after it.

Fumbling through that study, braving for a sign, elusive as it was, to explain what may or may not have happened, they discovered a clue by the freezer. There the shelves had collapsed and jammed a door – a door like a barn door, wooden and heavy. Its paint distressed into a shade of moss where it rotted. There the shelves had imploded so utterly that its shrapnel refused to yield. Its debris **did not budge** until they stomped it by foot. Freed, thus, by violence, the door that had been blocked for a decade creaked away from the abyss as if pushed. **Pushed** across time and space – as their flashlights revealed – for the door's other side had been gouged. Tools and claws alike tore tracts into the wood at frantic, desperate angles.

Peter and Cody stood under the door's frame.

A large round dumpster dominated the view. That fixture was peppered by decals and other, medical arcana. 'ELVIN' and a downtown Jeffersonville address were stamped onto it. Their flashlights scrubbed the site by the dumpster. It hadn't shifted, rather, its weight appeared to crack the floor. Over it, at the ceiling, they located the hole, **the hole** forced into the den.

Far from that rent, estranged by a slant of shade, lay the body. Garments very, very roughly kept its putridity together. Its hands fisted fingers where ears would have been. Its face shriveled – a scream had been punched into its expression. Whoever it was, they died, curled like a fetus, askew of that hole it failed to broaden wide enough to exit through.

"I don't like how that dumpster's just sitting there."

"Figured it couldn't be a dog."

"Who's gonna say what it is."

At the end they peeked into the dumpster.

Tarps, of lumpy, coarse textures, filled the dumpster to its midpoint. Each were amply tagged and stamped. Their labels blazed words like '**MEDICAL**' or '**HAZARD**'.

The boys stretched then recoiled their touch. It felt as if they stroked a fire. Their words failed to converge. Only the language of their eyes betrayed their glimmer of the tarp's contents.

Shock mounted as they realized what lay atop that pile.

Its head, twisted to a degree unnatural, rested between its front, crossed legs.

For a spell it merely looked asleep.

Then – **in front of their eyes** – as a gust rattled that house – that which had been lodged at the rent above tumbled below into the dumpster. A collar landed by the dog – **that collar**, it was what they had spotted jumbling and twinkling – its glint came from its medallion – it read 'Missie'.

★

Follow The Traffic

Officer – don't tell me – I know it – **I know it!** It's all over your face. I'm damned. If truth were a trillion times as strange, I'd be a trillion times as damned. I know it – oh – **I see it!** Right at the start, you figure, **I'm crazy.** 'Ya **spent how many hours drivin'?** Drivin'! Chasin' the **dynamic** duo. Honestly, part of me doesn't want to believe it – yet – how about that **evidence?** How's it denied, explained? You keep askin' 'n' askin' **'why won't ya remember their plate'?** – as if I or anyone would've! I don't, **just**, I don't remember their plate, OK?

So it's September – fall at NJIT – **not** Rutgers. Somebody said **Rutgers** – ah, ah – **N J I T.** It's gotta be Tuesday; my class won't start 'til 6 PM. I leave my apartment at 4 PM to beat traffic. What do you want me to say? – it's my habit to be early – I **hate** traffic. I drive to Newark from West New York. It's **all routine** and when it's **all routine** what do you remember? **Next to nil** – that's what you remember.

Except – as I exited the 'Pike at 15W – there's this, this **slow–as–heck** ado at **my** right-hand side. It's a gray car. It's old, **real, real** old. It's battered bumper-to-bumper – **amazin'** – that it's still movin'.

You're givin' me **that** look. Perhaps you've seen it too? – seen it – and, I wager – forgot it. That's the idea. Oh, yes. **That's the idea.** The car's a common, everyday car – **exactly** the kind you get tired of lookin' at.

Traffic's a crawl and thanks to its snarl I get a look. What a look! Damn, what a look. It wasn't the car, though. It was the driver! **He** made the impression.

I'm talkin' of a man who's gotta be seventy – na, na – older! Devil only knows how **older.** His face's as beat as his car's. He's dressed like he walked out of the 1960's. I mean it – that drippin' trippin' hippie stuff – head–to–toe 1960's. The shades were a piece of work – big 'n' thick – freakishly so.

Ah, already I forget the smile. I swear to you, **Officer**, it's a corpse's smile. No – don't get me wrong – that's not what I think he is. It's that he sported this ear-to-ear, lipless sort of smile. Hard to shake a sight like it.

I'm laughin', thinkin' – **'well that's a guy right out of a time warp'!**

The idiot behind **me** honks as if I'm the issue.

Let me spare you. My classes, yeah, they're not **popular** classes. Few study my field. Eh, **physics.** It's a tiny little community. We know each other. Go ask anybody. I'm there attendin' that evening.

It's a night class that ends at 9 PM. I don't leave 'til half an hour later. Newark – what do you want me to say – it's the not the place where you want to be caught in traffic. I wait 'til it eases. I take Raymond, left to McCarter, right to I–280. Traffic's a breeze. I tell you, I **hate** traffic. At the plaza, mergin' from I–280 to the 'Pike, that's my next **W T F** moment. My next! What do you think I see at **my** left-hand side? You got it! It's that old gray car and that old gray man.

'**Still sportin' that smile**', I say.

That night – I don't sleep – **insomnia**. Mostly, it's due to my imagination (**not an excuse**). Mostly, it's due to my addiction (**coffee**). I can't put it out of my mind. **Coincidence!** How many times in a year, **say**, in a year – how many times do we encounter the exact car, the exact driver? – at the 'Pike of all places? Well – alright – how many times **that we notice**? Could be that we don't realize it.

The next two days, Wednesday 'n' Thursday, my class is at 10 AM. The last day, Friday, my class is at 9 AM. I tell you so you understand I go to NJIT five days a week and my schedule's not identical day-to-day. Yet – **at least once per day** – I encounter the grays. It's to the point where I'm wonderin' '**did we cross paths Monday**'?

You realize it, don't you, how weird it is. 'Til I **noticed** it, how often was it happenin'? How many weeks or months or years were we intersectin'?

Look, you don't need to tell me, I said it, I got it. **Madness!** Try it, why don't you? See how many cars follow you around the state!

Of course, it wasn't **just** the 'Pike, north or south bound, eastern or western spur, where I kept seein' 'em. I see 'em at Broad, at Bergenline. I catch sight of 'em crossin' Tonnelle.

I needed, **wanted** to know – '**what's goin' on**'? Eh, but not enough to jeopardize my studies. That's why I wait 'til Friday to make my move. Friday, I leave NJIT, steadied, focused. I **hunt** for my gray friends. **Nothing!** Damn it all. The roads are clear. The week after that, the whole entire week after that, clear, clear, clear. **Everywhere**. Not an accident **anywhere**, you know what I mean? Not a whiff of traffic. Them? – they're nowhere to be found.

The next few weeks I got nil to show for it. '**Til** – oh – let's say it's Thursday? I'm sure it's Thursday. It's that day – **that day** – I take the plunge. Fate arranges for us to converge at the 'Pike, eastern spur, south bound, gettin' to exit 15W. I'm followin' the **dynamic** duo instead of goin' to class. I track 'em to see where they're goin', what they're doin'. I rationalize my act – it's the urge to know – it's too great to overcome.

My heart skips a beat – yeah – I'm doin' this, **I'm doin' this** – no retreatin'!

Well, then, it's exit 14. From the plaza we maneuver about the interchange. Then we're drivin' by the airport. Then we're mergin' into I–78, west bound. It's not long after that and we're drivin' the Parkway. It wasn't for long only a stretch – a mile so and so. Then it's Route 24. I tell myself, '**we're going somewhere, right**'?

For half an hour the two us we're drivin' through Morris County. I waver, gettin' a little close, gettin' a little far. It's frustratin' like you can't believe it simply to maintain that speed of theirs. I follow 'em about four car lengths behind. Other drivers – they don't get between us – we're goin' **slow**.

We detour across Route 10 then we switch to Route 46. You got it – it's clogged bumper-to-bumper at that hour. I gotta play it cool. Yeah, the distance between us, it comes and goes. I'm near enough – by-the-by – that I see their plate. All I remember – it's blue, **their plate**, it's blue. I should have jotted the tag but what am I gonna do about it?

After thirty minutes of agony at Route 46, we switch, **again**, we switch to Route 15. We reach Sparta and by then it's gotta be 8 AM. It's too far and too late to get back to NJIT for my class. At Sparta, we turn into a county road, **is it 517**? Yeah – eh – we turn into Route 206.

Ah – at first, it's clear, the road, **it's clear**. They **fidget**. What else am I gonna call it? Soon the road gets dense 'n' dense and they **relax** all the way into a standstill.

I gawk at my fuel. I filled my car earlier that week. It's readin' half a tank. I know my car; it's got a lot left, a lot left, enough to continue. I, though, I'm not doin' that good.

I'm sittin', it's Route 206, I'm sittin', **hours**, endurin' snarl after snarl. I miss lunch. I'm hungry and thirsty. For food I got a couple of chips and a thermos full of coffee. I take advantage of the standstill to feed. What I'd do for a stretch! My legs keep screamin' to go.

I drive and I ask – who, I donno – I ask '**what are the grays up to**'? – they won't stop.

At Trenton – it's almost 4 PM – we make the shift to the 'Pike. It's exit 7. There we switch to the Parkway – traffic's a nightmare. Why? – I can't say. Radio's lousy. Accident? Construction?

The sun's set, amigo, this drive of ours, it keeps goin' 'n' goin' past dinner.

We take exit 37, north bound. We start this stretch where we're wanderin' through byways. The roads, they're narrowin'. They're gettin' more 'n' more lousy. We gotta take it easy. That wild stretch, road after road of it, it doesn't matter where we go, it's simply awful **everywhere**. I keep thinkin' how dangerous it is.

Yes, **Officer**, I know, it's stupid. I just don't stop. I put so much time and so much distance – enough to sacrifice a day – if I stop, what do I show for it? Heck, how do I get home? I just can't stop 'til I know their secret. We're smack in the middle of nowhere NJ and I say to myself that we've gotta be **close** to their garage. At least **close** to where ever it is they rest at night.

Twenty miles of **that** and we're at Route 1 – it's 1 AM and we're at Route 1.

I hadn't gone to class. I got no food, no drink anymore. Eh, besides coffee. Sleep's 'bout to be the next 'no'. I'm followin'. It's a drive to anywhere at the slowest possible speed.

It's a miracle that I survived to reach 2 AM – that's when he pulls into an Exxon. Can't tell you where. **NJ**! I opt for the Mobil across the street.

The attendant services my car and I'm free to pace at the curb. A narrow two-lane road's what separates the stations. It's late but the stars are lit and I see everything above 'n' below. I see the driver – the driver who never exited the car – speak to another, unseen passenger by him at the front.

Look, he's talkin' to **somebody** who's in that car of his. OK – his attendant's standin' 'n' lookin' there straight at whatever that man's talkin' to. A child? A pet? I donno – it hadn't struck me that there would be a passenger. Yet – **something** moves right under my line of sight. The passenger's seat, you know, you know, it reacts like something's shiftin' about.

He whips a fist full of cash and pays – **then** – I follow.

Neither I nor the grays were givin' it up.

Where does he get that cash?

I pace the grays from night to day through Routes 1, 1 & 9, and 9 past Fort Lee almost into NY. Then – back, back, **again** – into NJ by takin' a bite out of the Palisades. We cut through twisty dusty byways of northern Bergen County 'til we intersect Route 4. We head to Paramus. Then it's down Route 17. Then it's up Route 3. Into Jersey City, we merge through the traffic of the Holland then the Lincoln tunnels. We cruise through Washington Street in Hoboken where I almost lose sight of 'em at 14th Street. We – **we?** – look at that – we climb the viaduct over to Union City, maneuver into Hilltop, then, circle onto Liberty State Park. That's where we get into the I–78 extension and reach Newark. Then, it's Route 21 to I–80, west bound.

I follow, and I gotta say it, it's my insomnia that saves me.

I tune the radio to 1010 – it entertains me with traffic reports – **those** are the forecasts. A truck jack-knifed at the eastern spur? – **to the 'Pike**! As I sit there I realize there's no pattern **yet** there's a pattern. The movements – the strange driver and the strange car – they go for the traffic.

See, yeah, every time I spotted the **dynamic** duo, the roads were congested. Circumstances didn't matter. Just that it's congested **with traffic**. It's when the coast's clear – like it gets every now 'n' then – that's when they **fidget**. You know what it's like when you really, really need to go but can't? That's what it's like with the grays. When it's clear, they're drivin' nervous, switchin' lane to lane. How do I put it into words? – **normal** people, when there's traffic, switch to the lane that's movin' fastest. Imagine **the opposite**.

Officer, listen, listen, OK, yeah, I get it. **But don't you**? How do I quit? What do I tell myself if I quit?

The grays, they're lookin' for the trouble.

In my imagination I formulate a plan. Eventually, the driver or the passenger or the car itself – **something's got to give**! They've got to reach a house. A hotel. A stop. A **whatever**! They've got to rest, don't they? When the driver pulls the car over, I gotta confront 'em. So I convince myself the end's near. I start workin' through what I gotta say to break the ice. I tense, ready to act, every time we turn into a town. But he doesn't stop. And I don't stop either.

It's 10 AM – it's been a day since I entered a restroom. **Officer**, you understand me – you know what I did, don't you? Right in my car. Right in my seat. All over my pants.

Two hours later he stops at yet another Exxon.

I enter it – **'this is my chance'**! And right as I'm about to open my door, I stop. I couldn't. I **just** couldn't. I just couldn't get out of my car with my clothes like that.

What do you know? – he, **the driver**, he exits **the car**. He goes into the shop. I donno what he does. He returns empty-handed. Could be he used the ATM? **Cash**, like that, wow, where does it come from? Pension? Lottery? I mean – is, is this, **all of this**, this drivin', is this the bucket-list? What about food 'n' drink? He wasn't out of that car long enough for eatin'.

Then – as my eyes follow the driver – my ears startle. The car's passenger side door **shuts**. I was so captivated by the driver that I forgot the passenger. I missed, **completely**, what the passenger had been up to!

We drive yet another half a day without intervention – north, south, east, west. There ain't a place we avoid. We scour the state, soakin' its vistas **of its traffic**. At night, it's the 'Pike, from exit 1 to exit 18, then, it's every byway 'n' alley throughout Passaic County.

It's morning – my concentration's a losin' battle. It's then – **then** – that it strikes me. At my least lucid, it strikes me. Come on, **Officer**, I don't – I can't – I could have followed the grays over every inch of highway and I wouldn't have understood anything. I wouldn't have faced 'em. Their secret? Forget it! There's no home for 'em to go. They've got to be the ultimate car and driver merely by their obscurity – a nondescript driver of a nondescript car – simply a part of the crowd where ever they go. They slip out of your sight 'cause their sameness makes 'em background not principle. I'm the random fluke – **to 'em** – if they notice me at all, I'm one out of a million to 'em.

It's clearer then than now. Now – I get it. Yet – as I connect these ideas into **something**, I fathom a way to get even with my rival. Yeah, he's the man of the traffic. Where ever there's a jamb, he's there, he's there – to **enjoy it** – to **revel it**. In the vastness of creation, there'd have to be something like it, wouldn't there?

We're at the 'Pike – it's a clear stretch of road past exit 13A. They're shiftin' lane to lane. That's where I go for it. It's not madness, though, 'cause I understand exactly what I want to do – **and why I want to do it**! It's the only way, truly, to stop 'em.

I speed and ram into the grays – our cars connect for what's like forever.

What're they gonna do now? **Complain**? I'm givin' 'em what they want – **an accident**! – to clog the traffic. Now **they** would be part of the blockage. They wouldn't be a faceless bystander, soakin' the misery, now, they'd be the **one** feelin' the traffic, front and center, star of the show!

Just like that, though, the grays release a superhuman, certainly, a supermechanical surge of speed. Through **their** rear view mirror I spy my last look of the driver – the passenger isn't even a suggestion. Me, I'm transfixed by his expression so, so utterly that even as I saw 'em speed, I fail to realize that I'm crashin' into an embankment.

Officer – look – that's the story. Fantastic! Unbelievable! But you got me out of that wreck. You noticed it? Didn't you? **You noticed it**! Same as I. How does insanity conjure it? – right there, right there – stickin' through the mangled trash of my car – it's their rear bumper!

★

Blue Beelzebub

For years, years, I wondered – 'why me' – you know, you know, kiddo – 'why me' – but there is no 'why me'. What? As if there were, you know, 'chosens', there's no 'chosens' – there's no all–seeing, all–knowing powerful nothing. It happened. That's it. I fell for it. I took its bait – hook, line, sinker. Didn't I do it to myself? Wasn't I the sucker? There's no 'why me' – and once I realized that, that there was no, that there was no, no any kind of justice what so ever, until I acted, that gave my existence purpose. And now I'm gonna fulfill that purpose. I don't want you getting involved. You're deep enough as it is. Don't be the sucker!

– Bobby Mortaren; famous last words

I raced from the house to the hotel, at Walsenburg, where I struggled to make sense of everything that transpired. I poured myself over notes and records that I had brought along. Only my laptop's glow illuminated the room. Every so often lights through I-25 swept across the bed. Every so often breezes stirred trees around the perimeter. Soon midnight passed. The world darkened, relaxing as it were into slumber.

A knock rattled the door – and I could have shrieked if it weren't for what remained of my nerves. All of a sudden, I felt so icy, so cold, that I stood, **frozen**, uncertain of how to proceed. Who was it? It couldn't be good. Not the FBI. Not the Thules. **Ache**, already?

I balked at chucking my laptop – whoever they were at the door, they'd find it, **they'd find it**.

'Twas the 21st century; evidence doesn't vanish without a trace.

As my heart pounded my chest, I reached that door and cracked it a notch. I braced for the kick certain to follow. It didn't come. The hotel's courtyard / lot spread, deserted except for my rented Wrangler. There wasn't anyone – anyone who may have been my visitor.

Yet – by my feet – at the edge of the threshold – I had been left a box.

I poked at it with my pole and turned it over and over. It wasn't postmarked. It wasn't addressed. It had been delivered by hand and, suspecting what it was, I yanked it inside. Leaning onto and drooping against the door, I tore its lid. The box contained two floppies, a CD, and a stack paper. It was **Blue Beelzebub** – all of it, every part of it. As well as instructions: a How–To–Guide for destroying your future, fetched onto my doorstep, white–glove–style to boot, as promised. It may as well have been a bomb.

How did **Blue Beelzebub** mutate into my obsession?

Worse – did I expect to find its truth remarked into code from 1996? **1996!**
There wasn't a lot to the internet way, way back when. But crime was crime no
matter its era. Was it crime? And did the game start this way or that way then
evolve into crime? Was it crime **from its start**?

The programmer of **Blue Beelzebub**, a hacker by the avatar 'ZuZu', claimed to
be legit. Their MO had been to create games not scams. Or so it appeared until
Blue Beelzebub entered the story. If it were a product of malware, why had
ZuZu devoted so much of their effort into its creation? Why had they boasted
of the game's nitty gritty details during its gestation? Why all of that trouble,
if only a fraction of it would have been appreciated by those who played it?
Even LVN, when they weren't laundering bitcoin, expressed what may be
described as **passion** for that game.

Was it a game?

By 1996 standards, its demos parlayed atrocious graphics and threadbare
mechanics. The way it affected the player's rig ensured nobody would be eager
to replay it. The game passed every scan available yet it twisted the OS and
hijacked the PC to serve as a node, a link into a yet-unknown and yet-
unnamed network for purposes every bit as mysterious as the game itself.

As I contemplated the reality of the situation, I settled onto the notion that
that game may have been a gimmick to cover truly malevolent intentions.
That had been the crux of LVN's <u>KickStarter</u> and <u>GoFundMe</u> rackets – they
always proposed plausible if lofty projects as if they were real, actual products
people buy. However, case after case demonstrated that their pretense
unraveled after scrutiny. Could it be, as far back as 1996, the creator(s) of **Blue
Beelzebub** conceived of such a deception? FPS (of the type **Blue Beelzebub**
reported to be) were the rage through the 90s. If so then their MO resembled
that of a typical bait-and-switch scheme – bait them with a game, switch them
with a virus. Then? What? Profit?

In the summer of 2017, Czech authorities in conjunction with the EU, arrested LVN at their apartment south of Plzen. They seized the hacker's laptop, PC, as well as their twenty thousand CD library. LVN was a hacker-for-hire; evidence presented at their arraignment demonstrated to the court that they had been paid by Russian and other Eastern European actors to pilfer bitcoin wallets. In addition to theft, the court entertained charges connected to a MeanRash heist of 64 million euros earlier that year.

It was the breach of MeanRash's security that brought my skills to the EU's attention. For a few weeks, between March and May, I played my part to aid the investigation and the conviction of its mastermind. We discovered that the breach had been directed from **inside** MeanRash. We split the work: 'brick and mortar' detectives ran interviews and stakeouts while my fellow 'white-hats' and I toiled at the forensics. To meet our end of the bargain, we created a model of that cyber-attack, in order to construct and deconstruct its operation. As we realized how the crime had been executed, we identified the party responsible for it and built the authorities a solid chain-of-evidence – a chain-of-evidence that identified LVN as the perpetrator.

LVN masterminded not just that MeanRash heist but a dozen scams at sites like KickStarter and GoFundMe. LVN traded **exclusively** through bitcoin. Their MO was to sow **fake** projects then to reap **real** funds submitted by backers – by backers who aimed to launder bitcoin via its exchange into euros. Projects were advertised to those who sought the service; they were fraudulent through and through yet they appeared real enough to fool the maintainers of those sites and the public at large who may have been tricked by the scams.

Under the supervision of the investigation at large, I pledged my dollars to a few of LVN's projects, to see what the response would be. Soon, LVN and I exchanged emails. They wanted to speak face-to-face. In front of the experts, I played to type and gained access to a roster of services from that hacker-for-hire. As a result of the communication, the investigation brought into play anti trafficking & exploiting agencies from around the world and accelerated their goal to convict LVN.

One of the projects LVN advertised didn't fit into the mold in so far as it felt like a genuine hobby of theirs. LVN sought investors to fund their (re)development of a game, **Blue Beelzebub**. The project listed at KickStarter – removed but saved to my laptop – included a lightbox of images and demos as well as snippets of code. It discussed such esoterics as: updates to its physics engine and its video & audio renderer; upgrades to its arsenal and its gallery of foes; changing its play – expanding its levels and ditching its linearity.

The details impressed me as they perplexed me. **Why?** I kept asking. What's the idea? What's the racket? Why create a game using twenty year old technology? I understood its esoterics perfectly for I came of age during the 90s. So much of what went into **Blue Beelzebub felt** familiar as it **was** familiar. An FPS – **first person shooter** – propelled by a fork of that fabled, 2.5D DOOM engine. Little wonder that its caps parlayed the look and feel of classic 90s PC games!

Maybe it was yet another scam? Or – **maybe** – it was a hobby of a gamer / programmer? Could it be that LVN recalled those early DOS games and wanted to re-create the era? But that wasn't everything. And as I mused & Googled I started to ask myself if there wasn't more about **Blue Beelzebub** beyond the haze of my nostalgia. I failed to connect the dots although it didn't shake the déjà vu that somehow, someway, I recognized that game.

Escape published my article about LVN's conviction. Against the advice of my editor, I stalked its commentary, to see what, if anything, the story drew out of the woodwork. Its aside re: **Blue Beelzebub** attracted attention. I wasn't surprised, to be honest, as I had inserted it into the text to draw reaction. And my rouse worked! But I wasn't the only one who felt déjà vu about the game.

A commentator, who asked for anonymity, posted a link to 4CHAN about **Blue Beelzebub**. LVN had advertized the KickStarter for the game at a group devoted to indie game developers. LVN never advertized their work at 4CHAN out of fear of exposure. So that thread where they didn't ask for money confirmed my sense that it wasn't, **necessarily**, a scam.

As I scanned that thread, however, I realized what a rabbit-hole the business would be. After LVN's post, anonymous replies went to and fro as they typically do. Then the tenor of the thread devolved into a war amongst those who were for vs. those who were against what LVN proposed to do with the game. It was a question about **credit**. At last – somebody revealed a truth I duly suspected of – that **Blue Beelzebub** wasn't the work of LVN – that the game, as it existed, **predated** LVN by twenty years or so.

The idea for **Blue Beelzebub** had floated about USENET c. 1997. The majority of the conversations extracted from the archives suggested that the game was vaporware. Its supporters countered that either a P/C or a DEMO existed and that a play-through had been uploaded to (early) YouTube. Everyone who added their opinion – pro & con – agreed that it was "inspired by Satan", "took its cues from Crowley's 'Thelema'", and that it included clips "replete with ever more corrupt" gore and snuff. A self-described player, whose rig they claimed had been "totaled" by the game, stated bluntly that it contained a "Chinese Sandwich".

Undeterred by the confusion, I kept at my search, ramming through the archives, pushing my way further back in time, from 1997 to 1995. USENET had been mirrored prior to its collapse yet its content wasn't indexed **completely**; a robust query of its posts required force and patience.... In spite of the odds, my effort worked, my persistence located the roots of **Blue Beelzebub**.

It was a post dated June 15, 1995 written by the game's **originator**, a hacker by the name of ZuZu. According to their missive, they claimed to have produced "a proof of concept demo" for their "latest and greatest" game, **Blue Beelzebub**, and that it was "a legit game catering to those who worship and admire Lucifer and everything that stands for". ZuZu listed, point by point, the substance of their creation. I wasn't surprised to see, splattered across that post, the verbiage LVN usurped for their own advert.

Except – they weren't seeking funding. According to their missive, the game had been bankrolled "by entities of a foreign sort, who don't want to be credited". Rather, they were seeking "experts" willing to alpha & beta test the product.

Blue Beelzebub and by extension ZuZu went rouge between 1997 and 2005.

Then – October 31, 2005 – ZuZu submitted their last, known public statement. Broadcasted through their usual, over-the-top flamboyance, they wished for their "fans to learn and spread the word" that they "secured an exclusive". They had convinced a devote of indie horror / FPS games to review **Blue Beelzebub**. The player they had snagged was famous for their day and their name I recognized as I read it.

Bobby Mortaren – an internet **pioneer** par excellence. Mixing reviews and play-throughs together, his format had been lauded as visionary and just as imitated. Tweaked a bit by-the-by it continued to find use. His name, though, hadn't been spoken of for a decade. Games had changed. Tastes had changed. He could have shifted into yet another venture so far as I knew.

Mortaren posted his works to YouTube – to YouTube **prior to** its merger with Alphabet. As I considered the changes that transpired across the years, I wasn't surprised to discover that all of my links to his works were dead. Eerily, though, it was impossible to locate his reviews **directly** via YouTube. So I tried Google and Bing. No result. Ditto with DuckDuckGo. Ditto with Wiki, SlideShare, BoardReader. Out of desperation I surfed into the remnants of Alta Vista – maybe its database saved the information? No. Futile – all of it.

YouTube's size was greater than USENET's size. My task's extent was altogether a colossal order of magnitude. If that which I pursued had not been deleted, then, it would be found **ad finem omnia**. So to dig further I opted for a quick & dirty hack – a bot. A bot scripted to sift and sort all YouTube's content that matched keywords Mortaren and **Blue Beelzebub**. I ran it and waited for days then for weeks then for months.

My extensive search corroborated the fact that Mortaren left the internet c. 2006. Assuming they may have continued via pseudonym, I enquired into the matter with colleagues who devoted themselves to games and / or to reviews. Only a few recognized their name; nobody was cognizant of their voice.

An editor from <u>ToplessRobot</u> directed my attention to a defunct fansite's messageboard where somebody asked why Mortaren vanished without a trace. To my shock, the reply was that Mortaren had been arrested by the FBI c. 2006. I couldn't fathom why. Nevertheless, if the revelation were correct, then, the resolution to the matter was tantalizingly viable. Arrests – and trials – were **public**.

The LVN / EU case brought my forensic skills to the notice of the DOJ and the Treasury / Secret Service. The FBI, like its European counterparts, wanted to understand everything about bitcoin and how it might (**might**) be possible to trace transactions to individuals.

As part of my freelance work, I already met and debriefed FBI agents re: the Czech hacker. Eventually 'large' talk gave way to 'small' talk amongst us. It was at that juncture that I broached the subject of **Blue Beelzebub** – namely, that LVN hatched a scheme to defraud investors (via bitcoin) ostensibly by promising to develop an update to that game.

"They got exposed by players who recognized the game's ill-repute," I stated. "Apparently, the game's infamy started after its reviewer, a fellow by the name of – er – Robby Mortaren? Bobby Mortaren? Well – they got arrested by the FBI."

Neither the game nor the reviewer elicited a reply – **immediately**, anyhow.

A (censored) document, summarizing a DOJ investigation, worked its way into my mailbox. Mortaren had been under FBI surveillance from November 2005 to May 2006. **Why** wasn't stated; just that the FBI obtained search warrants for computers & electronics. A federal judge issued an arrest warrant May 30, 2006; however, the DOJ withdrew the charges after Mortaren agreed to an immunity deal. Mortaren turned **star** witness at a trial that involved organized crime as well as rackets, cults, ritualized human & civil rights abuses and elements that suggested **Satanism**. The perpetrator(s) that the DOJ wanted to convict fled either to South America OR Eastern Europe / Central Asia. The trial evaporated; neither the charges nor the perpetrator(s) were detailed.

Mortaren's immunity deal with the DOJ wasn't negotiable or retractable and included a complete internet ban.

The document listed a PO BOX as Mortaren's **permanent** address.

To Mr. B. Mortaren:

Sir, I apologize. <u>Blue Beelzebub</u>. Were it not for the fact that you may be the only person left to recall that game, I would not have stretched my resources so thin to find you. If you aren't able to assist my research, is anyone?

*I was part of an EU investigation re: bitcoin, theft & fraud, as well as trafficking & exploiting vagrants. Through that investigation I came into contact with a hacker; they claimed to be working on <u>Blue Beelzebub</u>; they sought funds to upgrade it. While disturbing to say the least, that game didn't strike me as part of the hacker's MO. So I pried further into the matter and discovered, to my astonishment, that <u>Blue Beelzebub</u> dated to the mid 90s and that you reviewed & posted the demo at **YouTube**.*

I am curious about that game. I cannot get it out of my head. Who was the programmer? Who was the developer? Where did they get the money? What were their goals? What was the game about, if the game was about anything?

A DOJ document summarizing your immunity from prosecution was brought to my attention. I suspected, as I matched the timeframe of the FBI's surveillance and arrest, to the demo, that these matters are related. I wasn't able to find a link, due to the fact that all records, transcripts, etc., were sealed by request of the FBI.

If, for any reason what so ever, we cannot communicate about this matter, would it be possible to contact a surrogate or anybody with the information I seek?

With All Due Respect

JK

Due to limits that existed at YouTube's debut, videos posted from 2005 to 2010 were capped to 10 minutes. Both image and sound playback quality were kept low to spare bandwidth. A lack of (accessible) software and hardware to edit video forced vloggers to improvise. Mortaren's shtick was to use a webcam and mic from the 90s to shot their videos 'live', i.e., without edits.

YouTube retained the majority of Mortaren's content; however, after a check of the dates and the IDs, I determined that Mortaren's videos had been reposted c. 2007 by another user.

If the titles / numbers were correct then there were seven parts to the demo Mortaren recorded for **Blue Beelzebub**. Of seven, six remained. Specifically, the 5ifth – which must have been filmed as evidenced by the discontinuity between 4ourth and 6ixth – defied my ability to trace.

The reposter stated that "the 5ifth wasn't part of the review package". Yet, as I perused copies of replies they had saved, commentary that referenced material that doesn't appear anywhere **else**, I strongly suspected that a 5ifth had been posted for a while and, for whatever reason, Mortaren removed it prior to arrest.

1irst – details facts re: the game: the developer, the programmer, the system requirements, etc.

"If your rig's able to run DOOM, **Blue Beelzebub** works," they state then add: "although, prepare yourselves, kiddos, the game takes a very, very long time to install".

Passingly, he adds that a fan of his had ditched the game after they experienced "a catastrophic system failure" that they blamed "on either a bug or a virus or both".

The executable and its auxiliary files pass every virus and malware checker Mortaren throws at it.

2econd & 3hird – demonstrates game play or what passes for it.

"There's no backwards, I don't believe it! Did they forget to give us backwards? There's forwards and left, right. Kiddos, you gotta do a circle to go backwards." He continues to berate the game, adding: "Yeah, there's only forwards. And you know, I gotta say it, the programmer may think they're the monkey's nuts for it.... But it's so weird that going forwards causes the view to bob up and down or side to side. What're they trying to do? Are they trying to replicate a player's gait? Takes me right out of the game. Let me tell y'all why. Like I said, the programmer's got to be thinking they're the monkey's nuts but it's that bizarro attention to detail that's so jarring as I consider the **lack** of detail given to the graphics. Guys. Guys. Guys. You gotta think about what you present."

Mortaren piles his criticism of the graphics and the sounds, comparing both unfavorably to DOOM. Especially frustrating is the invariance of the black & white textures throughout the maze. He praises the **response** of the maze to the player as he notes, while attempting to draw maps, that passages shift at random. Then more and more criticisms were strewn at the game, including its lack of weaponry, its lack of powerups / extras, its lack of **anything**.

"A game can't be about going through the maze, guys, there's got to be a point – something to do!" Finally, he voices the suspicion that he had been duped by ZuZu.

4ourth – the demo gets interesting.

Mortaren finds an area of the maze where the textures **differ**. The video's pixilation – perhaps due to the webcam – perhaps due to the way the reposter preserved it – masks the bulk of the alteration. I detect a change of shade, though, from black & white to blue.

"Well it can't be for nothing that the wall is blue!" As he cracks the joke, to his shock (an explicative slips), the sounds became those of "eerie, drone-like notes fading into reverb" and the monitor displays a still-shot. Mortaren zooms into the image; I recognize it as coming from the shock–site, <u>ROTTEN</u>.

After that alteration, every blue–hued texture Mortaren faces produces other images, increasingly nihilistic and graphic, usually of the dead or the dying, often of celebrities, suicides, accidents, wrecks.

5ifth – ?

6ixth – the segment starts at an awkward jump.

It must have been split from the 5ifth video and while Mortaren doesn't state why, explicitly, the tone of the voice suggests that something serious transpired.

"Sorry, kiddos – a first – I guess ZuZu accomplished something."

When he returns the webcam to the monitor, it is apparent that in addition to tone the substance of the game itself altered.

The player stands at the center of a room Mortaren describes as "a vault with a hole at its floor". The 2.5D renderer prevents the player from gazing inside the hole. But by directing the player to walk the hole's circumference it is possible to catch bits of its contents. A sharp, blue light shoots out of the hole; the way it cast light at the ceiling suggests there might have been "water", as if the hole were a well of sorts.

What shocks Mortaren is that the room fills with children. The renderings of faces make each of the children unique. However: "the ghastliness of the imagery resembles how faces voxilate like with Delta Force games". Further, he notes, after a pause that echoes my own consternation and trepidation, "I've seen these kids. Yeah, I've seen these kids from those, those photographs the game stopped everything to show us!"

The children stand statue–like as the player walks about them. They serve as obstacles that block movement, otherwise, "they're inert, unresponsive", "not that the player interacts with the kids as there's no other keys available except A, W, D".

The video continues, then, Mortaren shrieks.

The playback jostles as if it were about to stop. When everything resettles, he speaks, calmly and evenly, that "there's a kid that's different ... **animated**. You gotta see it, kiddos, I can't say if it's **awful** because it's awful or if it's awful because it's **awful**...." The webcam zooms into the monitor; the child rendering appears to show it **breathing**, haphazardly, with their mouth agape. And then, then the child moves and the player like the viewer alike slip an explicative. "I take it back, everything, this is truly and utterly awful."

7eventh – the coda feels like the set's longest but is the shortest.

"Right now I'm running. I don't have a weapon! I'm running as fast as this keyboard allows but my health is shrinking." Mortaren stops and rotates the player to face backwards. The animated child is behind and striking the player using a technique that resembles "Hanna–Barbera laziness – or who knows – who knows, kiddos, it could be part of the style". Just as it is with DOOM, as the player's health decreases, the view gets redder and the avatar gets bloodier. Mortaren aims into the maze; there is no exit, there is no weapon, no upgrade, all that exists is the floor where the player drops, dead.

The 7eventh adds a post–script recorded after the demo. It shows Mortaren's PC, open and split to pieces. "The game installed a virus," he declared then described its symptoms.

"Immediately upon my player's death, the PC rebooted. After the BIOS, instead of going into DOS, it starts a telnet session and tries to connect via IP. Of course it doesn't get a reply since my PC uses dial–up. So it freezes, pinging and pinging a server somewhere that it cannot reach."

Mortaren concludes by theorizing that if **Blue Beelzebub** were a virus, it must have been designed to target high–end systems with LAN / Ethernet ports.

I jot the IP and attempt to connect to it. Strangely, it will not load yet it will not issue an error of any kind. Chrome, FireFox, Edge, etc., freeze. <u>WHOIS</u> isn't able to resolve the owner. Nevertheless, it yields the location of the server, a site approximately 50 miles north east of Trinidad, Colorado.

I reject the result; users of tracers already know that they rely on ISP databases to match IP / location – and how often are those databases updated? – and how often are those updates distributed? The decade that passed between today and the video, and between the video and the creation, assures that there must have been a drift re: the location of the server.

I won't reveal the particulars of when & where I received the call.

"Coordinates." Into my ear spoke a voice that my investigation made familiar. **"Coordinates."**

"Coordinates?"

"Blue Beelzebub."

"Yes," I replied and Mortaren implied we'd meet.

Mortaren had traced my whereabouts through the blogosphere. He wanted to talk about the game yet feared the government "and or others" eavesdropping. I admitted off-handedly that as I sunk into my work with the DOJ, my paranoia tipped.

"What's the deal with the game, anyway?"

"What do you want on your Chinese Sandwich?"

My impression settled onto a mixture of intrigue and trepidation. The matter felt so cryptic as to defy credulity. Coordinates? **Blue Beelzebub**. Chinese Sandwich? Nevertheless, even as we talked (brief as the conversation was) I put together that by coordinates + **Blue Beelzebub** Mortaren referred to the IP the game telnet'ed.

I didn't expect a reply to my letter.

Time – and deadlines – passed. My paying job took me through yet another cycle of crimes, forensics, trials. **Blue Beelzebub** didn't leave my imagination. I bookmarked then saved all of Mortaren's videos that had been reposted, and I watched them, trying and failing to find any clue to fit the parameters of what may have been the subject of the 5ifth video. I refined my bot and set it to mine <u>USENET</u> then <u>4CHAN</u> for everything that may yet be found about ZuZu and **Blue Beelzebub**.

Like every crazed and obsessed fan you encounter, I brought a cork board into my office to organize my investigation. Through it I spliced a timeline of events. ZuZu claimed they started the game's development c. 1995 after the original DOOM engine was hacked and released to a BBS. She used tools that I remembered from my own DOOM days to generate WADs and to serve as prototypes or proof–of–concepts. ZuZu detailed the work they put into utilities designed to assist their work – tools that transferred RCA signals into a digital format akin to AVI but thoroughly compressed. They went so far as to obtain a Commodore 64 to produce the music. She left trail after trail, tidbit after tidbit, detailing every aspect of the game's construction. ZuZu may not have had the letters after their name conferring degrees and whatnots but they were an expert–level and competent programmer of considerable talent. For better or worse the game **Blue Beelzebub** was their masterwork into which they poured all of their resources.

So I accepted the distasteful reality that the game demo'ed by Mortaren **was** the final product.

While evidence mounted of ZuZu's skills at game–building, I failed to find a reason let alone a motivation for creating that atrocity. What was their aim? Why devote so much time, certainly, so much money for a game that installed a virus into a PC?

2005, the last year anyone heard of **Blue Beelzebub** – until LVN's adverts – a plurality of the country clung onto dial–up. Scant PCs outside of government or university were equipped with LAN or WIFI. So why corrupt the average Joe's PC to telnet to an IP via LAN when few, if any PC, were so capable? Unless, if Mortaren's conjecture were correct, the game wasn't intended for the average Joe's PC.

I already mapped the server to a spot 50 miles out of Trinidad, Colorado: a spot abutting the quasi ghost town of Timpas. <u>Google</u> suggested it was a ruin by a railroad due south of the historical Santa Fe trail overlook. No photography of the area had been published so far as I determined. No reports of the ruins – or what may have produced the ruins – had been filed to any service. Chances were that that feature had been a part of the area for decades if not for centuries. Who would have put a server there? Who would have devised a game to connect to a server there? The rabbit-hole kept going. If only I had had that game in front of me....

You said that a fan of yours deconstructed the game and found videos inside it.

BM: "Yes, they reverse-engineered the code and as they sifted through it, they noted that up to about 50% of the original executable was devoted to these, er, these AVI clips. A lot of the files the game installed had to do with decrypting the clips. No, not decrypting, er, what word did they use ... decompress."

And those clips didn't play during the game at all?

BM: "Short, **say**, half a minute segments played. Not all of it. I'd say maybe 5% of the clips would have been seen by the player. The **longer** clips weren't referenced at least not directly. Amazingly, they inspire the bulk of the game's look and feel."

When you watched those clips, specifically, those *longer* clips, what did you think of them? Did they look authentic or rehearsed? Like, is the game a put-on?

BM: "Oh, if the game is a put on, kiddo. Didn't I want it to be fake, you know, you know what I mean? Yeah, like that <u>Blair Witch</u> flick. What wouldn't I give.... When I watched it, it felt real. It felt like, like I was watching something I shouldn't be. Like a snuff flick. Around me everything felt like it was shaking to pieces. It's real, though, what those kids were saying when...."

Mortaren stopped to wipe his brow with his sleeve.

You said that the bulk of the game's look and feel came from the clips. What do you mean by that?

BM: "The **longest** clip introduces you to the cult's leaders: Straniak and a woman, a woman I can't identify. She's an older woman, possibly of German descent, like Straniak. We see her direct the sex magic portion that starts the ceremony.

"Then there's actually a jump cut because that portion with the blood-letting, which Straniak is in charge of, that's its own clip and that's played during the game.

"After that jump cut, Straniak peels away the rug and under it, under where the pentagrams had been drawn, there's this hole.

"I don't think for a moment that the ceremony opened the hole. The ceremony must have consecrated it or whatever the equivalent is for that cult. The camera aims into the hole and it's like this dark space. Dark like space is dark.

"There's yet another jump cut and apparently the camera and Straniak are at the bottom of the hole where ever that is. It's obviously a cave or a mine that maybe the cult expanded and such. As the clip unwinds, the camera and Straniak reach the room – you know what I mean by that kiddo – the room where the player finds the kids. It's a real room."

So – let me get this straight – the journey the game's player makes is what's filmed at the end of that clip? [BM nods] Is there any audio? Are they talking at all about what they're doing?

BM: "The compression that ZuZu created preserved the images sort of, kind of at the expense of the audio. There's audio but it's twisted.

"Anywho, they're speaking German so I couldn't make heads or tails of it. It's subbed in English, though, er, somebody who knows German would be able to tell if the translation's good.

"Oh, they talk stuff about the echo, the weird, weird echo effects they notice. Stuff about the cold. Straniak, you can tell for sure, he was excited about that place. The camera kept talking about the walls and how the walls appeared to be changing or shifting.

"Kiddo – everything you experience playing the game, it came from that video."

It's crazy. Do you think the Thules or the followers of Crowley were ZuZu's backers? How else was she able to obtain that footage? I'm not ignorant about the occult, either, and the rituals, especially sex & sacrifice rituals, it sounds like it comes right out of the Thule's play book.

BM: "I suspect the money that paid for ZuZu came from folks connected to the Thules. And, I gotta say, I'm torn between two theories as to why.

"When it comes to magik [BM used air quotes] of that type, the **act** of re-playing the ritual through video and audio is enough to actually re-create the ritual. You know what I mean? So if you got the game installed and the game's playing that clip – even if it doesn't show it to you – the mere fact that it's playing that clip means that the ritual is happening **again**.

"So, look, they're not going to say, hey guys, wanna watch us have sex then kill a kid? Of course not. Nobody except the truly demented would be into that. But – if they package that experience as a game then they fool a whole lot of people. That's their logic. It's like they're magnifying the power of whatever it is they were trying to call through that hole.

"My other idea is to do with that IP, that server. Whatever **that** was about. We never got the game to interface with it properly. 'Though I suspect it's to do with compromising those who fell for it.

"I don't mean compromise because they take control of their PC. I think it's a type of **kompromat**, if you take my meaning, because of the content that's now on your PC and whatever the heck that IP / server might have contributed. Imagine taking it to the cops and the cops finding out what you're into. Well – look at what happened to me."

There are limits to what you can say about the DOJ investigation. From what I was given, it looked like the DOJ was ready to arrest – maybe ZuZu, maybe their backers – but that didn't go anywhere after the defendants escaped the country. What, if anything, do you know or are aware of?

BM: "Look, kiddo, you write about crime – ok, internet crime – crime is crime no matter what. It's so…. Argh! You know about that **Bulger** guy from Boston? That Mafioso who happened to be an FBI informant? The FBI let him get away with murder to keep him as an informant. **Blue Beelzebub**, maybe somebody realized what the game's occult ambitions were about and maybe just maybe let them get away."

The box that had been delivered to my hotel in Colorado contained a pair of floppies, a CD, and a stack of instructions. The whole of it comprised material that a fan of Mortaren's work delivered to the reviewer. To my knowledge it formed the kernel of an investigation into the nature of **Blue Beelzebub**. The instructions, replete with marginalia added by the fan and the reviewer, painstakingly detailed system requirements to run the game as its creators intended.

Out of an abundance of caution, I opted not to use a virtual machine setup. I wanted a rig that would be **extremely** isolated from the rest of the world – and which could be destroyed without impacting my work. It was quite a task to locate computers that fit the build; there had to be two of them; as well as a router to connect them to an ad hoc network.

The CLIENT, where the game would be installed, required DOS 5.0 to 6.2; it didn't require any flavor of Windows. The SERVER, where a suite of applications put together by the fan would be installed, required LINUX. The fan's suite had been designed to replicate the functionality of the IP / server **Blue Beelzebub** attempted to telnet. A router, which should not be connected to the internet, had to be programmed to redirect the IP address to the SERVER address.

Like Mortaren noted, the game's installation took an inordinate amount of time to complete. After it finished, I stopped everything to examine the CLIENT. The installation created a BB2 directory with the game; it came to about 5 MB of data. Unless the decompression scheme had been brutal to the CPU, those 5 MB of data and hundred or so files it created didn't account for the duration of the installation. I checked the DOS directory. As I suspected, the OS had been re-worked into an unrecognizable mess. The DOS directory contained a further 20 directories. Equally as disturbing, filenames for everything but COMMAND.COM had been renamed using extended ASCII characters.

I started the game and it went directly into the maze. There were no menus available; no save or load, no options of any kind, not even to quit the game. If **Blue Beelzebub** was a clone of DOOM, it had been radically stripped of its essentials. All that was left was the screen, the edges of the maze, and the player's hand.

I sat, face to face with my foe, that blasted **Blue Beelzebub.** My heart raced. I dared to disbelieve it, everything I went through to obtain it and to play it. It felt as if I were beside myself, disconnected to reality, a watcher, a gazer like a bystander to my very own life. I had gone to hell and back to satisfy a weird courtship and now, now past the nuptials, now I found myself alone with the bride. Knowing as I did, what to expect, that its end-game was hard-wired into the code, the shock of it energized me and I wanted to savor and document everything.

Mortaren's demos, hampered by the resolution of the webcam, scarcely gave the graphics any justice. The original programmer(s) captured the texture from the footage and re-created its vitality as photorealistic as 16-bit rendering allowed. As I progressed through the maze – and acclimated myself to its calamitous controls – I opted to draw a map exactly as Mortaren tried. I made my schematic larger, though, and filled it with notes where ever I encountered anomalous features that only playing the game one-on-one were capable of revealing. As my map expanded, I noted that its construction followed no rhythm, although from moment to moment the maze presented itself as exceedingly regular in width, in height as well as in texturing. Side passages, where they appeared as the player walked by, always spread at ninety degrees exactly as the layouts of early WOLFENSTEIN and DOOM were designed.

I added to my diagrams those spots where a picture or a clip appeared. The jumps started with the standard shock fare then escalated. Although Mortaren claimed that not a single image had been selected at random, I failed to note a pattern to their presentation – aside from the general trend of their becoming gruesome. Eventually, as the game dragged, the images featured its Chinese Sandwich **exclusively.** The clips, which flashed for a few seconds here and there and which never repeated or replayed, involved a scene that suggested an orgy with painted men and women shown writhing about a velvet floor.

It was at that juncture that I entertained the idea of shutting it off and walking away.

Having covered internet-based organized-crime for years, the sort of content I witnessed – as abstraction, so to speak – was always par for the course. Every so often censored content was displayed at trials I was privy to. It was yet another matter to have the raw imagery blasted in front of me on computers that I owned. All of a sudden I felt the enormity of Mortaren's paranoia. That's when and where I realized I was living through Mortaren's lost, 5ifth video.

I continued the game, if game it were, right into that spot where the maze ends at that chamber with the kids. At that juncture I noted activity stir at the network – the CLIENT system pinged the SERVER system. Acknowledgements, and a message that read "THRESHOLD", relayed from CLIENT to SERVER.

When the game shifted to its coda – that part where the player is chased to death by the animated kid – a sequence of numbers were exchanged between the systems. The numbers were always three digits, from 0 to 9, with no two consecutive repeats. According to the fan's instructions, the game used the player's keyboard input to select three digit groupings from a random number table included into the game and apparently based off the Golden Ratio. The game always came to an end not when the animated kid kills the player but when nine of those three digit groupings were selected. Again, according to the fan, the SERVER converted those 27 numbers into a 16–bit alpha numeric hash code which the CLIENT proceeded to check for validity. If it passed the game's check, it became the basis of a cryptographic network key unique to their connection.

Upon the player's death, the computer had been instructed to reboot.

When Mortaren reached that stage, of course, his computer wasn't connected to the internet so it ground to a halt when the telnet tried and failed to ping the SERVER. The way my network had been setup, though, that problem was circumvented. The CLIENT's telnet pinged and the SERVER's script replied. The key exchanged between systems then the network entered a wait state.

According to the fan's instructions, having experimented not just with the game's code but with the hacked DOS, the SERVER system had the ability to wake the CLIENT system and feed it a stream of data. The CLIENT system scrambled the data with its key and relayed it to yet another server whose IP would have been included as part of that original data stream. As everything would have been encrypted, "there's no way to predict what kind of data is passed from the SERVER to the CLIENT, let alone where it came or where it went."

The effect, however, was clear: "the game turns the PC into a node, part of a web within the web". Today we'd call that the dark–web. Likewise the data flow scheme resembled the torrent, typical of how the dark–web exchanges information.

Mortaren's appointment had left a slim window through which to prep. As a freelancer, I was free to travel across the country or the world for a story, so time off from work wasn't an issue that vexed me. I opted to fly to Denver then drive to Walsenburg – a city to the east of the San Luis Valley and a spot my travels made familiar over the years. By week's end, after a numbing but uneventful commute, I reached the comfort of my hotel days in advance – I wanted that buffer to breathe and to reconnoiter the site of our meeting.

The drive through US–350 was monotonous – mile after mile of farmland parched a uniform yellow. The only excitement, if such were the word, came from the prompts the GPS indicated which eventually took me onto a gravel road. The coordinates directed my route into a site too remote for satellites to remap every year; neither Google nor Bing ever sent cars there to photograph the area.

The route crossed a railroad. To my right was a farm. To my left was the overlook – a weathered and wizened hump of earth a geologist told me had been the remnants of a butte millions and millions of years prior. It stood by itself amid seas of grassy plains.

A road lurched onto the overlook's peak; there the earth had been pressed into a level (and empty) lot. My rented Wrangler was, to my impression, the sole visitor that noonday. It felt like the safest place to stop, (hopefully), out of sight and out of mind.

For a while I gazed westward. The sky was a vibrant shade of blue that smothered the distance. Across its haze I caught outlines of the Spanish Peaks. I let my eyes wander southward, toward that spot at the horizon where US–350 vanished into a point. I couldn't see a car anywhere coming or going.

A train roared as it approached the side of the highway.

Eastward and below – at what I gauged may have been a spur of the historical Santa Fe trail, I noted the ruins that had drawn me onto that stop. It had escaped my eyes when I drove by it and then, **then** I realized why. It was at the top of the overlook that the effect was appreciable. The ruins, through the years, had been cloaked by an orchard of junipers.

The ruins were that of a two–story house which had been built partially into the ground. I gawked at the style of it for it appeared so out of time, so out of place compared to the architecture typical of the area around La Junta. The closest match was Spanish Colonial. The eeriest aspect of it was that, in spite of everything, it didn't look like it had been abandoned for any lengthy period of time.

I approached the door – a slab of wood impressively resilient to weather – and stuck my head into the shadow beyond its yawning threshold. Its walls were tagged with an eclectic mixture of symbology, some of it Satanic, some of it native. Others defied my erudition.

As I grew bold enough to enter, my advance was stopped by a voice.

"Yeah, figured you'd check it out."

"Mortaren?" I turned to face the orchard, whose miasma cloaked the figure. "Wanted to see it for myself. Doesn't strike me as a place to stash a server."

"Exactly."

Mortaren, my erstwhile host, stepped out of the enshadowment and joined my stance at the door's threshold. I sensed by the familiarity he conveyed that he wasn't a stranger to its curiosity. I followed into the abode and almost immediately choked at a waft of putrefaction – urine and feces from sources unknown. Squatters – or worse – I started to suspect may have sought the refuge of its confines.

Still, Mortaren wasn't concerned. Nor was he curious about the freshly-minted tools strewn about the rubble. Gear, that I recognized from my years of hiking, had been folded into the mess as if to disguise it. I detected, too, the odor of gasoline – faintly and sublimely – like a suggestion stirred by the train that passed by.

"It hasn't been a residence since the seventies."

"If it's so, it's a mix-up."

"Little of that sort, bub, this," he said of it, swinging a finger around his head toward the upstairs, "this is it. Everything that happened, happened **here**. All of it was filmed where we stand. ZuZu or whomever they worked for, they chose this site not for the way it looked outside **but** inside."

"Is it booby trapped?"

"In a manner of speaking."

We worked past the foyer and the library that followed it. We walked: Mortaren at the front and I at the back. Could it be doubted anymore? My host splayed **intimate** knowledge of the abode which could have come only from a personal investigation. How many times had he stopped by? Perhaps he more than stopped by? Perhaps he more than investigated.

We entered a wide, tall hallway and paused. That volume was pitch except for a window at the apex of the stairs which blasted a square-shaped spotlight onto the floor at our feet. Behind us the hallway emptied into a kitchen. Light that filtered through its windows lent it a vibrant, green glow. A glow that came from the vegetation clogging that chamber. I noted flickering, whistling lights like fluorescents out of view but not of earshot.

Mortaren refused my help to unroll a tarp; "touch nothing, nothing – don't leave a print anywhere, kiddo, you gotta trust me, OK". He revealed a set of tools: pliers, machetes, rakes, and a crowbar. My host took the crowbar and aimed it at the stairs. "Let me give you a word of warning – if you insist you want that game – alright more, more than a word. Yes – I got it. And I'm far from the only sucker, let me say. I suggest, whatever you do, you don't ever install it, you don't ever play it, you don't even stick it into a drive that autoplays, OK?"

We ascended; the stairs were droopy and struggled to stay upright.

"Not saying that 'cause of what it'll do to your rig – you know what it'll do, I don't need to tell you what it'll do. It's the sort of stuff that'll bring the FBI to your door faster than you can say **Blue Beelzebub**. No, damn it, it's how that abomination tears into your soul. It'll compromise you and that's intentional not accidental. It wants to beat you into submission. The fear – that you'll be found, that you'll be trapped – imagine every day, every day thinking 'today's the day it happens'. It took a year to convince the FBI I didn't know what that game was about and then it was too late to save my arse."

Upstairs, my host drew my steps into a salon whose walls were a faded memory of yellow. Cracks formed like veins running the heights of the walls. The reek of corruption, like that of decay, attacked us fiercely. A hum issued out of the air; it was strongest at the center where the rug that cloaked the floor **bulged**.

Mortaren applied a streak of coroner's salve to his upper lip. I added a dab to my face. My host insisted I should be thorough; so I complied.

That area had been a vast, formal salon, a pit of "opulence and decadence" from the 70s. Furniture lay scattered to rot. An armoire waited at the far end with its doors wide, agape almost like arms outstretched to greet us. It, like the rest of the furniture, soaked the elements and charred into onyx as if burned. Slowly my eyes accustomed to the ambiance and as such I grew cognizant of a trove of esoteric details. Books strewn about. Mounds of salt. Blobs of candles. Pentagrams. All of that competed head-to-head with the scratches etched into the walls.

I found a fingernail embedded into those scratches....

"After I posted the demo, a fan – let's say they were a fan – contacted my office about it. They offered assistance and I – reluctantly out of curiosity – I complied. I sent them copies of the game. That was my downfall, kiddo." He stopped to take a breath. "The stuff of nightmares that destroys a man's life fits so perfectly into a pair of three point five inch floppies. Well, that fan reverse–engineered the executable. Dude sent everything right back to my house with a stack of paper. Never heard of them again. I assumed they were the first to contact the FBI. Can't blame 'em."

Mortaren pointed to the rug that spanned the floor.

"Is that hum under the floor?" I asked – he nodded.

"The sound isn't from the server, though." Mortaren lifted the corner of the rug with the crowbar. We cleared the furniture and rolled away the carpet. It decomposed into rubble just by touching it as we did. "It's a crazy layout. The house was built over a shaft. This room it's, it's right over that shaft. The hum comes from the way air works through it."

"So ... the server **is** real and it's here?"

My host nodded; "The game's a virus that turns your rig into a zombie. You work for them, now, now, you're part of something worse than anything you imagine. The events that created this mess, this wreck that you see – it was filmed right where we stand. ZuZu transferred the footage to AVI clips and used it to create the maze's layout and texture. My fan, when they broke apart the game, they found the clips embedded right into the code and I had to watch 'em, didn't I? I had to watch 'em. Look, it's not over, OK. The ritual they started, it doesn't end, it doesn't, **ever**, end."

His gaze as his eyes relived his memory of the video spoke volumes. I dared not ask what kind of ritual he witnessed. His whole entire body shook as if its violation were fresh. That was enough. **That was enough.**

"I tell you the strangest part of this business. The people who started it, they're a crazy kooky sex cult out of NAZI Germany. Yeah, they used Crawley's sex–magik. They never touched kids, though. It wasn't about the Cheese Pizza for 'em. But the Chinese Sandwich wasn't any better."

We walked into the center of the salon, to a spot where the rug had bulged. Removed, we saw what it was. A circle had been drilled into the wood and plugged by plate like a manhole.

Mortaren lodged the crowbar into the crack at the circumference of the plate.

"You'll never get it until you see it from their perspective. You gotta see it through their eyes. Twisted as it is. The game exists to re-create the ritual – to recreate the ritual **and make you part of it**. Simply by watching it, by playing it, you get tainted and that by itself makes you part of it." He tapped the crowbar to the plate that refused to budge. "Haven't I tried? It's not enough, is it? Am I too old, at the end? The server.... It's at the end of the shaft, a hundred feet below. I donno how it's powered. Maybe it's geothermal? I donno. It's there, idling, watching and waiting for a signal to awaken."

Cheese Pizza and Chinese Sandwich, to those not aware of 4CHAN and its vernacular, is code for 'Child Pornography' and 'Child Snuff', respectively. ZuZu and LVN used the dog-whistles of their day to advertize the game to a certain clientele. But the cult that bankrolled **Blue Beelzebub** abhorred the former as it embraced the latter. And the game itself contained tedious 90s **shock** – glimpses of death and its like – it never showed the goods, so to speak.

The CD contained the hacked DOS the game installed as well as a thorough, documented unraveling of the game itself. Mortaren's fan discovered and saved BMPs and AVIs that had been embedded into the code. I slipped that CD into a drive and scanned its contents with my virus and malware checkers. Not a single program detected a problem. Given the sizes of the files, though, I found it disconcerting that my checkers took minutes to complete.

Mortaren's fan had placed their deconstruction of the game's executable into a ZIP folder. The majority of it consisted of code that they converted from binary to ML to C. It was fascinating to gawk at the code which appeared so professional. Yet, as C was not a strength of mine, I found it vague and cryptic overall.

I dug into the multi-media directory and extracted images and clips that had been stored there. Saved to my laptop, I selected the largest AVI and played it. That film, whose sights and sounds were equally vivid and jittery, oozed the impression of an 8 mm production. It had been subbed into English and I (mostly) followed it.

Mortaren got it right – the clip had been filmed at the house by US–350, specifically, at its salon. I paused to check the layout and compare it to my notes of how I found the furniture and the other, macabre ancillary.

Amazingly, decades after the fact, everything matched.

The clip itself comprised a continuous stream formed of what had to have been a sequence of shorter segments:

1irst Segment:

At a couch sit three women – an older, frailer matron flanked by younger versions of herself. All of them are dressed by frilled & embroidered deerskin. They chat enthralled by action elsewhere that the camera does not depict.

2econd Segment:

The matron walks out of the frame and the camera pans to the opposite side of the salon where a man approaches the couch. The man is dressed in a style similar to that of Crowley's regalia – decked head to toe with shades of violet and onyx. The magik–man reaches the couch with the women and offers them beaded & boned necklaces that they accept & wear.

3hird Segment:

The matron reappears, trailed by a pair of older, wizened men, men sheepishly guised by their dress as to appear tribal American natives – except that they are, in spite of the elaboration, the headdresses and the breechcloths, of Caucasian stock, possibly, German like the women. They were **Indianthusists**, a fetish unique to Germany, that permeates into fringe, esoteric quarters of Thule magik. As the older men and younger women stand and co-mingle, the matron paints their skin everywhere with runes right out of the Thelema.

4ourth Segment:

The magik–man sits at the rug between a pair of circumscribed pentagrams; he lights a roll of sage (?) – a lack of definition masks the identity of the object. Smoke billows out of it as he waves it over the pentagrams. The matron sets & lights six candles – three to the left and three to the right of the magik–man.

5ifth Segment:

The camera drifts down and to the left, **down and to the left**, down and to the left, to reveal the orgy. Painted men and women are paired and writhe about the pentagrams. The females lay with their backs to the floor and their heads crowned by the candles. The males lay atop the females. Their limbs intertwine. Their bodies contort. All of it to the rhythm the magik–man beats into drums.

6ixth Segment:

The matron, naked and painted, sits in front of the magik–man and extends a chalice – the rest of this segment is cut into a clip that plays during the game.

7eventh Segment:

The magik–man pours the content of the chalice onto a loaf of bread. The camera zooms into that bread – it is shaped like a baby. At that instant the hands of the males and the females, their paint smeared and mixed post-orgy, reach onto the bread and yank it into four–quarters. They eat the bread.

8ighth Segment:

The magik–man remains at the salon; it's night, it's lit by torches.

After a spell, he folds the rug and reveals a portal into a shaft.

For a while the magik–man speaks to the camera. Subtitles state: "we consecrate the well – are you ready to see it again – to see it as it is enlivened by the spirit of [REDACTED] spurred by the ritual – are you ready – do you think you are ready", then, "it looks like a hundred feet", then, "as if a hundred feet were enough".

9inth Segment:

The bulk of the video consists of the exploration of the mine at the base of the shaft. The magik–man takes turns sometimes leading, sometimes lagging the camera. The narration is continuous although the German isn't translated throughout this segment.

The magik–man reaches a part of the maze that collapsed. Faded, partially in and out of focus, his baffle is merely a suggestion of the camera's aim. Yet, the pause and the silence that follows indicate that he isn't ready for the obstacle and so struggles to clear a way through it. The viewer notes, by the appearance of the hand low, mid frame, that the videographer is at last captured by their footage.

The magik–man pierces the collapse and reveals a vast, circular chamber.

The chamber is lit, awash by an eerie, hazy blue light. A crack crazes across the chamber. The light filters through that crack. The camera savors the chamber – it's adorned like the salon; it's a site where the cult practices its rituals. The camera sweeps toward the crack, prompted by a sound that startles the magik–man.

The camera zooms into the crack – it's like a well, filled to the brim with water. It's almost like an abyss, it sinks, on and on, hundreds if not thousands of feet; the limitations imposed by film and pixilation cannot do reality justice.

The water is upsettingly transparent through and through – and straight into the blur of light at where ever its bottom lay.

As the magik-man speaks off-screen and the camera continues the zoom, it's apparent that there are things, **things** of a sort not floating but swimming through the water.

I scream as the view jostles – it's not a jump or a cut, though, it's the camera's shake. Whoever it is that films that site, they had been startled by movement elsewhere. As the camera's view twists to the side, it pans by where the magik-man stands and captures a glimpse, just, a glimpse of something that had been standing at the other side of the chasm right as it jumps into the water.

The house off US–350 loomed abandoned in appearance only. Nobody occupied it since the 70s; however, it wasn't derelict. County records verified that its owners – **Ache Industrias** – paid its taxes year after year. **Ache Industrias**, named for a tribe of South American natives, was a company from Paraguay famous for its advances (and patents) re: GMOs. They were a partner to Monsanto but not as known outside of agriculture. **Ache Industrias** owned that house and the farms that engulfed it; a total of 500 acres.

BM: "Word is that the company wants to use this land for research.

"A lobby out of Denver, that represents a lot of cattlemen, filed a lawsuit working its way into the Supreme Court at this rate." Farmers and ranchers who would be, effectively, neighbors sharing their grazing rights of the nearby Comanche Grasslands objected to the idea, fearing the consequences to their business if their livestock mixed with GMO livestock.

"Meanwhile the acreage isn't dormant; it's rented and reaps a lot of profit from royalties."

Ache Industrias **wasn't the first owners, or, as it should be stated, wasn't the first incarnation of the first owners.**

BM: "An occultist, Straniak, was its proprietor of record according to my contact from Brazil."

Straniak, in partnership with two other expatriated Germans, formed a company c. 1930 then known as **Straniak–West**. Although the exact nature of **Straniak–West** wasn't advertised, it's suspected that they profited from the Chaco War and the partners became wealthy in spite of the Great Depression (which had been a world-wide phenomenon). As Europe verged into WWII, **Straniak–West** changed its moniker to **Ache Industrias** c. 1940. Around the tail end of 1941 the partners bought a thousand acres around the La Junta area; about half of the original estate was shed through the years.

BM: "Straniak and cohorts summered at their Colorado estate. Right up until they started to rent the land, the house had been the estate's only, permanent structure. They used its solitude to mask their rituals."

The cult / company was especially fond of that house and guarded its secrets.

Mortaren, as an aficionado of the occult, a passion that spurred him to review games of that genre, became aware of Aleister Crowley and the Thules, chieftains of bizarro, early 20th century mysticism, strands of which wormed their way into the works of Lovecraft, Blackwood, and a slew of other writers.

Straniak, and allies, were German mystics intimately linked to the Thules, "a society with their own weird take on Aryanism" whose forays into sex–magik, blood–magik, and **sacrifices** made them too extreme even for the NAZIs.

"He fled to South America before Hitler, if you believe that sort of stuff."

The house wasn't built by Straniak & Co, though. It already existed by the time they hired a crew to survey their property c. 1933.

That area of Colorado had see-sawed between Spain and France before it was ceded to the US after the Mexican–American War. Records from two centuries ago were hard to come by. Historians were reduced to combing through diaries and correspondences, however, the ephemera revealed a portion of history that otherwise had been lost.

The house used to be part of a hacienda granted to a patron of great wealth. Disagreements arose re: their identity as the sources used to piecemeal the history were themselves uncertain if the figure was American / English or French. Nevertheless, they built an extensive estate c. 1792. The house used to be larger; an earthquake c. 1820 reduced it more or less to the dimensions that Straniak & Co. found it.

What probably enticed the occultist crew was what legends claimed had been revealed after the earthquake. Namely – that the house had been erected over a mine from prehistory. The earthquake, as it leveled the house, revealed a shaft into that mine – which so happened to contain gold. The patron used its revenue to rebuild the house – albeit to modest proportions – with the novelty that the house hid or capped the entrance into the mine.

BM: "The cavity underfoot itself isn't the end-all and be-all. The cult was attracted to something else, something else not connected to wealth. A portal into cosmic realms of time and space heretofore unknown? It called to them. That's for sure.

"They recorded all of their rituals; the climax of which, which became **Blue Beelzebub**, if my timeline's correct, matches an earthquake in 1983. It wasn't much of an earthquake but it explains part of the video. It ripped a gash through the mine.

"The server's got to be inside that chasm, drawing power from geothermal. A system designed to work for ages without intervention while their poison spreads through the internet.

"Ah, but it won't be there for long, I promise you."

Night cloaked the house as we descended its staircase. It felt as if the structure somehow, someway gained a sort of sentience after decades of mysticism echoed through its confines. I fancied it understood Mortaren's intentions and shook at the foreknowledge.

If it goes, won't that destroy the evidence? What about the crimes they committed? Won't they go unpunished?

BM: "Kiddo, you're talking about people, people who will never be punished never, never, never be punished for anything. **Blue Beelzebub**, it's just the tip of the tip of the iceberg. And you know it. It's always like that. They regroup and reorganize. But they took me down. And I'm gonna take **this** much, **this** much if anything away from them."

My erstwhile host was adamant about their business and refuted my pleas to reason otherwise.

By destroying the house, they claimed, they would be saving lives, lives yet to be taken.

"Mark my words, they'll imagine another way to spread their filth. And that's where you and those like you continue what I start tonight."

A stark midnight moon loomed to the south west over the jagged grin of the Spanish Peaks. There wasn't a cloud to mar the sky. Crisp, summery wind stirred a floral scent about the air, then it faded, driven away to the ether by a tide of gasoline then of a char / smoke. I drove by the ruin where I noted how the orange escaped the house. It almost looked like a face, a skeletal face, buried into the orchard. I waved. Maybe the gesture was or wasn't returned.

I didn't stay.

That was the last I saw of Bobby Mortaren.

I dismantled the SYSTEMs' HDDs; I scraped the platters then I applied a welder's torch to them, fusing them, melting them, obliterating any trace what so ever of the data they contained. Later I shredded the floppies and the CD and the papers. For all I knew those may have been the last, extant copies of **Blue Beelzebub**.

My paying job resumed its malaise although I noted that my contacts with the FBI waned. Then my editors shuffled my workload. Cases I had been assigned to were re-directed elsewhere. Leads dried. I was shunned more and more. I recognized a familiarity to the pattern – to the way I was being isolated and overshadowed. I tried to squash the paranoia that may have transferred to me as I entertained the notion of starting yet another career.

I eked out a single article about the decline and fall of bitcoin. After that I put my thoughts together to form this record of my dealings with **Blue Beelzebub**. Partly to settle the history of it – as much of it as I understood. Partly to form a defense. I wanted to be transparent; there's such scant cover for journalists nowadays.

Earlier I received a call from a woman, a former FBI agent who claimed they owed me a favor.

They warned that "I had been flagged by an anti-virus software vendor that works with the government". Apparently, the anti-virus / malware scan had detected a rare item and reported it to the vendor's server for analysis. That's how the NSA discovered "the executable" with "embedded content" that "raised eyebrows". It wasn't just the government that started to investigate **Blue Beelzebub**, they continued, "a third party, a cryptic South American outfit", long suspected of trafficking and exploiting minors, "sparked a lot of chatter across the dark-web about you. You got enemies, son, lots and lots of enemies."

I didn't know any FBI agent, current and / or former who "owed me a favor".

I stated that in fact I had received a couple of floppies from a source familiar with the game. Naturally, I scanned the media. "I couldn't get the program to work **properly**. It needs DOS and there aren't too many PCs like it anymore. I destroyed all of that 'cause it gave me the creeps."

It wasn't entirely a lie.

Please Come Back

What say of it? what say of **CONSCIENCE** *grim,*
That spectre in my path?

– Chamberlayne's **Pharronida**

> Paper's* such an enigma. Even among reliable and go–to antiquers, it's rare to find a notepad full of paper and it's certain to cost a week's pay. The scarcity wasn't due to a lack of supply – although it's a luxury 'cause it's not manufactured anymore – it's just that few outside of government asserted a reason to write (or read). As the demand vanished, the supply retreated.

It's plain, simple luck that Dylan lived by Cheyenne, where paper continued to be a (relatively) easy find.

At the apex of a winter's afternoon, he stooped, armed with his instruments: the notepad and the pen. A bowl of soup stewed at the counter. The bar was a trucker's joint when Ault was a draw. Today it hummed in spite of that commune's slumber. There's the ruckus of feet shuffling about from table to table. There's the murmur of townsfolk prattling their business. There's the attendant tidying after everyone.

He turned a page and wondered: *where'd that idea fly to?*

It started as a poem. Stanzas oozed into his dream that night. He awoke and it's so clear, so vivid. Phrases were stuck to his lips. Only echoes of its vastness remained. Fragments.... He jotted a verse line by line then crossed it away.

No – that's not it – that's not it – damn! he reeled.

Resigned, as that verse slipped into oblivion, he grasped then devoured the soup.

He saved for that odd, spiral notepad. Its shape drew his gaze. Its color – a shade of orange – spoke of the ages prior to the troubles. Its cover promised a hundred 'leaves'; all had been preserved if yellowed at their edges. He didn't question the price. After a month, he yield those sun's and moon's pieces his work had accrued then took home his 2econd or 3hird most prized possession.

That must have been a decade ago.

---

* Contractions that end with 's' are non–standard past–tense.

What's there to show for it? Five pages and part of a 6ixth were written. That's it. They were lists or ideas. Anything to spark the imagination was represented. He hated to waste it – every scribble betrayed a fight. There's no return, no undo – as with life – the pen marched forward, onward consuming lines, spending pages. A lot of it's wisps of fantasies and appeared chaotic; before they would have been forgotten, after they persisted.

There hadn't been a convoy in or out of Ault for an hour. Then, by-the-by, a patroller stopped to refuel. A pair – too distant to identify – embarked from their ATV to pace about the lot. As their diesel pumped, they rounded his jeep, amused by its plate.

He yearned to ignore **that** development.

A crew of horsemen appeared. They were part of a convoy – a train of cattle – sent to slaughter at Ft. Collins. The trip's more or less ten miles west. However **routine** it were to them, they won't be careless about how they ferry that bounty from town to town. Ault reeked of cattle; it may not be a destination but its wealth could not be denied.

The patrollers at the lot scrambled to rejoin the convoy.

Away they went, all of them, all of them…. The sight of that parade resurrected a taste of life at Apollo. Albeit more impression than memory, he recalled how his parents worked security for the DeSotos'. They too rode ATVs while guarding convoys to and from Cheyenne.

Perhaps settling wasn't out of the question? It's not as if Cheyenne were so distant as to be unheard of. People kept shifting up and down that border – th'ought to be plenty of **Wyoming** migrants in search of **Colorado** jobs. He wasn't a stranger, like a rushbody from East of the Miss. He piled years of experiences at the DeSotos'. He understood everything about security. Well – he didn't ride horses – he did drive anything.

But that **idea** – no – that **panic** … **settling**! Settling? – **then** – to be normal? Wasn't it a defeat? He would be quitting a dream. Even if it wasn't his dream. Just what **was** his dream? It couldn't be to live for work moment by moment. No – it couldn't be, it couldn't be, there had to be **cause** to live for.

He withdrew his notepad into the duffel and his pen into the jacket – a rough, wizened leather jacket a size too large to fit properly. Few minded the garment's incongruence; or noticed the lanky, mute choker at his collar. He buried that pen into a pocket. There, among papers he kept at a finger's distance, he felt a tiny, little 2 x 2 photograph. He freed it, viewed it – a black and white image – its edges frayed by age. **How'd it travel so far**? That picture was for the wallet not for the jacket.

*He snips the picture – at the bottom of the strip – and gives it to me. I laugh, recalling the romp, enjoying the look of surprise made permanent by that black and white image. **He** yanks it away for his wallet whilst I pout.*

*He reaches to me, wrapping his arms about my waist, drawing me into his chest. I'm embraced by his warmth. **He** teases a kiss as if to mirror that picture. For a spell, we linger so entwined.*

"Dyl ... you wonder, sometimes, what if we didn't shoot the breeze that day? **At gym**. See – I itched to drop that day. I wasn't coming back, no, **I wasn't coming back**. Not to Armstrong." *He squeezes his arms around my shoulders and brings his cheek to rest by my cheek.* "Wasn't it luck? How **we** happened?"

"I wanted to drop. And I aimed to drop. Sooner. Later. But you stopped it. So – if you didn't and I did – we would have met at the ranch. Wouldn't we? We would have met – and talked – and maybe, maybe **you'd give me that smile**. Isn't that how it happened? It wasn't the kind of smile a boy gives a boy."

"You said ... oh, that you didn't care for dating or marrying that Jennifer girl. Yeah, I wondered about you. If you were **like** me.... Dyl, that day – if we don't meet, we won't meet. **Ever**. It's not like the ranch's a guarantee. You would've filled your head with books. I would've run with horses. Suppose, we didn't meet until later. **A lot later.** Later – like older, older guys. If we met like that, no way, no way we'd connect."

"We'd connect – just wouldn't be the way we'd connect as **kids**. I know it. **I know it.**"

"I don't remember why I stayed at gym. What a change a tiny, little act makes! Dylan, it scares me, you know. I want to believe."

*It's my house – **still** – cool and silent. I live alone except when **he** comes. Closest neighbors are a mile up and down the road. Too far to see what we're up to but they've got to remark about it. They don't like that I'm alone so maybe they don't mind, or, **they don't notice**.*

We gaze at a thin, wide slit of window right above us. Open – cool daylight filters into the basement, onto us. We're bedded side by side. The blanket rises to our shoulders. Our clothes scatter the floor.

*My house isn't like the ranch. We could have taken refuge anywhere free of fear. Yet we kept to the basement. It's **ours**.*

"I would've worked at the herd."

"You?" *he grimaces with that curl of a lip to set my heart racing.*

"Yeah, **me**. I'd work outdoors. I like it rough!" *He laughs at my declaration.* "I'd be dreaming for all of this. You'd be going there and there and realizing a part of what your life could have, would have been is missing."

I raise myself to be eye-to-eye. We work into a kiss. His skin is an island of hot against a universe of cold. **He** *smiles as I tug at his choker – does anybody wonder why* **he** *wears it?*

"Maybe we would've met, anyhow, Dyl."

Autumnal winds rattle trees – there's a scent of aspen to flavor the cool, dry air.

"We would've met as strangers and then – **and then** *– we wouldn't be strangers, like that, yeah, like that,"* **he** *speaks through the gaps between kisses that grow wider and wider.* **He** *stops to gaze first above last below: "If we're meant to be, then, it wouldn't matter, when or where or how,* **we'd meet until we'd make it.***"*

Dylan shoved the nozzle into the pump.

The jeep left Wyoming retrofitted for diesel. Gas's hoarded by governments. Diesel's fuel of the people, by the people.

"... pretty pretty plates there...."

Only the plates were a recent addition.

"Who wants to know?"

He turned: a figure stood by his jeep. That specter could have escaped a visage of the West that didn't exist anymore. His face reflected a shade of red and proved a curious mix: not quite old, not quite young. Braids dropped from his shoulder to his breast where they were tied by black fringe. A white bear skin cloak wrapped his torso. The hide's construction was asymmetric. There wasn't enough bear to fit his frame. Everything had to be used. A (diagonal) zipper kept it together. Yellow denim for garb completed the picture.

"**Me's** who, kid, I'm looking for a ride."

"Where you going?"

"Coast."

"West?"

"Keh, why not?"

His expression softened just enough to juxtapose ferocity and whimsy. Neither too old. Neither too young. He couldn't be five years older than Dylan. He couldn't be surfing the road for that long, for that far either. Migrants were few – and aged if not destroyed by their travel.

"That's awful far. You sure?"

"Yeah, sure I'm sure," the stranger cracked. "Isn't the coast where they hide the jobs?"

"I looked at the bulletins. At the coast, it's fishing, lumbering. Typical stuff, isn't it?"

"Where **you** going?"

"**Anywhere.** It's Dylan."

That figure, at last, flashed a wry and sideways smile then extended a hand: "It's **Ca**–yote."

Quickest exit to the coast was the #70 corridor. It stabbed into the Rockies. From there it split at Utah. From there either north or south bound corridors emptied at the coast. But #70 wasn't an option that winter. And corridors were left to convoys or horsemen.

Alternative routes could be spliced by following byways #24 or #50 else by tracing patchworks of roads any of which were subject to neglect. Winter didn't forgive.... Ah, matters about fuel and such had to be considered. Those tiny, little out-of-the-way spots always charged premium for a sip of their supply.

The interiors of Colorado were left to their devices. Communes struggled to keep afloat and weren't eager to share their resources. Places like that 'came distrustful even resentful of strangers.

"They're insular," Dylan explained.

"Aren't you local?"

"Nah, I'm from Wyoming. My family escaped Colorado **YZ**. I grew up, eh, not too far away though. Maybe not in body but in mind. With all of my family's stories and pictures and stuff like that.... It always felt like I came from here. You?"

"Keh, I'm from Wyoming, too," Coyote said, relaxing into the seat.

"Oh?"

"Apollo."

"Stop it, man, that's ... **that's where I lived**."

"We must've missed each other."

Dylan drove into the avenue marked #85. It's not a minute and the last of Ault reflected off the rearview. *Wasn't it just there?* As real as anything. Then – like a daydream – it's gone, gone....

"My folks forced me to stay in school. **Armstrong**. It didn't matter to 'em that all of my friends dropped."

"I couldn't take a year of Armstrong. Got left back, oh, **lots**. Look at me, why do I need a diploma? ... keh ... waste of time."

"I went too far to quit. That last year, wow, what a mess! Somebody stole the artifacts. Well, heck, I swiped a rock everybody said came from the moon. They shut that winter. Never graduated."

Coyote laughed: "I figured it's better to work at the ranch. It was. Then.... It wasn't. What're you gawking at, kid?"

"Would be something if we met but forgot we met?"

Coyote dropped a hand at Dylan's shoulder – where it languished.

"Would be something **if we got along**...."

Figments of winter littered rolling, wandering hillscapes at the sides of the road. At the left stretched a plain. At the right yawned the Front Range of the Colorado Rockies. The sky's a swath of gray. The sun's too weak to break that fog. A chill seeped into the jeep that its heater won't abate.

"We'll cut through New Mexico and Arizona."

"Ouch! We'll **what**? With **this** piece of shit?"

"It ought to work. Last I checked, well.... The tires' got another, eh, another ten kay miles. The engine's not giving any sort of trouble."

"What about you? You'll tire. You'll wonder – **where does it end** – **enough's enough**. Yup. You'll want to settle. Get a job, settle. They've got chicks, don't they? Get a girl, settle. Oh, I forgot. Settle – and dump **Ca**–yote at the road. **Jilted**."

Dylan, blushed, "Nah, that stuff's not for me."

Coyote raised an eyebrow.

"I pick'em, don't I? What's it for you? Giving strangers rides to nowhere without getting paid a piece to do it.... Seriously, I don't have a piece of anything, sun, moon, anything."

Dylan clasped the man's hand. "Are worse things to **don't have**. I'll take you, **Ca**yote. Coasts – or anywhere. I don't have a place, either. There's nowhere to go back, you know, you know **what I mean**?"

Coyote squeezed Dylan's hand.

It felt as if a weight were lifted and they were freed to be true by their ways. If and only if they went unnoticed! Protected by that jeep's sanctuary, by that road's isolation, they were safe, weren't they? They simply could not stray too far if enmeshed by others.

#85 widened into the city of Greely.

As cities went, it's **alive**.

YZ – nobody said Year Zero would be the end of everything. Society **survived**. Altered? Crippled? Of course.... It's only a shade of what the country used to be. Its distant, far-away corners were disintegrating by their isolation. Yet – people found a way to live. They preserved a body of skill fit for survival. They learned to grow and to fix anything, to create stock from what remained available. Many continued to invent.

Cities kept their markets where trade circulated. Roads extended the reaches of producers and consumers alike. Convoys spanned borders and knit a sense of country. *Wasn't that resemblance of America enough?*

They dodged a bullet – **so to speak**. Almost three generations after **YZ** and in spite of name-changes and power-shifts, life itself didn't change too radically. Yesteryear's simply an outlier. They expanded too fast and that's that. Life's always been what the troubles exposed: a fight to maintain existence.

To avoid delay, Dylan switched from the highway to the byway. He reached into the console and produced the GPS. He snapped it onto the latch at the dashboard. **What a steal!** The antiquers, they didn't understand, they didn't realize satellites **still** circled the Earth. A few were left. Enough that they empowered the GPS.

The device plotted a route from Greely to Denver.

A gang of youths gathered at the edge of the city. They gawked at the jeep. Travelers were rare and subject to amazement. It felt OK until they pelted at the vehicle – its soft top and windows bore the abuse of that snow. How much was impish or malice, he won't say. He sped at the sight of the horse.

Dylan hated horses; he hated their riders worst.

"I knew a boy, well, **a man**; he wanted to ride with horses. Like his ancestors. His family's a wild mix of traditions, not all of which were compatible. Either way he cut it, horses were a part of their past. Before they settled at sheep, I suppose. I'd catch him looking at bulletins; I'd read them, of course, **he**.... Anything to do with horses. Anything, especially, if it were west. Like **Oregon**. His folks wouldn't let truckers or horsemen post bulletins at the ranch for fear of losing men; didn't think they'd be losing sons. I'll never get what Oregon's about."

"You thought it was stupid?"

"No. My eyes were full of stars too. Books I read went to my head. After my parents died, yeah, I wizened. It capped my dreams. **He** was really, really into that stuff. **Horses**. 'Til he figured their cost. So his family gave him a bike."

"Where'd you aim to go? If I hadn't come by, I mean. It's not easy, is it, traveling without a lot of coin?"

"Denver, for a season, it's got jobs."

If we hadn't bumped into each other at gym? If we hadn't stopped ... everything ... just to talk a while? What would have happened to us? We were only at that school, together, you and I, only a day.

That bulletin at a junction outside Denver had to be the largest Dylan witnessed. Cheyenne's posts weren't anywhere as extensive **geographically**. Notices were organized by region and that assembly formed an impromptu map of the West. Adverts from Colorado dominated by volume not by variety – everything about Denver dealt with plows – so desperate, too, that they waived experience.

Dylan drove tractors and the like at the DeSotos'. He wasn't part of their blizzard rotation, although, from time to time, he helped the crew shovel. All of that was Wyoming. Experience didn't always translate. Especially if certain rivalries existed to complicate matters. He'd be forced by practicality to suppress what he knew and from where he knew it.

He figured it'd be like **everything** – he'd start low.

At the verge to exit, he stopped then scanned adverts from the coast. The Republic of Cali. The Oregon Commune. Greater Columbia. All of their notices were untouched. Somebody clawed a swastika into the gap between Arizona and Texas. He snipped contact after contact and shoved the strips into the jacket. *Tribute for Cayote....*

"Pacific's, wow, that's far, kid, that's far," blustered a woman – a trucker – who watched him feel the coast for its jobs. "You got any idea how far?"

"Months – with **this** weather," he tapped at the warnings about hazards throughout the #90, #80, and #70 corridors. "Is it just the distance? That's why nobody takes the offers?"

"It's a lot of country to cross for a blippance! Mostly, though, its **paranoia**. Look at Oregon. Cali's got a stockpile. GC's got **Alaska** – if you know what I mean. Oregon's got nothing. Nothing. Sure, agreements with Cali and GC, yeah. It's got that. And that's it. But Oregon's where a lot of **Nipponese** took refuge after China's genocide. They've got the notion that China's aiming to return and finish the job."

A murmur echoed about a crowd of truckers that gathered by the bulletin. China's and Russia's war brought about **YZ**. It wasn't certain, **yet**, if either aggressor survived or imploded into any of a dozen belligerents. As far as anybody understood, they wiped each other off the map.

Countries that survived **YZ** disintegrated to a certain extent. Some entirely. Some partially. It's said that the US and the EU deliberately downsized via a strategy put together at the zenith of the Cold War. It's too expensive to keep the West, the story spread, so states West of the Miss were scuttled to fend for themselves.

At the Denver Bureau of Transportation, a woman in command of testing would be applicants sat ready to work his form. 'Til Dylan took the task himself. Nobody prompted that gesture; rather, it happened by-the-by. He read and wrote as he filled his sheet; he didn't imagine it to be extraordinary. Yet, with eyes wide as saucers, **she watched**, transfixed by the hands that wrote consistently like a typewriter.

As the whole entire system of education the Feds produced collapsed, it 'came increasingly odd to find youngsters able to read (or write).

The West quit **the practice** a generation earlier. Ah, it wasn't so everywhere. **Where** it faded was determined by resources and priorities. Big states did better than little states. Big cities did better than little cities. Etc.

Wyoming's education wasn't respected. It took a hit after Cheyenne gave its funds to agriculture. Schools were recycled from town to town. Universities, too, weren't spared the axe. Armstrong's too proud to fold until, one by one, its volunteers either retired or fled.

The bulk of what Dylan wrote was true except at the periphery – as that would've alerted his migrancy. For **City,** he jotted **Greely** – Denver's too obvious and Ault's too obscure. For **DOB**, he jotted **July 1** but couldn't reckon what year – Wyoming's base was **AD** while Colorado's base was **YZ**.

Afterward: a visit with the crew master and a tour of the equipment rounded the interview for the application.

Was it their desperation? Was it his skill? Either way he got the job.

Work started **that** dawn.

"Dawn," he echoed the crew master, then, tucked his hat at his head and retreated into the lot where his jeep waited.

The bureau listed the address and the direction for its dorm then issued the token for its landlord.

That complex stood at the corner of Colorado and Louisiana. They used to be apartments – **skyscrapers,** by Denver's standards – when they were commandeered by the state. A circle of rises, either five or six stories, they were set apart by moats of dirt & gravel lots where asphalt had been stripped. Its earth's frozen like tundra; he feared slipping and crashing if he sped as he drove to where the landlord stood.

They exchanged the bureau's token through the jeep's window hand-to-hand. He's permitted to park only at a spot in front of that unit – **5ifth** unit. He's directed further and further into the complex, onto this unit. He's shown his spot. It's encompassed by bikes. There were scads and scads of bikes. His white and black jeep clashed against them.

He didn't like it. He didn't like it **at all**. *That clash!* It made people **notice** the jeep. No mistake's worse than trust. What's there to do **about it**? What's there to do?

He dislodged the jeep's solenoid and slipped it into his duffel to join everything of value to him.

Inside, the landlord showed him to his floor – **4ourth** – to his apartment – #406/4/2. Amenities were scarce – so – they had to be shared or rationed. Apartments were consolidated. Floors were reconfigured. All of that effort committed to maximize the dorm's occupancy.

A tram's scheduled to rouse the unit at 4 **AM** that dawn. He's told to relax – as if.... What's left of the day to enjoy? There's just waiting and waiting – and worrying. Almost everybody employed to work the winter clustered to mind the weather. They sipped tea as a radio at the end of the passage reported about the blizzard striking the state from south to north.

Traffic also trickled through that radio. Both the #25 and the #70 corridors were clogged by convoys that won't entertain that luxury of waiting. Traders camped at Denver itched to leave too.... The routes had to be kept navigable. In spite of that, there's only a skeleton crew of mixed talent to work the blizzard. The professionals plowed the interior of Colorado, west of Golden, east of Veil, after Grand Junction's equipment failed.

Snow dusted the lot with a sheet of gray. The shapes of the bikes and his jeep were softened. Their textures were smoothed as their forms were slowly, layer by layer, obliterated by the deposits of the tiniest, littlest blips of vacuum Nature put together.

The apartment faced south. From its window, he caught the sun's plummet askew. Sunset's revealed by a swath of violet that extended west to east and penetrated the gray of the blizzard. Through that cloak, the display kindled brilliantly. Right to the end, as the sun's face sank, swallowed by the grins of the peaks, the day fought the night to its last drop of blood.

Anxiety gripped his imagination.

"What am I doing?"

He retreated from the window to the center of the room. The chamber's large enough to admit a bed and a pile of comforts typical of a campground: matchbox, lamp, knife, canteen, and stove. The bed, though, reeked ... he propped that mattress against a wall.

He dropped sheets and blankets onto the floor then pounded his duffel into a pillow.

Lamplight illuminated his notepad as he wrote:

"I found a box with books at the bulletin this afternoon. Why didn't I see that elsewhere? Donated my Wells books. Didn't find anything to catch my eye. Oh, except, a notepad where somebody wrote a novel by hand. I argued about taking it. Don't think Coyote would've wanted me to if I wasn't going to read it. Want not. Waste not. So I let it be. Funny, isn't it, I'm not the only sucker with pen and paper."

He shut his notepad and wrapped it shape into the jacket – its leather felt warm from the drive.

The jacket's sized for a figure a foot atop his height. It had been through hell and bled scars to show its trouble. Traces of paint spotted the collar and the cuffs. Patches, where they had been sewed then ripped, holed up and down the sleeves. The DeSotos' logo had been embroidered onto its back; the needlework's preserved, amazingly, defiant of its experiences; the turquoise's vibrant enough to blind.

He recalled an age when its profile wasn't so battered. Where, indeed, the only violence came from braids whipping that leather like a frenzy spurred by the wind at the rear of the bike. **Those rides!** Three year's worth of riding to and from Armstrong. Three year's worth of exposed yet hidden intimacy.

It was **he** who kept the pressure not to drop: "*Your head's too full of shit to stop,*" **he'd** say. 'Til the school fell to pieces.

"Where are you? Riding mail to Calgary? Hauling crude from Texas? Did I pass you a dozen times since Cheyenne? Or were you there, rallying those kids along eight five? Look at you, erasing, what, **twenty years**? Admit it; you hurled that snowball, jerk. Or – could it be – you've forgotten? That's it, isn't it, you've settled. Made that family your mom and dad wanted. That family **I** couldn't give you. **You don't know I'm looking for you.**"

A shadow emerged into that darkness when he snuffed the lamplight. The figure's tall and broad; it lumbered into the chamber without a knock. By the totality of that January's night, he gauged only vague suggestions of a form of a man. Suggestions – that felt fuzzy at the boundaries. Wasn't that figment more imagined than real? 'Til Coyote slipped into the bedding, Dylan wasn't convinced, either way.

"Winters are best, keh, for sleeping."

"Cozy?"

"Yeah – I like the blanket – I like the company **better.**"

Dylan turned to where that voice emerged – Coyote's **intimate** voice straddled the timbers between a man's and a brute's.

It's an inadequate blanket. What a fuss to share it so! They rolled, spinning in then out, to tuck as tight as its fabric allowed.

Coyote poked a leg through its edge – a leg from foot to knee.

"It's a trick," he said, "to make it cold if it's too hot."

"For me, it's the pillow that's got to be cool."

"You a flipper?"

"Hope that won't be trouble."

Coyote brought a palm to Dylan's cheek – that paw traced a course from the cheek to the neck – where, without shirt or jacket as cover, he felt the choker.

"Big for a tiny, little neck, it's your ghost's, isn't it, kid?"

Dylan shut his eyes: "I didn't realize how careful we'd have to be. **Ca**yote ... do you ever think ... that ... **there's something wrong with us**?"

He felt the heat of Coyote's lips. They rubbed against his lips. It's a kiss as if they stumbled onto it. An accident that wasn't. A display of want whose haste exposed the shyness of its actors.

"What? Kid? What you're thinking? What you're thinking? It's dirty, isn't it? Keh, wow, ... it's dirty...."

"It's stupid," he sighed.

"You're stupid," he taunted.

The tease delivered by that growl/whisper served to elicit only a chuckle.

"We're not the problem. It's not us, OK? There's no dirty nothing – never was 'r will be. They keep making us, don't they? Got to be for reasons."

"You made it?"

He *holds it, raises it, studies it — that necklace I knotted out of smoothed polished bone — it rattles, chatters as it dangles.*

I grasp the ends where the straps are loose.

"They'll notice."

"Notice?"

My hands, gripping the ends of the choker, bring the straps into the veil of his hair at the back of his head. The choker yields a perfect fit. Tight like an embrace.

*"See, you feel **it**, you feel **me**," I say, tying the knot. "Even if you're lost, won't I be too? No matter what.... Remember, **I'm with you**."*

Dylan squeezed the choker – it wanted to fit like a necklace – a few bones were missing, randomly, throughout its length.

Above, the sky's misty. Below, the storm's dense. Snow, three foot thick, carpeted the #25 corridor.

He joined the company prompt that dawn – they got into their plows then jockeyed for position as dictated by rank.

He formed the left end. The crew master formed the right end. The bulk of them pushed into the middle. Together as a front, that alignment of plows surged forward like a comb to carve that road into five equally spaced, equally widened lanes.

That front travelled at its equipment's 1irst gear speed. He kept pace with his lot – that mixed talent crew. All would be well if he wasn't too fast, too slow. He let the lay of the road dictate what pressure to apply at the control. But the road proved uneven. And he feared breaking formation or worse. A struggle ensued – it was as if every inch of road were a fight that had to be wrestled free of fear. For a breath, he panicked. Claustrophobia? The cabin felt tight. It's shrinking, shrinking. Then – the effect passed as abruptly as it came. Yet the dread didn't lift: there were miles and miles of road to plow.

Were they going anywhere?

Convoys waited the front's advance uncertain if they were to idle or to follow.

The #25 corridor widened; the environment took shape as it came into view by degrees. Denver's a shell. What could be glimpsed of it at the edges of the road, wasn't it apocalypse? Much of the city's periphery had been abandoned; its structures were cannibalized; its remnants rotted away bit by bit. Skeletons of yesteryear haunted Dylan that night.

The road lurched uphill. He and his lot fumbled but didn't falter. They worked to match the pace of the crew master. They were told not to fan but to brake if they skidded. The convoys were a distant blip of light at the rearview. As they switched to a crawl, that blip grew larger **and brighter**. At the crest, the crew master yelled at them to stop. Then, together, they inched – link by link – into the maelstrom.

At that **sight,** he could have screamed.

The road's like a ramp, steep and unconstructed. It plunged a hundred feet as it banked to the left. There weren't barricades at the edges. There weren't signs to indicate where the via ended and the wild began. Too great a stray and they'd be off to their doom. As they lurched through that embankment, they caught a sight of the vista beyond the abyss – a valley majestic and ghastly.

He held the control as if life or death were a matter of accuracy. He wanted to focus only onto the road. He failed as his eyes roamed what they ought to avoid. Peaks of Rockies capped gray. Foothills distorted into mounds by the blizzard's wrath. Fire, fed by rubber, burned at the basin; a lighthouse of sorts to warn of danger.

As they completed the bank and the plunge, the road leveled, the sky oped: a vast display of starlight battled against the march of dawn.

A signaler directed that front to a ramp. They shuffled into a row led by the crew master. They followed onto a trail that spanned the road – then – plowed the other side of the #25 corridor.

By the 7eventh storm, Dylan learned to check his nerves. He worked up the chain, further and further to the right of the front, where the crew master directed their flow. By the end of the season, he accrued a tidy sum of suns and moons and a recommendation that would have landed a job at Eagle or Grand Junction, if he wished.

The pay's enough for fuel and food, maybe for lodging, too, if it were cheap. It wasn't enough for a plate – unless another kind of barter were possible. There's uncertainty about success. Antiquers around Denver didn't carry a plate appropriate for a jeep of its age. They claimed a dealer out of Walsenburg was certain to have what he wanted.

Walsenburg....

Weather and a want for coin derailed Dylan's plot. Denver's supposed to be a driveby. Rather, it went from January to March then May. It's not until they reach midspring almost June that roads were declared passable.

At night, while the unit slept, he resurrected the journey exactly as it started the midnight he fled Apollo. He packed his world into his duffel and volleyed out of the apartment, out of the floor, out of the unit like a man chased. Quietly, he slipped the solenoid into the engine – it started with a roar. Before anyone could have checked at the disturbance, he slumped into a deserted 3 **AM** street as the GPS mapped the trip east/south–east.

It started through Letsdale. Then it merged to #83. Then it paralleled the #25 corridor as it kept east of Castle Rock. The idea's to network sequences of byways onto the outskirts of Colorado Springs. From there it switched to #24, then, to #50. He opted to meander a trail from Pueblo to Junta. Ultimately to reconnoiter the antiquer at Walsenburg.

"There'll be plenty of fuel," he assured, "I took a map – a trucker left it at the bureau. It's got all of the cities with all of the pumps circled. There'll be plenty of fuel. I'm sticking to those communes that replenish their stock regularly. We can't take aye two five anyhow. I like byways, you know, we've got them to ourselves. Oh, we're roughing it. We'll be safe, mostly.... We'll be **alone**."

Coyote smirked – like Dylan, he grew then freed his braids that winter to let his hair catch the summer's wind. Somewhere he ditched the cloak for bare, naked chest. Dots of red painted the canvas of skin with patterns like stars.

The landscape, from the dark, to the light, sparkled at sunrise. The view ran a gambit from the populated to the untamed. The plains, east of the Rockies, were always sparse, weren't they?

As the journey approached the rear of (formerly) large settlements, ruins marred vistas. They were remnants reclaimed by traders or by governments and their carcasses furthered the impression of Armageddon. The display wasn't lawless as much as logical. It didn't make sense to let material rot by abandonment.

What couldn't be grown or dug was ripped off relics judged superfluous. The material that had been reclaimed was processed by hand into forms easily transported and sold. Tar's especially prized so roads were demolished. Both county and state roads were merely trails fit more for farming than for travelling. If it weren't for the GPS, Dylan simply wouldn't know the course to take through the wild that separated towns.

To the east, the plains were flat – at the horizon were suggestions of trees to break the monotony. To the west, the peaks were slanted, unbroken, as a line from north to south. Everything's decayed – the plains were yellowed, the peaks were gray. It wasn't taking as long for spring to root but temperatures hadn't yet reverted to normal.

Pike's Peak, visible by-the-by, loomed like a beacon. It grew out of haze in to reality as the jeep approached Colorado Springs. The radio tuned a broadcast from that settlement that verified stories passed by truckers at Denver. Colorado Springs 'came a haven for **cultistas**: a farce that remained of failed doomsday religions after their saviors refused to 'come'.

He opted to avoid entering Colorado Springs. Rather, at eve, he scouted what used to be a suburb. He stopped and waited by the jeep, with a map unfurled at that hood. He stopped and watched. **Listened.** Nobody could be heard coming in or out of that stretch of #83. As daylight waned, the vistas dimmed. There wasn't light from fire or smoke or any sort of activity to give the idea of occupancy credence. The whole entire area was left to itself.

At a roundabout, deep into what used to be a community, he located a ruin the size of a house. There's part of a roof intact – more or less – but walls were reduced to corners as they had been dismantled brick by brick. There's enough left to support the structure.

He parked the jeep at the front of the abode – a spot that could be reached by a jump, if he needed to escape.

Chief DeSoto gifted Dylan that jeep after he declared his intent to migrate. Apollo's a dot, stuck between Laramie and Cheyenne, a model that Wyoming promoted as the ideal commune. Everybody's connected. Everybody's eager to cooperate to survive.

They didn't waste time with that **cultista** bullshit.

Askew, between waking and dreaming, he reflected. Only as an adult, he realized how **complete** his childhood at Apollo had been. There wasn't anything he lacked. It's as if the last thirty odd years of history hadn't affected his life. Not so, of course. No, not so.

"Stupid, isn't it, **Cay**ote?" Dew collected at the roof like rain. It's rusted and the water splashed into the house. There's an odd sensation – a smell mixed with a taste together. It's water, spiced by iron, that dabbed at his face. "Didn't I make it difficult? Yeah, that's it, isn't it? I made it difficult. Everything that happened, it's a rouse. To get me out of Apollo. What I'd do to believe."

Pike's Peak, ever so melancholy, shrank then faded with a twang of unease as the journey switched west/south–west – to #124 – to #50. A straight road connected: Canyon, **to fuel**, Pueblo, **to sup**, Junta, **to bunk.** Or so Dylan thought. Junta's a disaster through and through. It's a rally for truckers and migrants and simply by the vibe he didn't want to stay. He opted for Purgutore where he camped by the jeep and the stars.

Dylan approached Walsenburg via #10. It's a late start; he figured, it wouldn't matter. It's not the destination, it's the journey. So, just free of Junta's reach, he pivoted out of #10. He drove across a track then parked in to a lot that appeared by the side of the byway. A signpost announced it's the Sierra Vista Overlook.

Centuries ago it had been part of the trail to Santa Fe. A segment of that trail connected the lot to Timpas further away ... if it were to be trusted. Posters at the perimeter of the lot preserved imagery related to its past. Exposed, as it was, to the air for decades, the UV almost burnt the paper crisp.

That dawn there had been traffic at Junta when he ambled by to fuel. At that lot, he listened then sighted a motorcade approach. He reached into the jeep for the map and caught the knife. He didn't spare a thought to pocket that weapon. The map, though, he took to the hood. He unfolded then pretended to read it. Tracing the route. Stopping to sip from the canteen. Eying the motorcade.

Dylan didn't like company at the road.

The parade's agricultural by the looks of it. Bikes were at the front. Tractors were at the rear. An ATV sped by the side of the train to be its lead. Their aim's business, transporting their wares, making their trades, perhaps, at Walsenburg too.

The motorcade passed while he bided – looking collected, he felt collected – he calmed.

Coyote, already out of the vehicle, rambled into the overlook itself – a mound too triangular to be natural.

Dylan followed, stopping every so often to gaze at the tracks.

At the peak of the overlook, the air carried a melody like a flute. The sun's overhead. It's noon. It's light enough to blind yet the day kept a chill that only at its periphery meandered into warmth. Ahead the world's a clash of blue above and yellow/gray below. At the horizon were faint shapes of mountains, misty not rocky.

"Ancestors of mine came by this trail. It hasn't changed. Important stuff, it doesn't." Coyote sat by Dylan. Their feet dangled over the edge of the overlook. "Or maybe it does – bit by bit – without notice. Can you imagine it? If the world only exists 'cause we're watching it. The act of watching it is making it. If we tried, couldn't we change it? Just by wishing it so, wouldn't it so?" He inhaled, deeply, the fresh air of spring then the shorter man turned to gaze at the taller man. "What are you gonna do, if you make the coast?"

"Float."

"If we don't?"

"Then **we** won't."

"**He** wanted that sort of life," Dylan confessed. "I must've intruded."

"Your ghost?"

Dylan shut his eyes; **my ghost**?

"Keh ... your journey, it's, **his** journey, huh?"

"Maybe I want to disappear, you know, you know **what I mean**? Maybe I'll drive and drive until the jeep breaks then I'll fade away."

"Eh? We got a problem, don't we? **Indians** don't fade away. Stop saying shit when you know better. What're you going to do? Cry, I suppose. I'll cry if it helps."

He and I escape the tent that night.

The moon is cracked. The sky is pitched. There isn't a wisp to hide stars. **Stars!** They twinkle like a rainbow. Their cool, eerie colors relax our eyes. Teachers say stars are suns. With worlds. **Like our worlds?** With people. **Like our people?** To explore the vastness – isn't that man's destiny? – **if folly doesn't squander fate.** Maybe thousands and thousands of years later we'd wander that sky. Maybe we won't.... That night, though, the stars follow **us**.

We flee to a trail then to a forest. As we hike, up and up, the sky 'comes a twisted patchwork of light and dark. The trees knit their leaves into a blanket. We feel frosty as the sights through that cover turn surreal. A scent of aspen chokes the air. The sound from the wild overwhelms the sound from the climb. We are shocked by a primacy that neither of us were prepared to face. Perhaps it is our excitement? Perhaps it is our isolation? Something heretofore unknown magnifies the intensity of the night we experience.

Aren't we fools?

We fear.... Still – we **hunger** more than we **fear**. Ah, so much, so much. Where'd it start? That fear we'd be caught? Aren't we free to love, if we wanted it so?

Our hike stops at the overlook in front of the valley.

Below us, the rhythm of the herd beats an ovine melody.

Isn't it the place where boys take girls? – for a while, it will be **ours**.

We fumble, uncertain of what to do, with ourselves, with each other. We struggle to express the fire that draws us together. Our lips break the ice not by their words but by their kisses. Their encouragement takes us from kissing to speaking. Soon strings of 'yes' and 'no' shatter the paralysis of our shyness. At last, braving our shame, we achieve a dialog of intimacy. We cross to where, from where there could be no return.

... **our** honeymoon....

He sighs as I curl by his side.

"I want to go everywhere, Dyl," **he** confesses. "Everywhere. Let me. Won't you let me?"

I want to reply, to echo. Intoxicated by the escapade, my reply is my smile.

After a spell, we tumble about the grass – what raw, naked exuberance! – our hands meet and our fingers zipper. We give into each other's fire.... The persistence of space and time, if they existed, disintegrate like the illusions they always were. Am I there? I feel it anew – the grass at my face – the weight at my back. **I am there!** – as if not a breath passed. Is the universe so vast that a fantasy might 'come a reality?

Coins, either sun or moon, were reserved for those commodities propped by the governments of the West. That's true especially of diesel and of water, which were produced by the states and allotted by that volume of coinage a community produced. Food was covered by coinage to a limited extent. For the rest, rates were arranged. Or bartered – goods and services were exchanged as like for like **effort**.

Plates were tricky – antiquers weren't allowed to sell plates.

Governments stopped issuing plates by about the period when the country ceased to produce vehicles. As corridors 'came venues for convoys, commoners travelled less and less, eventually, they didn't travel anymore. Journeys, long range, long term travels were thought to be a relic of yesteryear.

Vehicles weren't regulated. Licenses weren't issued. Traffic wasn't controlled – per say – by enforcement. Communes of importance adhered to a set of informal rules for roads. Away from civilization, it simply didn't matter.

The effects of a plate were psychological. Travelers weren't met by hostility if they carried a domestic plate. Authenticity's key, however, a plate's age ought to match a vehicle's age or the illusion's shattered.

Dylan fed the antiquer a tale about escaping that might have, could have been true from a certain point of view. The lady's sympathetic, to a degree. She wanted a level of coinage that would have burst his budget. He started to list, mentally, a series of objects that could be traded. She took a gander at the jacket.... Leather wasn't easy to come by. Even the embroidery, work that had been machined decades ago, fetched a hefty sum at the market. It's a collector's piece, she insisted, offering the plates **and a hundred pieces extra** for the jacket.

He shut his eyes and bit his lips ... then, hesitantly, transferred the jacket's contents into his pants pockets.

She examined the garment, growing more and more impressed.

"DeSotos', I remember that ranch from my days cutting through aye eight zed," she said of it. "It's quite a way for this jacket to go."

Her sons produced a bag of coinage and a pair of glossy if rusted turquoise plates. The metal's frayed at the edges. They were classic New Mexico plates she swiped from a 4 x 4 – a white and black jeep – that they spotted, crashed into a ravine.

He walked out of the shop then sat, breathless, at the gravel by the jeep.

"Wrong.... Wrong.... Wrong!" he screamed inside.

His body cooled, unyoked by the jacket.

Now it wasn't merely the insistence of space and time that separated him from what happened at Apollo. Now the very real, very tangible connections to that past were disintegrating. What would be left of it? He felt hollow and feared the squander of the jacket amplified the proportion of the tragedy.

"I'm not proud of it," his pen scribbled at his notepad. It's the 7eventh page. The 1irst through 6ixth sheets curled, dense with ink, deep blue and black. Scarcely a bit of white was left.

The notepad's edge fluttered, caught as it were, by the breeze.

Where'd your smile go? Dylan thought, studying the wallet's picture, its black and white image. *It's no more. No. No. No more. That even a worm has life....*

He sat on gravel and dirt in front of the jeep. It's the lot of the Rambler, an inn that abutted the #25 corridor away from Walsenburg. The lot's a refuge encased by that inn. He's isolated from the ruckus beyond; although, every so often, he heard the convoys pass the road to or from places unknown.

He's as of yet undiscovered by whoever minds the establishment.

"I never bought the official story. Most of it's the DeSotos' keeping face. Our relationship, it wasn't **that** secret. I can't put into words what it did to me. When my folks died, it was **he** who grounded me, pushed me to stay, trained me to work. He 'came my world. What am I supposed to do? Maybe just die somewhere, somewhere **Natural**. Away from prying eyes. I don't want to be slabbed."

The pen, like the awkward flow of reality, slipped free of his grip.

It's visceral, that reaction, as if it were happening again, again right there, right there. Nothing felt true anymore. Senses blurred into stupors. Was it nightmare? He thought – **if he'd screamed, he'd awake**. That miracle – it doesn't happen. There's no screaming, no awaking to break the spell. What happened at Apollo – it's not imagined, it's real.... It was, is, would be **forever**.

Dylan reclined at the floor. The Rambler Inn didn't stock a luxury like a mattress. Only walls and roofs were provided. There wasn't anybody to mind the place.... He had waited hours and hours without notice. By the lull of eve, he left a few sun and moon pieces at the desk then took a room for that night. #2B, the room, like the establishment, endured **silently.**

A breeze worked through gaps that had been its windows and its doors. That wind rattled strips of fabrics. They were what formed the curtains, the dividers between the outside and the inside. Their dance supplied the entertainment that night.

It's moonless, neither hot, neither cold. The night's shadow and darkness was interrupted by convoys. Trucks raced through the #25 corridor. Their headlamps swept right to left, left to right. Their lights flashed the chamber.

The truckers who stopped to fuel by the establishment grumbled about Raton's jam. They'd need to leave earlier than they pleased to beat its congestion. As sun set they formed a cue at the ramp that shortened one by one. When they fled, at last, it felt as if the entire town of Walsenburg's a ghost.

The solitude's profound and it bristled at his nerves.

Where am I going?

It's dangerous to be left with his thoughts. He questioned everything that led into that juncture. He kept replaying that afternoon when he realized **he's not coming back.**

He fled home. He couldn't, just, couldn't run fast enough. He burst through the door then into the basement. Their clothes lay scattered without a care where they had been tossed yesterday. He picked and picked at the evidence then crammed clothes into drawers. **Why did he scream**? *– he didn't know, didn't know what to do....*

Cool, spring air refreshed #2B. It poured through gaps as if it were water flooding a vessel. At the windows and the doors, it forced the curtains to flail like leaves. The lights kept coming – again and again – crawling from side to side. Some raced. Some lagged. Every so often a pair of headlamps lingered a while. There's no end to it.

He turned from right to left.

The Rambler's shaped like a ring with that lot at the interior of the structure. There's only a single access in or out of it. He judged it's a safe spot to park the jeep that night. Past the curtain's strips of fabrics, he noted the outline of the vehicle. Still where it's parked.

There's a woodsy scent to the air. Snatches, bits by-the-by, of a melody drifted through the breeze. Wasn't it like fantasy? As if it were simply dreamt?

"Aren't you getting a weird thought about New Mexico and Arizona, kid? Did you think about Durango? Maybe cut into Utah? Nevada! Don't the Mormons run a better state than the **cultistas**?"

"Yeah, aye seven zed ends at Utah," he mused, "Nevada's a wasteland, anyhow. Cali took its water. It's not possible to cross Nevada. We need to cross New Mexico and Arizona to reach Cali. It won't be so dangerous, if we stick north instead of south. I – **yeah** – I sacrificed too much to quit."

The blanket, wrapped tight and tight against them, parted the night's cold from their hot.

"You can drop me anywhere, kid, you know, anywhere, anytime."

Dylan faced at the window as it brightened – "No...."

Convoys took gravel from Colorado to a project deep into New Mexico and Arizona. A project whose extreme demands for material and labor brought rushbodies from East of the Miss like the good, old-fashioned West. It's state business; by the volume of the load, though, the truckers figured it dealt with a barrier. Texas always itched for a wall to secure the border with Mexico. Specifically – the **land** border that stretched between the Grande and the Colorado rivers.

Mexico gave into anarchy after oil collapsed. Its instability fractured into a war whose front shifted from Texas to Panama. Cali took advantage of the distraction to sweep Baja – that Colorado basin was easier to defend than a border through desert. Arizona's and New Mexico's borders were deserts but they weren't judged defensible.

Texan forces were stretched. It taxed that state to the point where its government considered cutting its clients if action weren't taken. So they resurrected that idea of a wall. A great, southern wall to rival China's.

"I won't try Raton's Pass, if it's going to be jammed. I'll take one six zed to Alamosa then two eight five to the border. There'll be a forest to cross. There'll be wilderness maybe fifty miles, twenty miles? That part of the border's like Apollo. There'll be a network of roads connecting farms. Too many.... So remote, too, that they won't have checkpoints."

Dylan stormed together an alternate route that dawn. From #160 to #12, thus, avoiding Veta's Pass. From #12 to Stonewall. According to his data, roads hugged at a segment of that Sangre de Cristo range. They're gravel perhaps forest roads but they'd take the jeep right into New Mexico. If they kept going, they'd gather at the Vermejo River then they'd converge onto #555.

Once the jeep crossed the border, the trip would be a race toward the four corners region. **That** would be a matter of feeling for the best route west. So long as the journey averted the border with Mexico, there'd be little to fret about other than fuel and food.

An hour of adventure later and the jeep made it through the junction of #160 and #12 by the ramp to Veta's Pass. He re-aimed the drive to go from Alamosa to Stonewall. At that switch it felt as if the land reacted and parted to reveal the clearest if remotest view yet of Colorado's interior. The San Luis Valley was a spring not completely, not fully awakened. Its basin bloomed yellow that at touches here and there burst verdant. Afar, from north to south, snaked a row of peaks still grayed by snow. Beyond it were vagaries, like a wispy, smoky haze, of more and more mountains. The vastness of it stretched the eye to the limit.

At first #12 started as an improvement of #160. Devoid of traffic, its isolation teetered from idyll to dreadful. Communes were rooted by that road. Their pumps were empty, unmanned. At the city of Veta he learned that diesel from Sterling hadn't and wouldn't arrive for a month. They're a modest priority to Colorado as their population dwindled.

The tank's over its half way mark so for a while there wasn't a cause to worry.

Then, out of the void, came the rises and the falls of Cuchara's Pass.

It's gradual so, so easy to miss. He felt it more at the head than at the gut. A sort of dizziness surged like a wave. It's too late to react. His ears popped. His eyes wavered. His mind struggled to keep focus. The road's gravel rotted into dirt. It's like a trench at spots as the jeep negotiates hairpins.

Did anybody travel #12 at all?

Beyond the pass waited the lodges of Stonewall. They embraced exactly the kind of life that sustained a commune. Theirs was a trade that produced and shipped lumber from the San Isabel forests to parts throughout Colorado. The state provided them plenty of diesel for their industry. Especially – as spring 'came summer – when they aimed to restart their harvest.

A tank of diesel quenched that jeep's thirst....

According to the map, the trip's last ten miles traced the eastern side of the Sangre de Cristo's.

Dylan left the jeep where the road forked then hiked a bit south. He sought assurance that the trail stayed navigable. The road's disrepair alarmed him.... He watched the grade, minded the width. It's ample enough for the jeep to pass **and not much more than that**.

Almost at the border, he stopped to inspect the vista.

The road hugged a narrow sliver of ledge between the range and the valley. He traced its trajectory to the extent that his stance permitted. The trail's framed by forestry; nevertheless, it wasn't obstructed.... To the right the ascents were too raw to climb via jeep. To the left the descents were barren, beginning shallow then ending steep.

Way afar and below he spotted the Vermejo River. It drained from a pool of melt and flowed to that gorge. Its water sparkled as its course twisted through the valley. A bridge crossed its rapids. Gates for livestock braced the ends of that span. Beyond that, everything had to be New Mexico.

He couldn't spy activity at the bridge. Nobody officiated its crossing either north or south. It may have been a relic from yesteryear that authorities forgot. Or, perhaps, it's frequented by ranchers. If so, there'd be trails. Livestock coming to and from that bridge would have etched trails at the dirt. Trails – that merged into roads – that merged into communes.

Sunset threatens as Dylan returns.

"It's going to be crazy," he warns.

He checks the map — his fingers blaze a trail more or less from the Vermejo River to #555. That north, north/west quadrant of New Mexico is close to Arizona and far from Raton. **Perfect.** Marryville, if it exists, will be the goal or **bust**.

He aims the jeep into the road. Uneven due to weather, the trail is a mix of gravel and dirt, eager to shred tires. The vehicle shakes as if to protest that abuse. The approach is torpid. The drive is jagged. Into that forest everything, everywhere is choked by shade. The sky is hinted not revealed until a mile of incline passes by.

The swatting of trees against tires adds a timbre unique to that journey — it comes as a reminder that the road is scarcely wide enough to admit the jeep.

After the climb, the road levels and winds. That trail is a trench too narrow to U–turn it. There was not, is not, will not be an opportunity to quit. The goal is only forward, **only onward.**

At 7,000 feet the forest retreats. Cover is either to the left or to the right. Overhead, skies are graphic streaks of violet. Then — the forest evaporates to expose the jeep. At the east there sinks the valley. At the west, there rise the peaks. The road is less and less of a trench but that victory is pyrrhic. At last, the trail is exposed as a ledge, narrow and rugged, without a trench as guide or as safety.

Dylan realizes the road is not level — it is banked ever so slightly from the peaks to the valley. It enters into the realm of the conceivable to stop and turn at the revelation. Except for fear that if the tires stray, the jeep topples into doom.

The bank is steady — so far, so good — yet he struggles to find the right speed to drive. He wants it to be slow. He swaps from **D** to **2**. He contemplates **1** just to keep control. The road's rattle is curtailed at speed less than **20 MPH**. Yes — he sets the transmission at **1**.

As the sun vanishes, an eerie, misty haze fills the vista. Twilight amplifies its gloom. He grips the wheel as if it were ready to snap. He shifts his focus. He keeps his eyes low not simply for nerves but for safety. Dangers would be right in front of the jeep if they were to materialize. Maps and GPS alike agree that the road as a whole is straight but neither were updated since **YZ**. And age is not kind to that path. In spite of that, not a sign, neither overt nor subtle, indicates it is avoided by loggers.

Four miles from the border, he crawls to a stop. The terrain flattens and widens. All is pitch above and below. Eyes, however, spot a disturbance.

"Didn't you always talk about sights like these?" he says. "That's Raton. Look at the lights; it's the convoys, weaving up and down that pass. We must be, what, three thousand feet atop that snarl? What a thing, **man**. What a thing."

Dylan drinks out of the canteen then speeds with the headlamps switched **lo** to **hi**. The GPS displays the crossing from Colorado to New Mexico. The **inches** of road waiting to be driven are life and death balanced — it will be so until the journey stops at the bridge.

The gut notices.... The foot races to hug then to kiss the brake. The head aches. The road — **it slants**. Down! Down! That slant came so swiftly he fears the GPS led astray. But the road is supposed to be a ledge. And not by the slightest, **not by the slightest** is he free to deviate. The only way is forward, onward.

The vehicle jolts.

The road that starts narrow ends wide. Without warning, he drives to where the trail had been swept by landslide. The GPS insists right. The momentum veers left. The path is simply a ride, rocky but steady, into abyss.

"We're almost out," he conjures that idea if just to keep his wits. "We're almost out...."

He lets his eyes gaze to where the light reveals the bridge. It waits ahead, below. A bump arrests the jeep's slip. The vehicle surfs the landslide and makes it safe to where the avalanche intersected the road **again**. It simply forges a straighter albeit deadlier path than it expected to follow.

Dylan **barks**.

At the end of the bridge, Dylan stepped out of the jeep then swept its perimeters to examine its tires.

He stopped to enjoy **life**. The night's starlit. The air's fresh. There's a scent of aspen. It's a mix of temperatures by what way the wind blew.

The Colorado plates had to be withdrawn. The back's OK. The front's stuck. Its top left screw refused to budge. That knife's tip wasn't enough to complete the job. A hammer's blow broke the corner. The new (old) plates were screwed into position – fully at the back, partially at the front. There it dangled at its top right screw.

Then, rising, turning, he's knocked by a punch to the chest – the knife and the hammer slipped out of his grips.

Against the road, he fought to breathe then to compute. He tried and failed to locate where the weapons dropped. Right then he scrambled to catch a view of the attacker.

There's a shade by his jeep's driver's side. It aimed a kick – it missed, slipped. The boot hit the bumper not the ribcage.

He took the chance and grasped then jerked the boot.

The movement sent the attacker onto the hood.

A shriek's uttered – it wasn't **his**.

That figure of a man staggered but got to its feet and made yet another attempt at Dylan. It set grips at his shoulders to push him into the grille. Then knee after knee bruised his sides. *Where's that knife?* he reeled. *Isn't it there?* He hoped the knife's glint wasn't fantasy – it's real not imagined – it's at the bumper. Then he made a motion as if he were to slip and fall ... but he grasped the handle and he lunged the blade.

Like a bolt, furious and crazed, he aimed that knife. **Stab**! He felt his hand wet ... **Stab**! Heat trickled through the gaps of the fingers ... **Stab**!

The attacker staggered then collapsed, spitting a word too faint to be heard.

At his feet, cool if shaken, Dylan peeled his shirt off his body, wrapped it around and around the knife. He wiped the blood from his hands to his arms. He flung the heavy, clotted bundle into the jeep. **Then fled.**

A mile into that race he noticed the headlamps were off. He slowed, stopped at the side of the road. He flipped the switch to illuminate the view. With the cabin lit, he turned to gaze at the trunk where the bundle rested by the tailgate. He turned then to his hands, to his arms. They were not entirely, completely clean.

He stepped out of the vehicle to spill the canteen's water onto the skin's stains.

Nothing had been taken from the jeep. Not the GPS. Not the maps. Not the wallet. Nothing of value. He had been attacked directly ere anything was stolen.

For a while, he loitered at the edge of the river, rapt by eerie and distant woodsy impressions. The world's a blur. He felt as if he were withdrawn. Separated. Parted. He judged everything that happened through a disjointed point of view. He relived the fight – blow by blow – until he put together a picture of what transpired at the bridge.

As reality settled, he felt weights at his shoulders, weights that took the impressions of arms then of embraces. It's a lock of warmth that tethered Dylan to that world. His body, battered, failed to resist the intimacy broached by the contact. Yet his mind retched.

"Please ... no, no.... **Don't. Ca**yote."

"**Don't?**" a voice growled/whispered.

He reached to his neck and shivered as his blood **iced – the choker! – where'd it go**?

"Don't forgive me."

> Chief DeSoto said it's an accident. I didn't see the body. Nobody saw it or admitted it – **not to me.**

"Where'd it happen?"

I didn't **want** to know.

"The pass east to the cities, north from the Market. That's where Jordan found his bike. He landed at the ravine."

The chief told me what transpired. I was stunned. For a while, I was frigid. There's a ceremony that eve. I wasn't involved. Didn't know how to be. Didn't know **if they wanted me** to be. Wrong tribe, I guess. His remains were burnt then scattered. The family turned the page, that's that.

There wasn't a will to dispose of. Still, the chief decreed **I** was the inheritor. A day after that I got **the box.** They left it at my door. They filled it; it's stuff I hadn't already kept of his possessions. The jacket he'd been wearing. The wallet he'd been carrying. **Somebody** took the old Federal dollars he'd stuff into the fold. Not saying it's **anybody.** The DeSotos' lack the want for cash anyhow.

The box.... It's my **finality,** isn't it? The moment it came I knew, I knew **he's gone.** Like that. Just like that – he's alive then he's dead. Now a body. Now a pile of ash. A switch, **flipped.**

The older generations, like the chief, they felt it worst. They remembered yesteryear – the age when the species tamed its mortality. The newer generations accepted it. Families, they **started** large.

Life's temporal – see – it's fragile, you can push it, you can push it, then, it's broken. Life – there's something **fake** about it. It's not real.... Death – it's real, it's natural. 'Cause it's forever.

"The pass east to the cities, north from the Market."

That pass doesn't get a lick of traffic. It's too narrow and too steep for trucks. Heck – **bikes** avoid it. Jordan only ever used it to shove tractors from farm to market.

It must have been the day they delivered the box that I travelled to the Market. It's sober. Everyone's upset. He **was** a fixture – there all the time, all the time. He'd visit often to hawk the ranch's produce.

It's where he was last seen **alive.**

Owner Calie – she said, er, she said it's sunset when he left. He rode out of the lot. She didn't know why he rode **fast**. May have been trying to catch somebody. No **other** detail's strange. To the contrary, it had been so normal a day that it's forgettable. Ah, they serviced a few riders from Texas, who came and went with deliveries. That's as eventful as it were.

The Market's where Apollo traded its mail. Horsemen were fond of the joint. **Everyone** in or out of town went there, didn't they?

I shuffled north from the Market to the road. That pass, it wasn't far. Most of Apollo's a plateau that's at worst a hundred or so feet over the plains. At its perimeter it's not much of a grind, you don't **notice** you're going up or down slope. Except at **that pass** – it's a cliff, a perfect, vertical drop so to speak. That you **do** notice.

The road starts and it's a sharp left bend. There's nothing to separate you and the ravine. The road sidewinds to the west for a quarter of a mile. At the midpoint of the course, it's a sharp right bend. The road continues to the north for a mile. That's where it levels onto the plains. Jordan's property expands out of there.

I always hated that pass. We'd ride through it from time to time. I'd sit and I'd hold **and hold** for my life. Keh, I'm sure that's why he liked it. As for me, I'd always fear he'd ride too fast and he'd slip and slide. **Damn him**.... Just, **damn him**.

None of it made sense to me.

Why he'd take that pass at sunset?

Where's he going?

Not to meet Jordan. Not to ride toward Cheyenne or Laramie. There wasn't any reason, any reason **what so ever** to go there.

The chief only said the obvious. That he sped into that pass. That a tire burst. He didn't wear a helmet.... The chief went on and on about that helmet like it mattered. A helmet? – there's nothing, **nothing** at the road to stop the tumble into the ravine.

It's so **empty** that I expected to find **fresh** evidence. The gravel's not going to record skids. Rather, it's apt to preserve rips and tears. There ought to be a gash where the accident **happened**. Try to picture that bike at its side plunging, scrubbing the gravel, maybe, exhuming the dirt. I don't find a gash. Not a sign that a bike and a rider separated. Ah, there were plenty of horsetracks. **Droppings** – lots and lots of droppings. Horses were there and were there **for a while**.

I crawled my way past the edge of the road. Well, **a tiny, little bit** past the edge of the road. It's a cliff. Er, it's not **straight**. Its got **these steps**, these ledges spaced apart just so to let you climb them up and down. It wasn't at the bottom of the ravine but at a wide, narrow ledge that they found him. They wouldn't tell me which but it didn't take a lot of effort to figure it. We were between seasons; nothing's growing so nothing's obscuring my view.

I hiked right to where the road leveled. It's where the droppings were worst. There must have been three horses. Not one. Not two. Three. **There must have been three.** They left a mess that reeked.

It's where I noticed....

I was a full mile ahead, below where they said the accident happened. Far from where the body's found. Nevertheless, that's where I noticed **a glint**. It came out of the gravel. I picked until I freed it. It's a bleached, polished bone.

Wasn't I pathetic? I hadn't put two and two together when they gave me the box. Both the jacket and the wallet were trifled! No by the DeSotos' though. The shock of it struck me. Yet – I couldn't **feel** – my mind stepped out of my body. I watched **not** reacted.

I combed the gravel and the dirt to patch the choker bone by bone. I fanned from the road to the edge where I recovered a strap that clutched the rest of the necklace.

The leather's cut not shredded, **not snapped. Cut.** Clean, too.

It's tough to throw **far** anything flimsy like that necklace. They kicked it? I don't know. It's night.... Maybe they just didn't see? Maybe they just didn't care?

That ride through the avalanche proved too stressful for the tires. The jeep made it a few miles east of Marryville then stopped. Firstly, the rear left deflated. Lastly, the front right exploded. It took a mighty heave of effort to exchange the burst and the spare then to drive the flat. Afraid that it's hurting not helping, Dylan opted to **drag** that wreck the rest of the way.

Marryville's a village whose proportions were sympathetic to Apollo's layout.

He identified and approached a market. He located the owner and enquired about anybody who may be willing to scrap a jeep with three out of five tires. A hand raised out of the crowd gathered to lunch at the cafe. Indeed, there's a rancher, Old Man Tapper, who would be willing, **if it were diesel**.

He kept by the side of the jeep for the remainder of that day, trying often failing to stay composed. To get his mind off the setback, he studied maps and plotted courses. Already he formed the outline of a tour to Cali.

As eve approached, he questioned if anyone were eager to trade with a stranger then contemplated the reality of leaving the jeep. He started to pack only those items he intended to keep – eyeing that bundled, clotted shirt, shoving it into his duffel.

Right as he felt hope fade, Old Man Tapper and four relatives appeared via ATVs.

While the grandchildren inspected the jeep, Dylan and Tapper conferred. The traveler explained his adventure through wasteland south of Alamosa. The rancher's impressed but low-balled the offer. Dylan wondered if an exchange for a bike were possible. Tapper stated that: "Bikes aren't available outside of the Navajo's."

They met at a deal that involved employment for a rate exceeding what had been offered for the jeep. The rancher's grand sons and daughters worked to scrap the jeep where it rested against the curb. Dylan, at the side of the ATV, watched the youngsters and tried not to betray a tear....

That night he slept at a cot at a tent abutting the Tappers' ranch – it may as well be the moon.

Marryville had always been a crossroads; folks from four states dropped by to trade. Even Texas. Many truckers to and from Arizona still swapped at the market. Few **stayed** when they tired of the road.

Corn's what the Tappers' and the village specialized. Every so often, they raised cattle. They wanted to mine but lacked the wherewithal. So long as everybody's employed, everybody's content. They were spoilt to a certain level of prosperity.

Old Man Tapper wanted the jeep's engine to assist the mine's restoration. The aim's to compete with Colorado's gravel. It didn't swallow well among cultistas how much **foreign** gravel funneled into the Wall.

Days spread into weeks. His grade increased job by job. He's fitted for security like his ancestors. He's considered educated thus treated as a commodity. There's promise of a future. Albeit a **tenuous** future. Only his **accent** not his introversion prevented a 'social' climb to match that 'economic' success.

The world's changed. It wasn't what his parents knew of it. Ever more distant and isolated, seemingly at the verge of collapse, ties between people – fostered by advances to technologies rendered impotent – were swept away by the immediate need to serve life from day to day. If not so by parts, then by whole, they were set to plunge into feudalism.

There's a strange sort of hollowness that reverberated through Marryville. It wasn't the town, per say, as it existed ages ere he stumbled onto it. The emptiness – it came from within not from without. Life had to it such promise. *Where'd it go?* He tallied his adventures, all of those mountains and valleys, all of those seasons of travels. Only coldly were they related into his notepad.

He reached for the wallet and flipped through its photographs. He filled it with scraps. Photographs of people and places from yesteryear. Then – then the last picture – then the only, real picture **he** kept there that nobody took away. A photograph, glossy yet rough with texture, its edges frayed.

It was them, at the remains of a fair, where they found a booth that took pictures. Amazingly, it worked in spite of its years. At the shock of its flash, he gave a kiss to that cheek. **His** look of surprise was recorded there forever and forever trapped by its 2 x 2 frame.

He fumbled to shut the wallet when others entered the tent. They stank of slaughter and that thought of blood churned his gut. They were older, his parent's age, if they lived, and thoroughly devoted (crazed) **cultistas**. At night, they argued, again and again, about China and Russia. Another truther poked their head into the tent to remind them of what the radio said, of India's war that the Feds were supporting. Nobody's convinced if reports from Asia were to be trusted.

Everyone fired. Everyone – **except the US.**

Throughout the world the reaction to **YZ** varied by continent. The Pacific fell silent. Africa erased its borders and its peoples settled into a kind of equilibrium – although skirmishes flared about the Sahara. Europe, like the US, retreated to hibernate – its governments downsized to its capitals. Asia's a mix of downsizing and warring. India's probably the only part of Asia that survived **intact**. Its agreeable land was and continued to be targets of attack by what's left of Russian and Chinese belligerents.

North and South America were spared the (early) wrath of **YZ** until the climate upended. Skies at dusk and dawn reveled across a spectrum that didn't match pictures from yesteryear. Soot cooled the world then winters usurped summers. Snows were black **Year Zero.**

Later he found Coyote at the market's lot.

"You're going to stay?" he spoke through that growl/whisper. "**Here?**"

"Why not?" Dylan turned. "Can't I stop?"

"Cultistas! They're not **your** people, kid."

They were silent a spell as the breeze kicked sand.

"Where are you going?"

"Coast."

"I'm sorry, **Cayote. I couldn't help**. It's a shit town, isn't it? **Cayote**, why'd it need to be this way?"

"Hey, kid, stop that. Stop that! You dumb, stupid kid. You're free to drop me anywhere, anytime. Always were.... Look how far you took me. Keh! Farther than I prayed."

A tear welled and that tall, broad man stopped to give a kiss, lips-to-lips, a flagrant expression to challenge whose eyes might have, could have spied their scene.

Dylan watched coolly if achingly as the figure turned to hike the road, dust sweeping his tracks, fading him into deeper, deeper shades of yellow, then, wiping him out of sight entirely.

"What did I do?"

He ambled into the market at the end of the lot. The front's a cafe frequented by the labor. Nary an eye followed as he approached the bulletin. Its notices had not been updated. As he dug into their posts, he realized their dates ended when his journey began. It's a testament to how remote an eon it had been since that area touted its importance to commerce.

His gaze shifted to the patrons, to the walls, to the windows that faced the dusty wispy road west.

Voices bawled about that night's broadcast and conspiracy. That Mexicans were (apparently) stealing jobs. That China or Russia were set to invade Cali for its farms. Ah, they weren't unanimous about that.... Others persisted the notion of America's safety 'cause of its oceans.

He looked from table to table but found only the trapped not merely by geography but by thought heretofore alien to his psyche. Marryville's isolation and depression incarnate. Its economy was controlled by the Tappers' who held the cards. What were the chances he or anybody could have broken free? If he stayed, that's his future, right then and there, that's his future.

Dylan pined at the windows – **why did its vistas appear smaller, ever more and more distant?**

Go! That's the word. At the idea's onset, his mind accepted it, his body accepted it, together they replied with a revulsion that cut the paralysis. **Go!** – his spirit wailed until he reached the door, his duffel pounding his back.

He struggled to escape the crowd – their irksome burst of discord impeded any notion of a straight trajectory across the market.

That town – **it wasn't for him.**

Had it been a minute since he watched Coyote vanish? A minute for feet to walk curb to market, market to curb.... Had it been so far? *Where'd he go? West* – yes...

Their separation – it had been short in time yet long in distance. Dylan sped to the foothills west of Marryville. At their summit, he gasped, stunned by the miles and miles of road that exploded beyond them. The valley between ranges soared to the horizon. He struggled to grasp the immensity of the vista. Coyote could be anywhere.

Was there enough time? Was there enough space? How'm I to search all of that? Dylan raced into that expanse. Coyote wasn't lost. *It's the road!* He'd follow the road.

At a ridge, where it swerved like an 'S', the road flaunted pavement: a jet tar vividly against a frost sand. Yellow stripes glistened as if fresh at the middle of the via. He surged through its bumps, its gentle peaks and valleys. As the road straightened into a view of crimson sky, he caught his breath – there's a scent to that desert and the way its wind stirred its sand reverbed like notes too fragile to sense as music.

He feared that any fault, even a word, if uttered, would have shattered the mirage like a needle to a bubble.

So it's that, step by step, the vague notion of a shape condensed into the proportions of a man.

"Hey, um, you going my way?" he asked.

Coyote stopped to flash **that** smile. "Where **we** going?"

"Coast."

Coyote grasped Dylan's shoulders. "I always believed you, Dyl."

It's ten miles west of Marryville. They stood, cloaked by the vastness of sky and land. There's not a hesitation as they sink into each other's warmth.

"If something's meant to be, it's meant to be? People fated to be together, yeah, they'd find each other. They'd keep crossing paths. They'd keep seeking...."

That night's sky – and its eerie, cool light – revealed the site. Yesteryear it had been a rest stop. Age reduced its structures to foundations. Weeds, thick and reedy, enmeshed its ruins. Tonight that rest stop would be a camp.

"**Cayote**," Dylan sighed, tucking the picture of themselves into the wallet. "How'd you stand it, **me**, a dumb, stupid kid?" He stopped to gaze west – the highway's straight through bare, naked land. It's silent; not a trace of activity was betrayed by its tranquility. He should have been afraid; strangely, he felt, he felt.... "**Cayote**! Are you by me? In Denver that winter. Across mountains and valleys. Weren't you there **that** night too? **I want to believe**. At that road after Marryville – say it wasn't as real as anything! Isn't that enough?"

His bike stood parked about the rubble. At the north, there's a stretch of highway. At the south, there's a track. Earlier, a train dragged its shipment of coal from Colorado to Cali. Later, he wondered how prudent it would be to jump and ride away.

Pipes jetted by the sides of the tracks. They gathered dew that trickled like rain. Funnels collected the water into the canteen. Thirsty, he sipped – its flavor echoed metallic timbres.

It's time to swap plates. He rummaged his duffel – lighter as he travelled farther. He dug – **where's it, those plates, those tiny, little plates**? His bike's plates ... they were easier to afford – mostly 'cause of size – they were easier **to mislay**.

Desperate, he yanked away treasure after treasure. There's that notepad with the kernel of the novel. There's the GPS. And a few maps. And a few bulletins. He's at want of a job as that bike cost a fist's worth of coinage.

At the bottom, he found the bundled, clotted shirt. It's heavy with the knife. Far, at the weeds, he unfurled the shirt. Everything tumbled. **Everything**? It had to be **just** the knife – yet – there's something, something **other**.

Dylan pulled it out of the grass – **the choker**!

"**Cayote** ... you come back." He brought the choker to his neck. He didn't need to imagine Coyote any more than he had to conjure up the sun or the moon. **Coyote was there** – in the drift of scents – in the lure of melodies – the hot against the cold – everywhere, forever it's so. "I would've died if I lost you. But I never did! ... you've never, never been beyond my reach. Even now, you're here, **Cayote!**" A breeze rattled through that gossamer webwork of leather and bone. "You live 'cause my journey makes you live."

★

The Jeffreys

Cat tumbled onto the remnants of **Tallas**. That ghost town, forgotten a century ago, waited at the end of a five hour hike, alarmingly if not unsettlingly deep into uncharted parts of the **Dominguez**. The geologist had ventured through terrain dotted by collapsed and abandoned mines and labyrinthine tracks – eerily traversed yet absent from any of his descriptions – all just to reach **that** destination. Even as he celebrated the achievement, he mused or joked, if it had been wise to veer into that oasis of solitude right at the cusp of a wintry holiday. It was far, far too late to retreat, though, which ever way the verdict went.

The administration at **Grand Junction University** didn't provide funds to pay for expeditions. Geologists ought to be at the field, he protested. Safety undercut his argument. Undeterred, every so often, he brought students into the wilderness. Summer usually proved to be the optimal season except class wasn't always offered. That left winter and its desolate playground to whet his skills.

That day's target shot to the top of his **to-do** list after he learned of it by osmosis. A lecturer of **Ute** tribal history had been invited to **GJU** to discuss tradition and folklore – and how together they preserved **Colorado's** known and (yet) unknown history. To the professors, a particular story sounded as if the people of that lionized past were witnesses to a meteor's strike and aftermath. To the Utes, that event spurred cataclysms that revealed the existence of the **hive-men**. The **hive-men** labored underground to harvest silver that Utes exchanged with **Navajos** and **Apaches** and, later, with settlers.

Natives and **industrialists** alike prized that silver for its purity. Science noted its unique mixtures of isotopes and its exotic thermal properties. Fantastical jewelry fashioned from it were rumored to circulate among inventors like **Edison** and **Tesla**. A trip to Denver's **Museum of Natural History** revealed that samples of it were extant although seldom presented to the public. Further research brought him to Golden's **School of Mines** where he discovered a scrap of paper, **a map**, of where it was said to come – a town erected then abandoned by the miners who or what ever they were – a town called **Tallas**.

Tallas was a rare portion of Colorado's west, whose legacy had been obscured by a trove of other, famous treasures. Maps didn't list its whereabouts – nobody visited, nobody explored. Only tales passed about by locals, generation to generation, teased of its history.

At last Tallas was his, if his it could be. Yet strolling its street, which a century ago had been its thoroughfare, it felt as if not a day passed by since Tallas **lived**. As if in particulars **not** in generalities the ghost town remained **somebody's** home. Details vivid to the eye – like paint fading and wood rotting – revealed its age and the extent of its disrepair. It was rather through the intervention of aspects too nuanced to note at first glance that sparked notions of its recent tenancy. There, were the well–trodden paths. There, were the tools oiled and stacked. There, were the functional doors and the unbroken windows. There, **everywhere**, a foetal odor that pierced the air as wind stirred.

At the town's square, Cat stopped and asked, aloud, if he hadn't wandered onto a live **John Wayne** set and was due for a lot of explanation when its crew returned. Or perhaps it was more not less likely that the crew fled for the holiday. Yes – **that** felt appropriate. As he learned exploring **Ault** and a few other scattered locales, former western colonies were ripe for **Hollywood's** lens.

While day approached its peak, he noted the emergence of a climate whose roughness prickled a sense of dread. The sky assumed a peculiar shade of gray; its vistas splayed the violence of clouds crashing into clouds. Lightning accompanied that fury as well as a faint grumble of thunder. Gusts of bitter, cold air only served to make his jacket feel thinner the longer he stood about. But there had **not** been a speck of blue since, **since** Grand Junction. And the memory of a pleasant hike felt so distant as if it were imagined.

The land everywhere reflected the gloomy visage of deep, autumnal November – a kind of forbidden middle between the exhaustion of life and the carnage of a truly, vibrant winter world.

The decay that waited to be found everywhere required a rare mood to appreciate. The worst of it was the silence and what that hinted of the vastness of the isolation. Its omnipotence intensified the wind's arrhythmic howl as it echoed throughout the skeleton that was Tallas.

Past noon, as daylight wasted, Cat accepted that his odyssey left his car **stranded** twenty miles and a river away. As it was far too, too late to embark a **return,** he would have to camp at the ruins for the night. It was a prospect he relished. To that end he scouted what had to be the perfect, Hollywood location – a tavern's 2econd floor – a spot where only three generations ago miners came to unwind and, if they were lucky, to live yet another day.

What had been the tavern's stock depleted into an array of empty, glass bottles. Their labels radiated color and text **sharply** in spite of decades of grime. Amazingly, while the establishment had been abandoned, its contents had **not** been entirely smashed or littered. The bar wasn't dusty. He noted, to amusement, that the tables were upright and propped by cinders in order to be half a foot taller. *A trick for cameras?* Except that the stools were shaved more or less to half their original heights. Or that the chairs had been deformed by regular, consistent patterns of usage – their legs were bent inward, their arms were bent outward, and grass had been crammed into their seats.

At the joint's recess, its piano preserved what had to be its singular if, else **disregarded** abnormality. Its keys had yellowed like a pirate's smile – yet a few, **only a few**, five or six or so, weren't dusty. They weren't dusty but **stained** by a grime not unlike the bottle's. The patina sported fingerprints where ever it had spread. He thought the passage of time would have solidified the detail; so he reached and pressed a finger onto where a print lay. *It was wet.* He smudged the grime as if it were fresh. A thick, tar–like grease, the grime proved a chore to scrape off the flesh.

"Where'd they get pianos, anywho?" he asked to nobody or to everybody.

The piano's keyboard retained its functionality except the 'E' of its 3hird octave. Pressed, it sunk and clacked against its frame – not a note issued out of the instrument. Its cord must have snapped and languished so **unrepaired**.

Upstairs, the tavern settled into the pitch of the abyss, which scattered only at its windows. At its windows a twisted sort of reality crept into view and struck the eyes as it juxtaposed the void. That war battled by the clouds came to its end with the dominance of a single, thick haze wrapped around the heavens. Into that twilight the sun gave its last, primal shout. It filled the horizon with streaks of vivid, ochre hues that nevertheless failed to penetrate the cloak. Then, **then as it bled to its death**, the sun vanished into the earth across a display that matched the eldritch mythos of Egypt.

Cat found a chamber for that night's roost. It faced the street and its window cast a perfect view of that sky. In front of a fireplace, he propped a lamp onto a table. By that a chair lay tattered where it had fallen into pieces. He hadn't given a thought to fetching wood, calculating that the enclosure and the sleeper together would be enough to buttress the chill. Looking at the mess that became the furniture, though, he realized that a great portion of it went missing and could **not** be accounted for – and thus he entertained a wild conclusion.

A search of the 2econd floor produced an ample pile of scrap – enough to last the night.

The fireplace itself was clogged – a fact he anticipated. Clearing its ash wasn't pleasant but necessary. He reached into its chute and located its valve. After a century to rot it wasn't ready to budge. No worry, thought he, current flowed through it anyhow – and with air oozing in and out of the tavern like so, the chamber wasn't about to suffocate its occupant.

The professor assembled a pile of debris; lit, it glowed a somber, dusky orange.

Satisfied by the fire, he barricaded the door with the furniture, to prevent an interloper's breech were they to get curious about the warmth. Signs of life (wild or otherwise) had been scarce. Prey usually went about dropping hints of its presence. Predator, however, hid its existence.

Cat set the transistor by the lamp at the table. The signal out of **Montrose** couldn't break through static. Nothing from Grand Junction. Nothing from **Gunnison**, **Telluride**. A Denver station – that always tuned **perfectly** – skipped the weather for the state's extreme west. He failed to locate a **Utah** station. Only a signal out of **Durango** was strong enough for reception; he kept the radio so tuned, perhaps, to fill a void that otherwise would have been warped by silence.

Night recast Tallas. Or, could it be, that its melancholy had been present, always? – subdued at the fringe of awareness? – revealed only to the vigilance of the slumbering mind's eye? At that instant he arrived, had it not exerted itself, perhaps not physically – for it may have been too feeble – but to that and only that part susceptible to suggestion for it, too, thrived at the moments, the aeons between conscious impulses? Now, it surged. Now, aided by night, its suggestions penetrated into the conscious unencumbered by mere notions of reality that otherwise temper imagination's enthusiasm for spooky and entwined connections – ever among the rarest of coincidences – all of which naturally portend doom.

He cataloged a train of observations to report later. The piano and its broken 'E'. The tavern and its bottles, its tall tables and short stools. The mixture of repair and disarray. The tracks etched into the dirt. He dismissed that litany as artifacts of a Hollywood production. Yet as he settled to slumber that night, amid the ruins of the ghost town, he felt obliged to reinterpret what it could be, if it could be anything.

As he supped in front of the fireplace, a gust of air jolted the window. Currents yawned in to the chamber then funneled out of the fireplace. They surged and as they did so sparked crackling, blistering life into that pile of wood he had lit. The flame beat an unsteady if bright light to equal that of the lamp. Then, at the ebb of the stir, as he stared into the fireplace, an object that had been hidden by the masonry, loosened and dropped out of the chute.

It must have been what jammed the valve, he surmised.

Instantly he poked it free of the fire.

That which tumbled into view was a wrapped, leather docket – rectangular and thick. His reflexes saved it further injury although the damage it accumulated was evident. It wasn't burnt, per say, only seared at its edges. Its hide bled a strange, oily tar accumulated by years of exposure to smoke. Its content felt solid but he couldn't say either way if they survived the ages.

A buckle kept its cover shut so tightly that it wouldn't budge. It succumbed to a knife, however, without difficulty. Inside, Cat found a trove of curiosities – chief among them a trinket like a pendant. It wasn't hot to the touch, in spite of its metallicity. He lay it aside to soak the light and as he studied its shape, his layman eyes came to a **Mexican** conclusion for its origin. Or could it be Navajo? Or ... wasn't there something altogether modern to its design? Something, perhaps, that only by-the-by evoked the impression of jewelry? Yes, its construction had to be the work of **natives** even as its design reflected patterns not akin to jewelry. Its arrangements of stones and filaments resembled **circuitry**.

Exposed more and more to the fire's light, its gems sparkled, as if they contained a cosmos. A scent like ozone wafted out of that trinket. Was it driven by a power unknown to ionize the air?

The rest of that docket's innards amounted to a bundle of maps and documents. By their uniformity he judged that they had been ripped out of a journal. They weren't numbered; he reworked their order by tracing their tears at their edges. They were thoroughly written and seared due to their storage.

Under the lantern's gaze, he struggled to read. Wasn't it a chore to unravel that narrative? The frustration wasn't the hand (as it was steady) and wasn't the script (as it was familiar), rather, it was the ink's **fade** that hindered progress. Often – and throughout passages – the ink had been reduced to a scratch etched by the stylus. A rubbing may have revealed what was written. Such as it was, without tools to analyze the papers, their full decryption awaited at GJU.

Nevertheless:

"I must inform the Commissioner of my survey xxxxx xxxxx were I not at the mercy of these forces xxxxx these xxxxx pages suffice as my testament. xxxxx xxxxx fact I suspected but could not prove xxxxx is that xxxxx xxxxx xxxxx not safe at Tallas. Tallas is not ours! It existed prior xxxxx xxxxx xxxxx frontier shifted west, perhaps, earlier xxxxx xxxxx summered at the plateau. The region's True Power felt content to hide then to let us occupy xxxxx xxxxx xxxxx for reasons xxxxx only their minds comprehended. xxxxx xxxxx xxxxx what is Tallas but a refuge for xxxxx and what the Jeffreys left behind.

"Tallas only feels tiny considering xxxxx xxxxx volume of wealth flowing in & out of it, all of which is concealed by the roughness of the plateau and the machxxxxx xxxxx of the Parcel, that homestead xxxxx I was sent to investigate xxxxx xxxxx economic vitality xxxxx xxxxx is apparently disconnected & unaware of the settlement's purpose. The state was right to suspect xxxxx xxxxx xxtaxed revenue generated by the Jeffrey's xxxxx xxxxx neither the state nor any, earthly power will succeed at extracting a penny of what is due xxxxx xxxxx.

"The Commissioner provided a dossier compiled piecemeal by a train of researchers hired prior to my arrival. It had been my 1st priority to interview xxxxx xxxxx xxxxx predecessors as part of my venture but leads xxxxx their xxxxxbouts dried at Tallas where few talk xxxxx compxxxxx xxxxx xxxxx xxxxx Mr. T E Xavier convalesced at a sanatorium south of Las Cruces. His mental derangement sparked the train of experts who followed and of whom I am the last. What I found xxxxx xxxxx Tallas xxxxx only partially xxxxx xxxxx with mines and little if anyxxxxx xxxxx about the Jeffreys.

"xx'x greater portion xxxxx settlement is populated xxxxx brutes xxxxx xxxxx xxxxx xxxxx are inscrutable, their features, to the extent they were visible, did not strike as xxxxx xxxxx typxxx of the area. Rather, they xxxxx xxxxx as transplants from Eastern Europe else xxxxx. Physically, they were large, xxxxx limbs oddly proportioned and spaced. They spread a xxxxx xxxxx amalgam of pastes onto their skin where ever it xxxxx to sunlight. Their eyes are unique enough to baffle xxxxx xxxxx. Townsfolk simply do not know what to make of them except that as far as anybody recalled the brutes were always at Tallas.

"I xxxxx posited their prevalence xxxxx xxxxx xxxxx thereabout revealed that they were the town's originators and maintainxxx. Tallas may have been xxxxx xxxxx specifically to contain them. Indians and Settlers alike simply latched onto xxxxx xxxxx that included, perhaps, the throughput of the mines.

"Of that lode xxxxx xxxxx I inspected xxxxx xxxxx what my predecessors were thought to have xxxxx their reports were not compxxxx, understandable as mines were not xxxxx xxxxx. Immediately I xxxxx xxxxx mines were ancient and xxxxx xxxxx depleted by the onset of setxxxxx xxxxx their modest output corroborated that who or what xxxxx xxxxx them they took what they required and xxxxx abandoned xxxxx.

"I gauged its ancient xxxxx xxxxx by the obtuse xxxxx xxxxx of their construction xxxxx xxxxx xxxxx not xxxxx xxxxx xxxxx xxxxx what it meant xxxxx nobody buttressxx xxxxx their mines xxxxx such standards, if standards they could be called. xxxxx xxxxx their passages xxxxx xxxxx have been carved by xxxxx xxxxx as they exhibitxx xxxxx hexagonal symmetries and it was not an accident xxxxx xxxxx xxxxx xxxxx nothing about their construction was haphazard, it was intentional as it was industrial. Neither the Utes nor any other tribe yet known to us mined xxxxx xxxxx voraciously as who ever it was that xxxxx xxxxx xxxxx xxxxx.

"xxxxx xxxxx be understood, in spite of the Jeffrey's departure, their danger is not past. It may be worse as xxxxx brutes xxxxx may not be controlled anymore. They xxxxx xxxxx xxxxx appear to be creatures of habit, without the oversight of their masters they may not confine themselves to this region. Without the stability xxxxx xxxxx xxxxx the Parcel's True Power to curtail xxxxx xxxxx loathsome prowess, our status is imperiled until xxxxx xxxxx xxxxx xxxxx xxxxx xxxxx are they not flesh and blood?

"xxxxx xxxxx.

"The Jeffreys, as so they were named, traded exclusively with a xxxxx xxxxx band of Utes other tribes xxxxx suspected xxxxx xxxxx xxxxx. Through that exclusivity, ores mined at the Parcel xxxxx xxxxx freely tribe to tribe xxxxx xxxxx toward points southwest xxxxx among the Zuni or the Navajo the trail ended. xxxxx could be xxxxx it traveled further xxxxx into Mexico? From that the whole of Spanish America xxxxx xxxxx xxxxx trade was omnidirectional and it rooted firmly into my speculation that the silver and the jewels produced by the Parcel returned xxxxx xxxxx xxxxx xxxxx as fully formed and ornate wares xxxxx xxxxx hoarded by the Jeffreys.

"The survey from 1856 which is xxxxx xxxxx xxxxx that of the Jeffrey's homestead is not entirely wrong. Putting aside questions of xxxxx xxxxx xxxxx pedigree, it abutted to known Ute territories in xxxxx xxxxx xxxxx that none of the signatory chiefs professed its annexation xxxxx. xxxxx xxxxx xxxxx conceded only that the Parcel's inhabitants were neighbors with whom they enjoyed a longstanding xxxxx xxxxx relationship xxxxx xxxxx as well as many other exchanges.

"My asides to xxxxx xxxxx xxxxx and missions revealed that the trade and xxxxx xxxxx xxxxx (marriages, a few of which were recorded to the mid 1600's) attested the notion (and gave xxxxx xxxxx to xxxxx) that the existence of the Jeffrey's Parcel spanned the greater portion of Spanish Possession. If so, their homestead represented the oldest, continuous habitation of a European family settled so far west or so we were intended to believe.

"Despite their ancient residency and relation, few were directly aware of the Jeffrey's overt existence. xxxxx xxxxx that ostracized band of Utes whose connection to the Jeffreys spanned nearly three centuries if not longer. Others meekly inferred that the Jeffreys occupied that Parcel and left it be. If what a missionary at Durango intimated were accepted as fact, the status quo that developed along the plateau may have been the culmination of a protracted stalemate betwixt the Jeffreys and a majority of tribes. A stalemate of hostilities that caused that band of Utes to be shunned by their kin.

"Colorado entered into statehood vexed by the lawlessness of its western territory. Yet, as the Parcel affected only the Indians and their trade, its business escaped notice. It was only after Tallas became a destination for speculators that the county inquired into the nature of that plateau they assumed xxxxx xxxxx xxxxx xxxxx it was only by accident that the xxxxx xxxxx xxxxx reviewed treaties and surmised that a great xxxxx xxxxx wealth flowed xxxxx that Parcel untaxed.

"For all anybody suspected, the Jeffreys were simply a family, perhaps of Hapsburg origin, vast in number and connected to peoples throughout the southwest. For reasons more political than nefarious they self-exiled into that Parcel of ten thousand acres.

"What if the domicile were older still? **xxxxx** if their origins were not **xxxxx xxxxx** by their assumed appellation? Nothing akin **xxxxx xxxxx** Parcel existed **xxxxx xxxxx** prior to 1856. Treaties **xxxxx xxxxx** at the end of the decade demarcated it simply as being the Jeffrey's homestead **xxxxx** survey had been **xxxxx xxxxx xxxxx** by an associate to the Parcel to cement its claims **xxxxx xxxxx xxxxx** boundaries. Except for **xxxxx xxxxx** routes and **xxxxx** anecdotes **xxxxx xxxxx** records of marriages there was no formal assumption of a claim.

"**xxxxx xxxxx** turn**xx** to **xxxxx xxxxx xxxxx** of **xx**56 **xxxxx xxxxx xxxxx** its inconsistencies there remain**x xxxxx** truth to its design **xxxxx xxxxx** legitimate. Except **xxxxx xxxxx xxxxx** not identified, the dates were not recorded – 1**x**56 had been a guess **xxxxx xxxxx xxxxx xxxxx** employed to measure **xxxxx xxxxx xxxxx xxxxx xxxxx** not standard. **xxxxx xxxxx xxxxx xxxxx** assigned to dimensions and elevations were added by another hand after **xxxxx xxxxx xxxxx xxxxx** already produced the map.

"And there was something else, **xxxxx xxxxx** that left me at a loss **xxxxx xxxxx xxxxx** as I examined the **xxxx**inal survey I not**xx xxxxx xxxxx xxxxx xxxxx xxxxx xxxxx xxxxx xxxxx xxxxx xxxxx xxxxx xxxxx xxxxx xxxxx xxxxx xxxxx xxxxx xxxxx xxxxx** only made its lack of **xxxxx xxxxx** identity so tragic. **xxxxx xxxxx xxxxx xxxxx xxxxx xxxxx xxxxx xxxxx xxxxx xxxxx xxxxx xxxxx xxxxx xxxxx xxxxx xxxxx** 1856 **xxxxx xxxxx xxxxx xxxxx xxxxx xxxxx xxxxx xxxxx xxxxx xxxxx xxxxx**.

"I applied my loop to it. Instead of pen*xxxxx* *xx* *xxxxx* *xxxxx* continuous *xxxxx* arranged throughout the document as if it had been *xxxxx* *xxxxx* *xxxxx* *xxxxx* matrix *xxxxx* *xxxxx* *xxxxx* none of which were larger than a tenth of a *xxxxx* *x*eter. *xxxxx* ultimately *xxxxx* *xxxxx* the methodology we employ to transmit images over wire may in decades match the quality and the workmanship flaunted by that survey *xxxxx* *xxxxx* *xxxxx* *xxxxx* 1856 *xxxxx* earlier, of this I am certain *xxxxx* *xxxxx* no facet of industry is able to produce that page as it exists.

"Startled by the manner of its construction *xxxxx* *xxxxx* *xxxxx* *xxxxx* I was baffled by *xxxxx* it contained.

"I alluded to units and non-sensical measurements. *xxxxx* *xxxxx* *xxxxx* *xxxxx* *xxxxx* like elevations and contours. I concluded that much of what it was may have been added to overwhelm a layman. Topography via a cursory inspection demonstrated that the map did not match the Parcel's boundary or contents — a hill that stood a dozen miles interior and tall enough to be seen at Tallas did not appear *xxxxx* *xxxxx*

"*xxxxx* *xxxxx* *xxxxx* expressed doubts as to *xxxxx* *xxxxx* that survey and concluded as I did that its *xxxxx* *xxxxx* *xxxxx* *xxxxx* irregularities were *xxxxx* *xxxxx* *xxxxx* attempt to obfuscate *xxxxx* *xxxxx* a lode responsible for *xxxxx* *xxxxx* and the influence of the Jeffreys.

"I *xxxxx* *xxxxx* and add at this lateness *xxxxx* *xxxxx* *xxxxx* *xxxxx* yet another reason too fantastical to utter.

"I am not unreasonable or prone to fits xxxxx xxxxx. I was a man of science before xxxxx xxxxx xxxxx xxxxx xxxxx only that curiosity mounted and without an outlet to resolve the paradoxes xxxxx xxxxx xxxxx xxxxx xxxxx xxxxx xxxxx I determined to gather facts xxxxx mysxxx. I interviewed xxxxx elders who frequented the posts xxxxx xxxxx xxxxx through mutual understanding of Spanish my efforts xxxxx xxxxx xxxxx xxxxx of the Jeffreys met with diversions xxxxx xxxxx xxxxx xxxxx already spoke of xxxxx xxxxx xxxxx that a network of trade extended xxxxx xxxxx xxxxx through southwestern tribes to the Aztecs and possibly to points further xxxxx. Trade xxxxxed up and down xxxxx xxxxx across boundaries and the bulk of it involved the silver and gemstones xxxxx xxxxx not native to the Americas nevertheless emerged from the Jeffreys and returned to the Parcel ostensibly as jewelry.

"xxxxx xxxxx from a Zuni artisan who happened to xxxxx xxxxx spoke of designs xxxxx xxxxx provided, sketched onto curxxxx xxxx–like parchments xxxxx

"I made an attempt to speak to the brutes xxxxx xxxxx effort after effort failed. I shudder to devote xxxxx xxxxx xxxxx xxxxx of words to describe the ordeal xxxxx xxxxx xxxxx xxxxx xxxxx If they xxxxx xxxxx aware of any part xxxxx xxxxx xxxxx my insignificance may yet spare me their wrath? Already Tallas is strikingly and unnaturally deserted, frustrated xxxxx.

"Ixotiz!"

Cat shrieked, aware – then and only then – of a **visitor**. Earlier he had not probed the attic so he overlooked a defect at the roof's distant, rear portion. For a while, jostled and perplexed by the intrusion, he froze and watched, **watched** that area uncertain of exactly what to do. 'Til a trickle like a stream of rain drew his eyes to what might have been the cause.

At that corner the crossbeams protruded through the rafters. Rotted as they were by weather, most only sagged, fatted – like a pig's belly – except that a single crossbeam snapped.

"It could **not** have **just** happened," he said of it, "I would have noticed. Wouldn't I?"

The **snapped** crossbeam rested at an angle; its jagged end onto the floor; its other, unseen end into the attic. The alarm – so to speak – crackled out of the hole it left.

As he gasped, aiming the lantern at the source, the alarm, again, mauled his ears and urged his shrieks.

It was the flapping of wings!

To his eyes, the feathers were white, iridescent against the pitch of the night that otherwise engulfed the bird. Its wings folded and wrapped about a sturdy body. Its head spun into view. The strange, eerie glow of its electric eyes revealed its crest to be an owl's.

At last he laughed.

The bird perched itself onto an intact crossbeam as it gawked into the chamber.

Even as it felt ordinary, wasn't there something altogether ominous about that visage? Its talons clung onto a crossbeam that drooped heavily, **heavily** enough he feared its wood may snap. All the while that crossbeam didn't sway, didn't groan as the bird spread its wings about the hole. Its wings – its feathers at its tips – how they spread so evenly, so evenly **like fingers** – all of it had to be **deliberate**. A deliberate and intentional display of what, though, he couldn't say.

"Ixotiz?" he asked as he obeyed the urge to look away from the bird.

Returning, then, to the document, he realized he flipped onto a page that comprised a pair of sheets latched onto each other as if glued. They were out of sequence anyhow. Separating that pair, he discovered that between them there had been pressed a 3hird sheet, **a postcard**. A stave had been formed of its margins. A tune had been etched into it. The author claimed only that the music was dominated by **octaves of E**.

Cat leaned into the table – it had **not** been propped or altered. Gazing to the rear of the chamber, its pitch softened only by the dusky, orange glow of the fireplace, he asked of the bird if they were alone. It felt alone and imagining the hike and the car and the snow certain to cover that terrain by dawn, he felt, too, a shiver of gloom.

Throughout his travels, perhaps, **perhaps** beyond what he cared to imagine, that he always lived to tell the tale, wasn't it a matter of luck? Anything could have happened anywhere thereabout Colorado's vast interior. Why, if his car was to breakdown at such an inhospitable spot as the **Uncompaghre**, he wouldn't, he couldn't fathom what to do.

"To dinner," he spake to the owl and bit into the sandwich. The radio pushed static. "So much for all that," he declared and off–handedly, reflexively, **switched it off.**

"I followed a **xxxxx** *Ute men* **xxxxx** *by horse toward the* **xxxxx** **xxxxx** *southern perimeter. At a rise* **xxxxx** **xxxxx** *to the north, north west, they directed my attention to* **xxxxx** **xxxxx** **xxxxx** **xxxxx** **xxxxx** *singular, obelisk, about a yard tall, it* **xxxxx** *the start of a trail* **xxxxx** **xxxxx** *led to a swap–meet.* **xxxxx** **xxxxx** **xxxxx** *toward their encampment whilst I navigated the crooked* **xxxxx** *that switched to and fro* **xxxxx** **xxxxx** *a forested ridge.*

"As I approached **xxxxx** **xxxxx** *the terrain widened and thickened* **xxxxx** **xxxxx** **xxxxx** **xxxxx** *the trail I followed vanished under a carpet of growth. A sequence of those obelisk / cairns stood* **xxxxx** *clear of that litter* **xxxxx** *the periphery of vision and* **xxxxx** **xxxxx** **xxxxx***. The terrain,* **xxxxx** **xxxxx** **xxxxx** *level perhaps half a mile* **xxxxx** *a sharp rise where* **xxxxx** **xxxxx** *thinned* **xxxxx** *into a neck.* **xxxxx** *the forest rec***xxxxx***, there, as I rode* **xxxxx** **xxxxx***,* **xxxxx** **xxx'x** **xxxxx** **xxxxx** *my eyes and grew keenly* **xxxxx** *of unobstructed views into a* **xxxxx** **xxxxx** *south and west of the plateau.*

"It was the Ute encampment; crossing that neck, I kept myself as invisible as geography allowed. I **xxxxx** **xxxxx** *setup* **xxxxx** *at a hinterland clear of their* **xxxxx***; not that I expected* **xxxxx** *as I told my* **xxxxx** *guides I simply wished to trade* **xxxxx** *with the Jeffreys and they reacted as if that were* **xxxxx** **xxxxx** **xxxxx** **xxxxx** **xxxxx** *at that distance I noted how the Indians kept busy and* **xxxxx** **xxxxx** *work* **xxxxx** *aided my effort to hide.*

*"***xxxxx** **xxxxx** *into a wall of trees whose* **xxxxx** *age endowed* **xxxxx** **xxxxx** **xxxxx** *heights and widths. Into that veil I dismounted* **xxxxx** **xxxxx** **xxxxx** **xxxxx** *a distance away from the trail where I thought* **xxxxx** **xxxxx** **xxxxx** *safe to wait and watch* **xxxxx** **xxxxx** *my vista afforded* **xxxxx** *of the plateau to* **xxxxx** **xxxxx** **xxxxx** **xxxxx** *my position and everything indicated a gradual thinning and dispersing of the forest* **xxxxx***. If I were to make camp it had to be* **xxxxx** **xxxxx** *stop.*

"Settled thusly I crept **xxxxx xxxxx** south, to the rim **xxxxx xxxxx xxxxx** and spied the Utes taking note of what I **xxxxx xxxxx xxxxx** increasingly **xxxxx xxxxx xxxxx xxxxx** hypocritical as that might have been. I suspected that **xxxxx xxxxx xxxxx** the band that shared **xxxxx xxxxx xxxxx** with the Jeffreys **xxxxx xxxxx xxxxx xxxxx** aware of their **xxxxx** or at **xxxxx** least cognizant of its periphery. **xxxxx xxxxx xxxxx xxxxx xxxxx xxxxx xxxxx xxxxx xxxxx xxxxx xxxxx** of culture, as wit**xxxxx xxxxx xxxxx xxxxx xxxxx xxxxx xxxxx xxxxx** what I knew of the Utes and **xxxxx xxxxx xxxxx**.

"By the 3rd day of my vigil I located **xxxxx xxxxx xxxxx xxxxx** swap–meets between the Utes and agents from the Parcel.

"I grew bold enough **xxxxx xxxxx xxxxx xxxxx** it was a gate, five or so feet tall, held together at odd intervals **xxxxx xxxxx xxxxx xxxxx xxxxx xxxxx** to the obelisks / cairns I tracked. I was not met by any sort of hostility; the Utes **xxxxx xxxxx xxxxx xxxxx xxxxx xxxxx xxxxx xxxxx** I tried to exchange signs or words with them **xxxxx**. They were waiting, as **xxxxx xxxxx xxxxx xxxxx xxxxx xxxxx xxxxx** a burst of excitement at the other side of the gate when a pair of brutes **xxxxx xxxxx xxxxx xxxxx xxxxx xxxxx** the Utes; rather, without even an exchange of any kind, they dropped a trove **xxxxx xxxxx xxxxx xxxxx xxxxx xxxxx xxxxx xxxxx xxxxx**.

"Of the brutes, they were dressed awkwardly; their fashions were larger than their already exaggerated frames suggested. Their faces were enshadowed **xxxxx xxxxx xxxxx xxxxx xxxxx xxxxx xxxxx xxxxx xxxxx xxxxx** stabbing of their eyes where ever they zeroed **xxxxx xxxxx xxxxx xxxxx xxxxx xxxxx** if I simply **xxxxx** froze, their gaze ceased and turned onto a myriad of disturbances like **xxxxx xxxxx xxxxx xxxxx xxxxx xxxxx xxxxx xxxxx**. When their hands escaped their pockets I noted the slender almost deformed character **xxxxx xxxxx xxxxx**. Their joints swelled to ovoids **xxxxx xxxxx xxxxx xxxxx** yet I surmised **xxxxx xxxxx** was a deliberate attempt to hide truer facets of their being. **xxxxx xxxxx xxxxx xxxxx xxxxx xxxxx xxxxx xxxxx xxxxx xxxxx xxxxx xxxxx xxxxx xxxxx** but as the Utes left and as I stood, alone, I noted how their manners altered as if they felt freer. Only when I shifted about **xxxxx** were again aware of my presence that they **xxxxx** into **xxxxx** of what they were.

"At the 4th day, to my astonishment, there had been a **xxxxx** alteration to that area of the Parcel. In the middle of the night, the Utes (**xxxxx xxxxx xxxxx** spied) shifted their activity a dozen miles to **xxxxx xxxxx xxxxx** the crux of the plateau setting themselves into a sort of invisibility between **xxxxx xxxxx xxxxx xxxxx xxxxx xxxxx xxxxx xxxxx xxxxx xxxxx xxxxx xxxxx** act was due to their ways or if it had been spurred by my **xxxxx xxxxx xxxxx xxxxx xxxxx xxxxx xxxxx xxxxx xxxxx xxxxx**.

"The trail and its terminus at the gate were stifled and **xxxxx** innavigable. **xxxxx** It had to be my intrusion and the brute's reactions to it. I was not a stranger anymore. I was a known **xxxxx xxxxx** to the Jeffreys themselves.

"**xxxxx xxxxx xxxxx xxxxx xxxxx xxxxx xxxxx xxxxx** On foot I penetrated the Parcel intent to explore it so far as safety allowed.

"I am not a daydreamer and I write **xxxxx xxxxx** aided by the fortitude of sobriety. The instant I crossed the threshold, that gap between obelisks where the gate stood only hours ago, I was arrested by the stir of the wind. A cool gust of air like the ozone of a bolt exploded into **xxxxx xxxxx xxxxx xxxxx** was bright and the sun cast its light yet in spite of summer I felt a wintry omniscience. Somewhere ahead a bird **xxxxx xxxxx xxxxx** and jostled **xxxxx xxxxx xxxxx xxxxx xxxxx**.

"They – everything – **xxxxx xxxxx xxxxx** they knew of my intrusion and the disturbance that engulfed my position became the alarm **xxxxx xxxxx xxxxx xxxxx xxxxx**. Was I not watched? Studied? **xxxxx xxxxx xxxxx xxxxx** they let me get near? I wonder **xxxxx xxxxx xxxxx** I write, the weight of the world at my shoulders, **xxxxx xxxxx** what they wanted of me.

"Miles into the Parcel **xxxxx xxxxx xxxxx** their cover melted **xxxxx** into a dusty high–desert **xxxxx**. Judged by its features – that I compared to the environment encompassing it – **xxxxx xxxxx** the area to be artificial. **xxxxx xxxxx xxxxx** too perfect **xxxxx xxxxx xxxxx** to have been carved naturally. Men, **or their like**, constructed that field for reasons entirely and uniquely their own.

"**xxxxx** to be certain of my impression, I produced the survey of 1856 and verified a discrepancy. The lay as it existed spread flatly where the survey displayed a rough, rugged terrain. And yet another issue vexed me: at the north–western end of that sandy field the land dipped into a valley — it was not deeper than a hundred feet — its walls were wide and steep like a 'V'. Its facades were **xxxxx xxxxx xxxxx** vitrified as if its substance had been scorched into obsidian.

"Perhaps, unwittingly, preposterously **xxxxx xxxxx xxxxx xxxxx xxxxx** mistaken for a dry river bed — if not for the perfection of its walls, **xxxxx xxxxx xxxxx xxxxx xxxxx xxxxx xxxxx**.

"The sides mirrored each other and did not meander as it carved its **xxxxx xxxxx xxxxx xxxxx xxxxx xxxxx xxxxx xxxxx xxxxx xxxxx xxxxx** valley terminated at the distance I noted the hill. I observed it ear**xxxx xxxxx xxxxx xxxxx xxxxx xxxxx xxxxx xxxxx xxxxx xxxxx** but it had always been shrouded by forest. And now, now **xxxxx xxxxx xxxxx xxxxx xxxxx xxxxx xxxxx xxxxx xxxxx xxxxx xxxxx xxxxx xxxxx xxxxx** distance, its features gained a reality it **xxxxx xxxxx xxxxx xxxxx**.

"The hill was a conglomerate of debris **xxxxx xxxxx xxxxx** pushed into a mound. **xxxxx xxxxx xxxxx xxxxx xxxxx** of it was not sculpted by weather — although the softening **xxxxx xxxxx xxxxx xxxxx** ages **xxxxx xxxxx xxxxx**.

"I could not avert the intuition, tenuous as it might have been, **xxxxx xxxxx xxxxx xxxxx xxxxx xxxxx xxxxx xxxxx xxxxx** connected to a singular event that created these discrepancies as **xxxxx xxxxx** heretofore unseen careered into the Earth. **xxxxx xxxxx xxxxx** of the survey **xxxxx xxxxx xxxxx** pedigree **xxxxx xxxxx xxxxx xxxxx xxxxx xxxxx xxxxx xxxxx xxxxx xxxxx** a glimpse of what the terrain had been?

"The valley's eastern rim was desolate save for the spare Juniper. While its western rim retained a thick forest cover. I kept west as I approached the area of the hill, whose grizzled textures and unsteady shapes I struggled to keep out of sight.

"**xxxxx xxxxx**

"Of **xxxxx** the valley's path was not a perfect arrow; it rocked ever so gently side to side. **xxxxx xxxxx xxxxx xxxxx xxxxx xxxxx xxxxx xxxxx xxxxx xxxxx**.

"I emerged a step out of the **xxxxx** forest to gaze over the valley. It **xxxxx xxxxx xxxxx xxxxx xxxxx xxxxx xxxxx xxxxx xxxxx** just as I satisfied my curiosity, I noted a feature, a sparkle of sorts at the oth**xxxxxxx xxxxx xxxxx xxxxx xxxxx** familiar hexagonal aperture pushed into the surface of the cliff.

"**xxxxx xxxxx xxxxx xxxxx xxxxx xxxxx xxxxx xxxxx xxxxx xxxxx xxxxx** – I caught that tune – it escaped from the aperture. It was a tune the Utes played the other night.

"**xxxxx xxxxx xxxxx xxxxx xx**ickering, swaying light of torches that set the aperture aglow.

"That tune became **xxxxx xxxxx xxxxx xxxxx xxxxx** their bearers lurched onto the surface. Voices uttering words of a language I could not fathom pierced **xxxxx xxxxx xxxxx xxxxx xxxxx** as the reality of my capture became tangible.

"I fled into the woods yet I kept low to **xxxxx xxxxx xxxxx xxxxx xxxxx** rush of activity but it was not to fetch me – it was, perhaps, the simple act of shifts replacing **xxxxx**.

"Of the creatures that crawled out of that hole, I q**xxxxx xxxxx xxxxx xxxxx xxxxx xxxxx xxxxx xxxxx** for the shadow and the darkness that then obfuscated the valley but because **xxxxx xxxxx** itself so conspired to crush the impression of my memory. Clothed, their bodies could have fooled **xxxxx xxxxx xxxxx xxxxx xxxxx** men.

"But without the padding and the shapeshifting the largess of their clothes provided, naked as they were, there was no place to hide the anomalies. Limbs were longer, thinner and curled as if extended they might have doubled their stature. Arms were joined to broad and straight shoulders whose backs splayed a kind of triangular frame. Legs were split at a point where the abdomen ought to be. I might have mistook them for malnourished were it not for their torsos that gripped together the bulk of their corpulence.

"Their heads spurred a shock **xxxxx xxxxx xxxxx xxxxx xxxxx** my words cannot capture **xxxxx xxxxx xxxxx xxxxx** of their features. Faces were recognizable as such and distinct from figure to figure and that I am free to state without struggle.

"It was only in the periphery, in the impressions of aspects that identities remotely human could be asserted. They were utterly pallid as if bloodless until they slathered that balm onto their skins. They were the brutes xxxxx xxxxx xxxxx *were they the family? The Jeffreys?"*

Cat set the sheets aside.

The tale's disquiet felt quaint – **tempered** – as if robbed of its vitality by the intervention of decades and the struggle to read what remained of its script.

Wasn't it past time to quit, if he still entertained the notion of an early hike to the trailhead. The trek through the canyon would be arduous until enough daylight melted the snow. But night was long, **long and deep**. And day was a flutter of eyelids. Already his body ached at the thought of what awaited.

A chill stoked the air. Then a sound. A sound like a trickle, a splatter. Like a stream of rain, perhaps, striking the floor. It came out of that hole. What had been misty then, now was thicker, heavier – it was snow. The owl fled, no doubt, **no doubt** to seek warmth elsewhere. The perch it had formed of the crossbeam drooped as heavy as it had been. As he stared into that vacancy, the attic over the hole assumed a haze. It was the night's vista oozing through gaps chewed into planks.

Returning from the hole to the fireplace, Cat became dismissive of a feeling that a subtle yet profound material change affected the content of the chamber he commandeered. True, the door and the window both remained firmly secured. If there had been any change, any change **how so ever trivial**, he himself had been its cause. Save for his pacing or his exploring – lately, of the hole into the attic – he couldn't determine why the table shifted toward the window or why his gear had been hastily and incorrectly re-packed.

For a while his eyes darted to the window. Flakes hit against its glass. As he stared away, afar, night faded into the recess of consciousness. Reality as conjured by the senses withered into a stream of random and jumbled impressions. Out of that blur came signals spurred by fear that could have been interpreted as activity. Activity – at a ghost town.

Wasn't it music?

Exhaling, drawing free of that trance, the music – if music it was – melted into the atmosphere.

Snow poured onto a mound right under where the owl had perched.

The excitement that had been spurred by the discovery of Tallas softened the edge of the situation he thrust himself into. As events resumed their course, however, a weight grew steadily into a burden he couldn't mask. It was the snow and the distance and the vastness of it all that magnified how **he** was the outsider.

The narrative – presently his only, real point of human–to–human contact – re–ignited his imagination and curiosity. It felt safe to be wrapped by its confinement. For the alternative was to be alone yet not alone.

> "I waited until sunset to slither out of my cover. The brutes continued to work either above or below the surface. Circumstance impelled my silence as I crawled a retreat toward that flat, sandy field. I realized xxxxx xxxxx xxxxx my position lent a vantage over it and to my dread xxxxx xxxxx torches throughout its perimeter lit its expanse. xxxxx xxxxx xxxxx silhouettes reveled but it was not the Utes, it was them, they copied Indian ceremony. Just as their appearance mimicked humanity, so, too, their culture borrowed what they came into contact with.

> "I cannot say if I caught them at the apex of their revelry or its onset. Of what I witnessed xxxxx xxxxx xxxxx xxxxx Jeffreys. That tune of theirs, xxxxx xxxxx tearing its xxxxx xxxxx xxxxx xxxxx xxxxx, jotting its notes only makes it real xxxxx xxxxx xxxxx words xxxxx xxxxx xxxxx.

> "I was trapped and perplexed at what to do – how was I to exit that situation?

> "I retreated and scanned the other rim. My plot, then, was to crawl down then up that valley until I spotted a pool of xxxxx gathered at the rift. They had been xxxxx xxxxx xxxxx xxxxx and enshadowed as they stood audience to their fellows' ceremony.

> "I came to accept that my exit went straight through the Parcel – past the hill, past the river."

Onto the floor, that spot where he intended to sleep, Cat stopped – stopped moving, stopped breathing. The only sound to reach his eyes came from the flickers of the flames – and the snow. That snow hitting the window. That snow growing and expanding its pile at the floor under the hole. All the same, he froze alerted to a disturbance. Music – dulled and muffled by distance – bore into his ears. It was a singular melodic sprawl, repeated and repeated, verbatim, like a mantra. What so unsettled the mind as to its immediacy was its imperfection – **its lilt**. It felt as if a piece of it were missing and his mind struggled to find the sound required to fill its gaps.

A creak? Why, wasn't that somebody lurking about the tavern?

A whistle? Why, weren't there voices deep into discussion?

The remains of a wild, western frontier reanimated as if it were still somehow, someway alive. The night wasn't simply a canvas but a mirror to reflect the psyche's underbelly. Such as it were – ghost towns were haunted because people made them so.

> "Farthest from the revelry, I felt as if I were spared detection. Still, I could not shake the reality that I stumbled into a realm where men were not permitted to venture.

> "xxxxx xxxxx

> "I should have been disturbed to find the hill resonant with a vivacity akin to life. The cause of its xxxxx was not yet evident to my senses as I xxxxx – xxdeed – to discover the totality of its artifice. As I surmised, the hill was a conglomerate shaped by the violence that tore the valley at its foot. xxxxx was the debris that had been ripped away from that gouge.

> "Worse was to come – as there were xxxxx xxxxx xxxxx facets of its construction only proximity revealed.

> "A protuberance jetted out of the hill's base. Jetted out as if it were lodged and xxxxx xxxxx xxxxx xxxxx xxxxx it slanted, its right edge above its left edge by no greater than forty-five degrees.

> "That protuberance xxxxx xxxxx xxxxx xxxxx xxxxx xxxxx xxxxx xxxxx xxxxx extended out of the hillside by a hundred feet and xxxxx xxxxx xxxxx xxxxx tx xemalx so perched, it must have continued into the rubble xxxxx xxxxx xxxxx xxxxx. The hill's own weight kept the object steady xxxxx xxxxx xxxxx yaxxed xxxxx xxxxx xxxxx valley.

> "What I detected of the object's surface gave the impression of a layered, rugged skin. Its facets were metallic and accessorized by pipes, valves, and hatches. All of it together indicated a fantastic industry the like of which intimated the impossible.

> "Tempted as I was to flee its immensity, a flicker of curiosity took the better of me. Had I not been watched since I camped at the Parcel? I could have been stopped at anytime they wanted. I was allowed to venture as far as I did for reasons I could not fathom.

"**xxxxx xxxxx xxxxx** stoke **xxxxx xxxxx** I noted that a hatch had been left ajar at the right spot where my entry would have been a trivial matter. The hatch conformed to my dimensions and permitted my passage unencumbered.

"So blindly if not foolishly **xxxxx xxxxx** the object.

"It was the deep yet vivid azure that struck me. Inside, it was alive with light neither from a candle nor a bulb — and from where it came I could not say. Its source must have been ahead, further **xxxxx xxxxx xxxxx**.

"Across the stretch of tunnel I trespassed came that rumble which drew me onto the hillside. **xxxxx** I recognized it — **xxxxx xxxxx** what **xxxxx xxxxx xxxxx xxxxx xxxxx** the hum of a dynamo.

"Due to the angle and **xxxxx xxxxx xxxxx** to grasp at, my ascent was not easy. I persisted in spite of slips that could have shot me out of the hatch I breached. I try to string together the images that linger about my mind yet I struggle to unravel the order of events. **xxxxx xxxxx** my recollection **xxxxx** jumbled: sensations, more imagined, less real.

"I persisted **xxxxx** and reached into a chamber **xxxxx xxxxx xxxxx** Apertures at its walls promised to lead further into the object's interior but the angle simply worked against my progress.

"I stopped to catch my breath **xxxxx** my **xxxxx**. I had not found debris. Dust. Dirt. Not a trace to imply an animal's den. Not a cobweb. Could it be that **xxxxx xxxxx xxxxx** of its steep **xxxxx** the tunnel if not the object itself continued to be occupied **xxxxx xxxxx xxxxx xxxxx xxxxx xxxxx xxxxx xxxxx**.

"I shrieked and — **xxxxx xxxxx xxxxx xxxxx xxxxx xxxxx xxxxx xxxxx** tunnel. Ahead, at the start of a passage, I noted movement. An object large enough to cast **xxxxx** against the floor arose from the base **xxxxx xxxxx xxxxx**. Its movement mesmerized my eyes as I struggled to gawk away.

"It gained shape as it formed itself **xxxxx xxxxx xxxxx xxxxx xxxxx** was round and as it continued to rise its contours spread then dropped then merged V–like into a point **xxxxx xxxxx xxxxx** where it arrested its motion.

"I could not get a sense of scale; **xxxxx xxxxx xxxxx xxxxx xxxxx xxxxx xxxxx xxxxx xxxxx** and it was white, then, **xxxxx xxxxx xxxxx xxxxx** realized its head turned to gaze eye to eye.

"I laughed as a kind of euphoria struck.

"It was an owl. My intrusion must have startled it. It perched itself onto xxxxx xxxxx xxxxx xxxxx xxxxx where a doorway had been left ajar. Yet – its eyes – those eyes, those eyes, I swear, I cannot bear those eyes the way xxxxx xxxxx.

"That interlude so disturbed the sequence of events that I failed to realize a material change xxxxx xxxxx xxxxx. The chamber I stopped at expanded xxxxx xxxxx xxxxx xxxxx xxxxx xxxxx xxxxx xxxxx xxxxx xxxxx xxxxx doorways xxxxx xxxxx passages appeared to stretch at all directions. xxxxx the owl's perch vanished and for a while I was grateful its eyes did not follow my steps.

"It was xxxxx xxxxx what the chamber became xxxxx where I noted the light's xxxxx originated.

"Walls xxxxx covered by panels – most of which xxxxx xxxxx smooth, glassy, and cool to the touch. A few were jagged and kissed by fire around its edges where many xxxxx xxxxx shattered. A majority were repaired – their gaps filled by what looked like xxxxx xxxxx the jewelry. xxxxx jewelry not unlike what the Indians produced of silver and gemstone.

"The work – original and patch – possessed a modularity at once industrial and organic. Inspecting their panels with my limited resources xxxxx xxxxx I found that xxxxx they contained xxxxx amazingly complex although from panel to panel they were built of identical components and identical arrangements. xxxxx xxxxx xxxxx xxxxx xxxxx electrical xxxxx xxxxx xxxxx xxxxx but their character betrayed engineering at a level beyond our capacity. The azure came from the xxxxx xxxxx the panel's components, that rainbow of xxxxx.

"I contacted a panel only then xxxxx xxxxx cognizant of the slanted gravity and its conspiracy against my motion. Something beyond my anatomy restrained my action xxxxx I found the strength to act. I simply had to touch a panel. It dangled at the periphery of my grasp. With my fingertips I dislodged a trinket from its socket. It slipped into my hand with a spark that coaxed a scream. xxxxx xxxxx xxxxx xxxxx xxxxx not my scream.

"xxxxx xxxxx xxxxx xxxxx xxxxx xxxxx xxxxx xxxxx xxxxx xxxxx xxxxx recall? I cannot shake the sense animated by my mind as I sit to sort and write this sequence of events that I was aboard that object for longer than my coherent memory admits.

"I chase fragments of other, rarer moments that due to time, due to exhaustion, due to fear, slip past even the realm of certainty.

"I recall **xxxxx xxxxx xxxxx xxxxx** that involved the owl running to my hand. Elsewhere I spoke to a sentience that replied to my inquiry. Pieces of a conversation that feel more and more random **xxxxx xxxxx xxxxx xxxxx** escape **xxxxx xxxxx xxxxx**!

"As I am certain, too, of vistas, of experiences that must have been of **xxxxx** intensity crumble like a dream. Only sights of myself, reaching and grasping, breaking that trinket from its panel and of that owl's reaction remain solid, if for a spell.

"**xxxxx** I **xxxxx** slipped then **xxxxx xxxxx xxxxx** I pushed **xxxxx xxxxx** onto the edges of the tunnel through which I breached **xxxxx xxxxx xxxxx xxxxx** I felt gravity **xxxxx xxxxx** down, down to a pinpoint of light I understood to be the exit. I was not fast enough so **xxxxx xxxxx xxxxx** into the struggle, writhing as I **xxxxx xxxxx** advancing **xxxxx xxxxx xxxxx** through the hatchway.

"I tumbled onto the ledge. After a scramble to my feet, I clung at the hillside and turned to the valley. It was the dead of midnight; the stars above were unnaturally bright and distinct whilst the earth below slumbered. Then, one by one, from the distance and amassing like an avalanche, were torches.

"The brutes, alerted no doubt by the Jeffreys, approached. Amid **xxxxx xxxxx xxxxx** enormity of that pile and the object lodged into it, was I not too irrelevant **xxxxx xxxxx xxxxx xxxxx xxxxx xxxxx** running from danger to danger **xxxxx xxxxx xxxxx xxxxx xxxxx** as I retreated, a rumble **xxxxx** urged through my body. I froze and rooted my feet.

"I had achieved a distance great enough to be safe — **xxxxx** so I judged — yet I caught sight of the earth tremble as if it liquefied. **xxxxx** transfixed as the hillsides split and spewed its innards into the valley. **xxxxx xxxxx xxxxx** dusk like fog spread far and wide; I feared everything verged into cataclysm; the sensation of slipping **xxxxx xxxxx** had to be imagination for I did not move save to spin onto my back, my face to where the sky would have been. **xxxxx** out of that imponderable fog the object glowed **xxxxx xxxxx**.

"xxxxx xxxxx xxxxx the sight of it. Fear was the only, sane response that visage should have inspired. The reality of how it rolled xxxxx xxxxx xxxxx with the voracity of an animal snatched my breath away as much as its violent destruction of that hill.

"xxxxx xxxxx xxxxx its incomprehensible sound xxxxx the sound of it, splitting and rolling away but of that object's xxxxx xxxxx xxxxment of that I was not prepared to grasp. xxxxx xxxxx xxxxx machine whose movements were not damped by inertia.

"Rather, its movements came with the agility of the living and so shook itself clear of the hill that had entombed it. And by so doing destroyed what had been its tomb and the valley and the mob advancing through it.

"As that xxxxx visage filled the sky xxxxx, the ground xxxxx xxxxx resonated to yet another terror. The brutes who had split xxxxx xxxxx xxxxx mines and fillxx xxxxx xxxxx started to climb against the avalanche like insects grasping, reaching yet failing to stack themselves far enough to stop the object's ascent. xxxxx xxxxx xxxxx their voices echoed syllables – tiaz – queh – tia hueh – tia hueh – ixotiz! – words whose intonation magnified their futility.

"What could it be but a craft? It exposed itself as larger than what I suspected. It yaxxed xxxxx completely free of the xxxxx and the hill imploded its innards onto the hoard of brutes xxxxx the lot of them away. I could not help but feel as I witnessed xxxxx xxxxx xxxxx the way its scree flowed into the valley, the way its avalanche crested and shattered like foam at the beach, the way it erased the valley so efficiently, was it not intentional?

"At once the Jeffreys erased the valley and their brutes were not to be seen or heard, drowned as they were by the violence. All that remained was the azure that clung onto the skin of the craft that itself faded out of sight into the fog it lifted. Then – with a flash that rivaled daylight – was gone to join the uncountable stars.

"I lack a coherent memory of what followed. I wandered until the Utes (who had been drawn to the Parcel by its ruckus) caught and drew my path toward their camp. By a firepit, their elders – who I recognized from Tallas – attempted to interview my experience. Their own expressions were a mixture of emotions although, perhaps, they were dominated by melancholy. I did not detect surprise, however.

"I must have been left to wander. Or was I led away? xxxxx xxxxx xxxxx xxxxx the site xxxxx xxxxx xxxxx and I the other way to xxxxx xxxxx xxxxx.

"A chill blanketed my body. I could not sleep. Not with the sight of that night sky and that pinpoint of light that seemed to me out of place, out of time, wobbling as if unstable, shrinking and dimming into unimaginable oceans of emptiness.

"Echoes of Ixotiz continued but was it real or imagined? I wanted to believe what I witnessed and survived had been only a fantasy and that morning held the promise my wish would be granted. To my surprise dawn came sooner not later.

"What had I misjudged? How long I had been detained by the Jeffreys? How long it took to destroy the hill and the valley? How long I xxxxx xxxxx xxxxx gazing at the stars feeling as if I were shrinking in ways xxxxx denied xxxxx xxxxx forever.

"The early gray twilight pierced the trees and lifted a fog xxxxx xxxxx xxxxx xxxxx. When at last the sun blazed ahead, I stood, battered, and sensed that my world or my perception of it had been jolted to the core.

"I retraced my steps through the Parcel. It felt dead everywhere. The eyes it casted upon me were not felt any longer.

"When I reached the field whose proportions disturbed my senses earlier I felt awed at how the peculiarity of the terrain had been erased. Nevertheless, I grew aware that their plot did not go as they planned. Had my intrusion into their craft ramifications I neither realized nor fathomed?

"I shuddered at the savagery and at my helplessness in the midst of it. Because if the Jeffreys were capable of such indifference, what chance do we have? We take comfort that advancement tempers us as a race, that improvement and progress – our mastery over the world such as it is – ushers a vast era of prosperity and enlightenment. What if the opposite were true? Or if one did not necessitate the other? If those who already possessed power of that magnitude were no better than us at wielding that power, what terrors wait to be unleashed by man himself?

"xxxxx Utes xxxxx xxxxx and xxxxx xxxxx I found Tallas this way. I have watched and waited for days. xxxxx xxxxx xxxxx xxxxx not xxxxx."

Cat flipped the sheet, the last of the bundle. *I found it this way?*

> "Poor devils — blotted as if by shame by those who created them for their own ends! But they were not all wiped away — certainly — not all. Maybe the originals, those who had been stranded for centuries, maybe they — the Jeffreys — left to where they came. But not the chimeras they devised.
>
> "Those brutes, whose existence was to work, were they accidents or necessities? Employed to exert their master's will just long enough for man's skills to sharpen to a level of sophistication they required?
>
> "The wait must have been agony. While artisans bore the skills, society lacked the industry to automate their craft's repair. When at last humanity advanced and inadvertently assisted their efforts, they fled, erasing their occupation.
>
> "But I say to you, to you who finds this, I say, they did not all die that night. I hear their chant. **Ixotiz!** They shout it under the rubble that filled the valley. Their cries do not cease. Their bodies were not human enough to die so easily. They have not yet found me but they search. They search for all of us to avenge themselves.
>
> "If I do not haste—"

So it stopped.

Cat folded the document and stuffed it into the docket. That trinket, which sat in front of the fire, exhausted its life. It fit into the emptiness of the container and rattled a bit as he put the artifacts away. He was tired and touched by delirium – and not in any condition to ponder that curious testimony for what it was or might have, could have been.

Thoughts of rest flooded his mind. He sat propped against the table, with the lamp and the radio by his side. The fire's light turned a dusky, abyssal orange. *Another scrap of wood?* he thought and then, then – as he spun to fetch the fuel xxxxx xxxxx xxxxx his body froze, his mind reeled. A xxxxx paralyzed his movement. That sound – a stilted broken melody – **a sequence of notes** – xxxxx as if there were a part of it missing.

It must be the weather, he said of it. Clearly it was way, way past the station's hour.

Cat reached for the transistor and shrieked – the radio, **it was already off!**

★

Ogden's Domain

Bryer leaned into the window. Caged by that tiny, little bedroom, which he revisited after a decade's worth of study elsewhere, he forgot how weakly its walls resisted the night. That summer's chill, breaking through the glass, streaking across his hair by his face, brought to focus a scent that transported his imagination to adolescence. An episode from childhood, perhaps, a dream of what life would have, should have been.

With that flood of memory came not the intimation but the certainty of activity beyond the homestead. Not a sliver of solitude was to be found in spite of the midnight that snuffed the cove. Why was Nature so preoccupied by foreboding where ever he gazed, in or out of his mind? Where hid the sleep? Where came the anxiety?

With his hands at its frame, his face at its glass, he gawked through the window, past the perimeter of the yard, into the wilderness that constructed much of Canada.

A single blade of grass fluttered – danced, as it were – the wind breathing life, spurring madness.

Then a sight he almost ignored caught his attention: a shape formed itself out of shadow and darkness at the borders. From that shape, which fancied itself a man, features of a face so familiar emerged where it ought not to be.

"Whose ghost is't?"

To answer, the figure attained substance enough to scatter moonlight.

"Logan...."

The pull of what the senses beheld sparked an instinct to shriek.

Ten years abroad were breached as if not a breath passed since the events at Ogden's Domain.

Bryer escaped the house like a man waking out of a nightmare. He fled passingly almost forgetfully grasping at his clothes. His mixture of running and dressing was a chaos of action. Still shoving feet into boots, he made it out of the door and tripped in to the yard.

There, at the spot where Nature envisioned Logan, he found only panic.

For weeks after his graduation (before his escape), the vision of Logan running and vanishing ripped into Bryer's conscience. Afar, always and forever out of reach, it felt that his friend wanted to be followed. So he trekked through Ogden's Domain a dozen times.... How Bryer wished Logan kept ahead, ahead if not in flesh and blood then in spirit. And was it not so? Was that not how it really, actually happened? Logan at the front. Bryer at the back. Right to the bridge where the trail crossed the railroad. But there, who or what ever that specter's reality embodied, it vanished and the fever lifted.

What else remained of their friendship but its disintegration and that vanity of tracing the hike into the mine?

Again, Bryer followed. Again, Logan led. Without words. Indeed, without acknowledgements. They walked from the yard to the street. From the street to the cove. From there: the park. A lot where the jeep had been towed away somewhere, sometime. A field where the school celebrated its graduates. Past grandstands – yet to be disassembled – stood the signpost welcoming visitors to Ogden's Domain.

As the forest thickened to blot the moon and the stars, that lure into the void became more audio than video. Logan ceased to be an image and became sounds. Branches swaying. Leaves falling. Twigs breaking. As such that recreation of his friend was as real as anything could be.

Their warmth aside, a gulf that their affection could not overcome remained a feature of their friendship. Its severity only magnified how their relationship rubbed their families. What happened that summer cemented distance into permanence. Still, when they were young, they thought it was possible to bridge that gulf. What separated them were borders set by others anyhow. Then, at least, it was so. Now....

Was Logan there?

"Futile, even if you're there. I can't reach you. Go. Go ahead.... I'll find where you'll be."

The gap widened.

"You wanted to escape – south or east – where life called ... and that's that isn't it?"

After what transpired at Ogden's Domain, Logan was not seen or heard again. Little, if anything, spoke of his fate. Life just continued as if it meant nothing. Then, when his study pushed him into Toronto, when his work prodded him about Canada, his friend and their adventures retreated into a kind of memory that merged with fantasy. Bryer came to wonder if anything happened. If the whole, entire episode as he recalled it was real or imagined.

Dusk loomed ahead when Bryer caught Logan by the cuff. The friends gathered their supplies in front of the jeep by the signpost. Trails, everywhere, snaked in to and out of Ogden's Domain at that juncture. They were ready to go.

Bryer: "Should've come earlier?"

Logan: "We're just in time, don't want to be too late or too early."

At a spot where the gravel turned a shade of gray, they stepped right onto the remnants of a railroad that had been laid but not used. From that point its width expanded like a mouth ready to scream. Exactly where fangs ought to be, the trail settled into a defined, constant shape.

They tread through a relic of industry certain that it promised to lead them further and deeper into Ogden's Domain than they ever penetrated. It was a forgotten path and the encroachment of Nature proceeded without restraint. Shoots at its borders disrupted its symmetries. Assaults, though, came from above not from below. Branches with ivy dangled at the edges and scrapped their faces as they walked by. Those veils were so thick the boys were forced to hike single-file. Logan at the front. Bryer at the back. Intermittently tethered by a grip from one's hand to the other's hand.

"Still don't like jackets, eh?" Logan teased.

"Weird at summer.... What if it's too dark?"

From what Bryer gathered, the sightings and such always came either at dusk or at dawn.

"Dark doesn't mean anything. It's not about time. Could be day, night. It's about who trespasses and why. Intent matters. Karma matters. You'll only ever see what you want to see."

Two miles into their journey and already the canopy obscured the sky. They were enshadowed if not outright entombed. The air assumed a cool, breezy character unseasonable even at that geography. It carried a subtle woodsy scent. It echoed random chirps, fragile echoes of gossamer activity.

After an hour's worth of rising, falling terrain, the trail leveled. Trees retreated and let them walk side by side. As miles lapped by tenths, they noted interruptions to the path. Yellow cairns appeared here and there with arrows north or south. White driftwood, blazed black and red, marked other, well-defined and well-used trails. The landscape had been carved by footpaths used by natives. Such passages descended onto the coast. Logan recalled a few of them to Bryer where his family fished at the channel.

Of course there were easier ways to reach the Pacific but none as isolated or as picturesque as the trail to the mine.

"It'll be sunset when we reach the bridge. We'll get this whole, entire place to ourselves, Bry."

Bryer gazed with a sly if wicked smile that Logan returned with a thrill.

That area of Ogden's Domain was not travelled often. Its isolation was due partly to folklore, partly to the nature of the land. Their remote, costal village seldom endured a genuine summer. Its natives were concerned more with surviving day-to-day than indulging frivolities. Its transplants were opposed to development for their own, peculiar reasons. So, it languished, returning more and more to its virginity.

Every now and then the cove was upset by the notion of opening Ogden's Domain to sport. Usually outsiders from Vancouver kindled that topic. The opinion at the village simply detested the matter. Natives did not want their land disrespected and feared the influx of tourists such a move would have provoked. Others, themselves exiles from the affluence of the dominion, objected as they felt the cove was their oasis from civilization and did not want to jeopardize its solitude. Everyone cited Little Vail and Maple Leaf as proof of the worst.

Of course, the truth was that the legends (and the disasters) of the past capped any attempt to exploit the reserve for gain: the land always fought back.

A clamor alarmed through trees and their ears echoed its ruckus.

They fled, playfully, if teasingly. Their boots sloshed the gravel and added an arrhythmic scratch to what the wind stirred. As they started into yet another ascent, the sky sighed: the day waned and the night rooted. Just like that there came a sound they stopped to appreciate – a howl, more imagined than real, like the breath of an organism immense enough to drown that region.

Ogden's Domain inspired their excitement.

Legends prowling its dawn and dusk were a mix of native and foreign origins. Shapeshifters. Tricksters. Creatures of the night. It could be anything it wanted to be. Stories were told of its exploits that dated to the origins of the tribes: who or what inhabited that area, it had to be older than man.

The mythology only took its final form after the quake of 1964. The sightings, disappearances, and other, eerie happenings spurred people into accepting its reality and respecting its boundaries. Officially, isolation was not imposed. Anybody was free to come and go as they pleased, provided they followed blazed hikes and posted guidelines. Unofficially, legends dogged that territory and sufficed to keep outsiders away.

Only Ogden braved its wilds. The man who carved the trail they followed died after a fit of madness sparked by the quake. What could be said of it? That he caught a glimpse of its truth and its reality was too deep for the mind to endure?

Ogden hailed from pioneers who stocked Oregon. Although a century separated him and his ancestry, he could have stepped right out of that era. Fittingly, he procured via poker the deeds to the homesteads that would have been carved out of the domain. He intended to start a mine and to harvest that timber – efforts backed by the impoverished who struggled for any kind of employment. He laid the bedrock for a spur railroad. He contracted the Pacific Northwest Co. to ship ores and woods to Seattle until the quake of 1964 put ambition to rest forever.

Exactly what transpired when he raced to check the mine will not be known. Tales were told later. A legend had to be invented if just to make sense of the cove's fate. Man's arrogance, executed to perfection by Ogden, was matched and defeated by Nature's monsters. Maybe it was the sasquatch. Maybe it was the wendigo. Werewolves, too, could be invoked with impunity.

The trail curved to their right – to their left the gorge became more and more pronounced – even at twilight that canyon was impressive.

The path they trekked was carved out of a ledge perched between rocky upslopes to the south and alpine downslopes to the north. Although they could not see it, they heard it – a channel at the base of that gorge – its water roared into the Pacific.

Elders who recalled the quake spoke of fishing Ogden out of that channel. Either he slipped and skidded into its current or he was flung, by what, they could not say. There were gashes to his clothes and tears to his flesh that spoke of an encounter. Or it could have been caused by the tumble from that height.

Logan and Bryer stopped to water – and as they sipped they felt the ground rumble.

Light approached from the north. It started at the distance where its glow revealed trees – tall, slender and aged beyond reason. Through the bleak mist of dusk, they swayed as the light – no – as the train sped. The locomotive wore the livery of the Pacific Northwest Co. It probably came out of Juneau with crude destined to points south of the border.

The gravel at their boots rattled – they sunk an inch into its bed. They retreated onto the upslope as the worst passed. Minutes ticked without abatement – until the train snaked into the bridge that spanned the gorge. Topography amplified the exertion of the bridge and sparked the thought of its collapse. Then, one by one, the cars made it across. Then, when the train vanished out of eye and ear shot, the land resettled. The intrusion diminished into an annoyance then into an afterthought.

"I hear. You?"

"Yeah...."

The old men who were young men when they found Ogden at the gorge swore they witnessed a figure lurking about the bridge. A figure that could have been a man or a bear. A pair of miners separated from the pack and dashed to the bridge intent to reach who or what it was. They were seen entering the near end, running through the gaps of the frame, exiting the far end. When a pair of lumberjacks reached the bridge, though, they were confused at the emptiness – they walked its length to and fro, they explored the wilds by the tracks, they found nothing. Nothing of the miners. Nothing of the figure. Nothing – not a footprint.

When Ogden awoke at the hospital, the staff struggled to restrain the madness, a frenzy of screaming and laughing and crying. He rolled about as if his skin were ablaze. Sedated, his tendency to harm ebbed by a fraction. For stretches of calm, though, he whispered. It was a voice too gravely to be human. He spoke of the mine, an event that looped, again and again, although the details were not always identical iteration to iteration.

"He fled," Logan claimed. "He saw what people weren't meant to see. It's not all ours, you know, this world ... it wasn't just meant for us. When you go too far into places not for you...."

The dying light of day filled the gorge red.

A journey that started at a park miles and miles away became at last a physical and mental danger as they plowed into the heart of Ogden's Domain. The terrain itself overtly magnified not only the hostility but their meekness in the midst of the wilderness.

In spite of that peril, what remained of the hike to the mine amounted to a mile, a mile to pass the ridge, then to pass where the trail crossed the railroad, then to pass a hill to the east.

At the area of the bridge, they were greeted by a skeletal, incomplete barracks. It was started to house workers for a dam project further up the gorge. It had not been finished. Neither was that dam project which had been designed like a mine to extract not ore but power from the land.

The project was spearheaded by a movement to revitalize the region after the quake of 1964. As before, so after, the impoverished supported the plot and volunteered to man its construction. A change of government c. 1978 led to the dam's cancellation. Somewhere between lips and ears, the word that spread was altogether ominous. Blame fell onto the superstition of the cove. Workers vanished never to be seen or heard again. Tales spread about screams echoing out of the wilderness. Wails from those who left. Warnings to those who remained. To flee or join, their feet afire.

Truth, if it existed, would have pointed to the mundane as the spark of that disaster. The site that straddled a path between the gorge and the bridge may have been expedient but proved to be the worst location to house workers anybody could have thought of. Not because of those trains that passed north and south daily. But because of the drop from the ledge to the channel. It was not survivable. Men got drunk, careless. They fell then vanished. The raw wilderness and its power of suggestion drove the sober away.

Deconstructed by Nature, the barracks were more of a frame and less of a building. Walls were erected only at its mid-level. A single window remained unshattered where it had been installed. Holes yawned where others may or may not have been fixed. Doors were not to be found. Stairs attempted though often failed to connect features above and below. Strangely, there was not a hint of defacement.

"Inside?"

"Why not?" Logan smiled as he clasped Bryer by the wrists. "It's roomier than my jeep."

"What's it up to if there's nobody around?"

"Dream? We don't know," replied Logan. "They must be old, ancient people. We can't imagine what they do."

Bryer passed the canteen to Logan. It shook, still heavy with water, spritzing drops onto thirsty, acrid earth as it exchanged from hand to hand. Thus they took turns sipping and passing the bottle.

They faced a steep ascent and, to be certain, they were not anywhere finished. Everything they experienced at their coming-in awaited at their going-out. If they wanted to return, they would be forced to hike that whole, entire trail to the jeep – backwards not forwards – in the middle of the night.

"It's just stories, you know," Logan continued. Bryer scooted by his side under the doorway to the barracks. "Everything's stories. You afraid of this?"

Bryer took a second to drink. "Course I am." He passed the bottle, sinking deeper and deeper into warmth. "Aren't you?"

Logan did not see the risk. He understood the situation and the parameters set by the world of the straight and narrow. How much to show. How much to hide. Resentment of what others imposed as normal drove a streak of impatience. His people were a part of that area for more generations than history accounted. Yet their ways were dismissed as if they did not matter.

Bryer was ready but uneasy. His awareness of nature extended as far as memory allowed. Its call was sharp but, ingrained as if by instinct, he kept its urge at a distance. He thought it safer to experience only a tamed and civilized version. Not that he would have been adventurous. He was not quick to make friends. When it came to companions, book people were safer than flesh-and-blood people. 'Til the family moved west.

They should have clashed; rather, they echoed. The deficits of the one were the abundances of the other. So they complemented.

That tiny, little cove they inhabited was a noose. Eons past it might have been different. They might have been free. Ogden's Domain, a window into a vast if lost reality, recreated what life used to be. There the judgment of the detestable fled away to die.

Light filled the voids of the barracks. Fragments of colors washed their faces. As they gazed west, they watched their memory of the day fade. At its loss, that land transformed fully into a new and different reality. At last its true existence emerged, free to exert itself. All of a sudden activity assaulted their senses and tantalized their imaginations.

Was it a reaction to finality? That future whose dimensions were not grasped until its onset proved too late to reverse. Was it just senselessness, recklessness? A defiance of fate! A youthful dash to enjoy everything the senses offered.... So they veered into the barracks to explore its passages just as they wandered into Ogden's Domain to share its mysteries.

Not a trace beyond the obvious could be ascertained of its occupancy. Workers simply stopped and left everything as incomplete as they found it. Since the 1970s it had not known a visitor.

Their footsteps stirred a scent like rain. Creaking formed as wood rubbed wood to stab at their ears as they rambled from room to room. Visions inspired by their torches danced fevered, maddened cadences in front of their eyes while they explored from floor to ceiling. Such were the impressions of their dalliance with the structure.

The creaks of stairs announced their decent. Their swaying, jiggling torchlights illuminated that distance. They seemed to be falling into the abyss of the unknown. Their trek led them into that basement and a strange chill, a familiar scent. A spring's morning? Of laying awake while the world stirred. Not wanting to leave. As if denying the inevitable were the power to obliterate its existence.

Lights dimmed as batteries died. Only the filtered starlight shined through the gap of the ceiling. Aided by the glow of distant worlds, they explored with touch what sight was denied.

Wind, whipped by the train, almost knocked Bryer into the gorge. He tumbled onto the ledge and reached into the gravel. The earth shook and loosened the security of his grasp. Only friction, amplified by the texture of the trail itself, arrested his fall. Safe, he sat while the cars passed by.

At the wake of the train, moonlight revealed a spot ahead, beyond the tracks, where the world was still and calm. A shudder marked its significance. He recalled its particulars: neither age nor distance appeared to alter its proportions. It was that spot, that spot, where it happened.

"Logan, why'd you go?"

They were at the cusp of adulthood. Their future was set to diverge after graduation. Their plunge deep into Ogden's Domain was their strike at the world before it conspired to convert fantasies to regrets. Could it have been different? Not the end but the beginning? The crux of a fate of their own design?

Bryer stood where he chose, not the hard, but the easy way out of the cove – the way his family arranged. It was the spot where any chance of happiness shattered to pieces. It was the spot where, precisely, he last gazed at Logan. Bryer dared to believe then and there, not in the whimsy of a mind grasping at figments, but in the certainty of reality that Logan remained or returned as if not a day of the last decade passed. Then, breath by breath, the illusion melted.

"Logan, what'd I do?"

Were there no answers only more anguish?

Little if anything was said of Logan after that summer. Simply: he dropped out of sight. His family continued its business about the village; he, never met warmly, never stopped to ask what became of his friend. That irked Bryer; especially, the guilt he felt for his cowardice. It denied them any sort of farewell.

That hike through Ogden's Domain – it must have been a part of Logan's ploy to escape the cove. Maybe, if he would have dared plunge past the railroad, maybe, if he could have followed....

The trees stirred at the other, far side of the tracks. Out of that frenzy of activity – the dancing of leaves, the interplay of light and dark – the suggestion of a shape presented itself to the eye. A face. That face....

"What do I follow? Logan – you dream? You dream, now."

The figure's braids whipped like the tails of kites then drooped, then skid to settle across what appeared to be shoulders. Something like remembrance sparked at the eyes. A smile like he knew so well urged a thrill.

"Let me follow you."

Nothing....

Nothing.

The image he willed to be Logan did not answer – only an echo of his wish came into his ears.

The roar of a train shook them out of their sleep's embrace.

"Didn't mean to doze like that."

"It's alright, Bry, I'm exhausted...."

"Yeah," he said, slipping off, away, "You dream? What'd you dream, Lo?"

Logan stretched – then nestled his arms around Bryer's shoulders – then aimed his eyes past the jagged, broken ceiling into the veil of skylight. Quickly: "We follow the tracks south. After a while we find the jeep. We drive through the graduates – OK – that's not true! We drive ... and there's a town and we're lost. Everyone's driving somewhere and it's crazy. Scary crazy. We escape and it's night. We're going up and down these valleys. Mountains, everywhere. There's this valley by a coast that's a forest with a single, large house. It feels like we know who's inside. We kind of want to stay. No, it's a fight. We escape and keep driving and driving. South – there's this plain that just goes on and on forever. It's a town and they're building a tower into the ground. We're hired to work. We're getting trained, getting ready. Then, I don't know why, I can't find you. I searched everywhere ... and then I felt – I remember this Bry – I felt as if it were real."

As day intruded their interlude, they stopped and simply let the world turn.

"What if there's a spot where we'd find ourselves? Like, if anything happened, you know, we'd return to that spot. We'd meet again somehow."

"Here," he did not waste a breath. "Where the trail crosses the railroad by the bridge. No matter what, Bry."

"No matter what, Lo."

At the distance, north or south they could not say, the train popped the whistle.

"Is that whistle heard if there's nobody?"

Logan chuckled, "does it matter?"

"I think it needs a somebody."

"Maybe it wants a somebody...."

"I dreamed about that pageant. Again. Only this time, this time I couldn't tell who was who. Everyone's just so painted, so painted that they didn't have faces anymore. Maybe they had masks? But then, and I don't know what it was about you if it was anything at all, but then I found you. You didn't have a face, so, maybe it was the way I imagined you that formed you out of the crowd. Your feathers twining into your braids. Your beads beating onto your chest. Or maybe it was the chaps at your legs – yeah, well, alright – it was the chaps at your legs. That's where I figured it was you. I couldn't get to you anyhow. The crowd exploded and you got distant like tiny. I ran to you then I fled so far that I stopped and there was no one, no one. Why aren't we ever together? Our dreams – what do they know? – what do they know, Logan."

Logan's kiss stopped the quiver of Bryer's lip. For a spell they resisted even the urge to part. There would be time, years for distance to accrue. They stole that moment. For a while. Then – for another while. For as long as they might.

When they stepped out of the barracks night lost its battle to day although the sun did not yet rise above the eastward grin of the Rockies.

Anxiety, the like of which they evaded throughout their hike, entered into their essence.

They wandered to where the trail crossed the railroad. To their left was the bridge. To their right was a mile's worth of hike to the mine. A walk that would have taken them to the crest of the hill straight ahead.

"There won't be another chance to live, Bry!"

"Wait!"

"Come on! Come on, Bry. Just, come on!"

"Wait!"

Bryer struggled against his stiff, heavy feet.

Logan fading into a curtain of trees was the last glimpse of his friend.

"Damn it, Logan, wait," he wiped a tear – he could not move without a twang of pain and a trace of blood, blood working its way from his thighs to his knees. "I can't get up that hill."

He crawled into the barracks where he stood then sat under its doorway, determined at least to wait his friend's return.

As he waited, he dozed – until a disturbance jolted him out of a void in to despair. Why? he wondered, aloud. It had not been Logan but the crackle of leaves, the tremble of branches.

The sun was not yet overhead but the air warmed to its early July normal. Its light exposed the crossing, the gorge, the bridge, the hill, all of it, everywhere, still as if nothing happened. Were they so unaware of the goings and comings of men?

Defeated, he waited an hour – then another. Strength returned slowly. He found a long thick stick and used it as a cane until his body cooperated. He thought about that hill and that mine and how simple it might be to go but he required every bit of strength just to get home....

Then, he felt it at the pit of his stomach, hollow, empty, he felt it creep like a shiver – and he knew Logan was not there anymore.

As the smoke of a train came into view, he retreated and retraced the hike through Ogden's Domain alone.

Bryer crossed the tracks then froze.

"Why'd you be so real?"

He caught sight of Logan's face at the trail beyond the railroad. A figure, that specter, defied reality like the unnatural. Its face! It conveyed not a remnant of emotion. As he stared, amazed by its likeness, its fidelity, he was struck by the notion that it was more like a mask than a face. Yes, if only it were not such a perfect recreation of youth, he might have believed it entirely true.

"You vanished. Nobody said why. Nobody asked why. It was like, like you stopped existing and they reacted as if it were normal. But I get it. Yes, I get it. Lo, you chose to escape and they understood you weren't coming back."

As reality unraveled, impelled to do so by the magic cast when Bryer's thoughts transfigured into words, he trembled.

"Damn it, Logan, told you I was scared. Weren't you? Not even a little, eh? No, not even a little? Our last adventure; the bravest we'd ever be. 'Til I.... Not everything's fated to be, is it; but; I would've gone if I could've gone."

That night a train's whistle pierced the solitude of Ogden's Domain but nobody heard it.

★

The Girl in The Window

The **Crew** – Lex, twins Jason & Paul, and **I** – assembled at the cross of **Mississippi** & **Federal**. Spring's semester concluded and we advanced yet another year. So we opted to celebrate that success by immersing into a haunt of equal parts mystic and tragic.

The site we zeroed onto wasn't vacant – a reality that complicated **everything**. We faced **real** not **imagined** risks of capture. Our approach had to be the opposite of what years of travels throughout Colorado ghost towns and ghost mines taught us.

We rejected as impractical the luxury of taking internet or equipment into the hotzone – it would be just us, just the lot of us.

We kept the investigation and its particulars away from our channel's fans. To spur hits, we planned to drop hints, then, to reveal evidence at a date past statute. To deter enmity, from either in or out of the community, the episode would be formatted as **audio** not **video**.

Lex, our apt **journalist** & **Jersey** transplant, reconnoitered a site – a site that abutted corners of Denver not friendly to outsiders. **Little Berlin**, as it used to be called, sprawled over a five square mile area. Roughened by its stormy gentrification, its eerie folklore, it simply wasn't a place to seek diversion. So it wasn't a surprise to learn of a haunt buried amongst its tenements – only at how **far** and how **deep** its connections permeated the occult.

Our target, the warehouse – formerly the **Lux Haus Autos** warehouse – boasted of a complex history. Constructed **c.** 1919, ostensibly to store surplus, the facility exchanged ownership every so many years 'til captured by that stated **foreign** company. Between wars it thrived as a go-to **Ford** supplier. At the apex of the depression it swelled, occupied by employees, workers who claimed years of backpay.

Of its squatters, there was a girl, a girl named **Vilma Carolina**, aged sixteen, and – to junkies of this art – heretofore known as **The Girl in The Window**.

We pressed into midnight awake and alert as if it were noonday. Our excitement stoked at the promise of the haunt. Electricity pervaded the air as though, **as though** by wizardry we strayed into realms of vast, cool **if ambiguous** sentience. Or was it that this our trespass–to–be amplified the malevolence of the city we trampled? Its hostility stirred premonitions of calamity, **of doom** that may or may not **yet** await us.

As we strolled through **Zuni,** we crossed a vagrant's sights. We swore they were typical of that confused, bewildered tribe of walkers – except – they were elder to a degree not often encountered at the street. That figure eyed then footed at us as we hiked block after block of urban sprawl. Who or what they might have been, in spite of everything, they kept a steady, calm pace adrift to ours as if to mask their advance.

We weighed options to either admit or deny their entry to our **Crew** – then – we thought better of it. We sped. **They sped.** The stalker proved wise not only to the neighborhood's layout but to the trajectory toward the warehouse. That they fathomed our route so perfectly unsettled us beyond anything our imagination produced. Did they know of us? **How** did they know of us? **Our plot....** Why wasn't it easy to fox that interloper?

Crossing **6ixth & Sheridan,** we startled into a panic, a blaze of fear. The vagrant shouted to us. My hair stood as I tasted their ire, their warning perhaps threatening that we ought not to go further. **Run! Run! Run! Fools, you still gotta chance!** – and other, eerie ravings colored by a battered, crazed accent prompted us to escape.

Was **The Girl in The Window** still a draw?

Vilma Carolina was the daughter of veterans who served (and died) during the First World War. Her father (**allegedly**) was a Frenchman named **Auguste d'Carolina** – he died at **Somme.** Her mother (**allegedly**) was an American named **Lementine** (nee **West**) – by affluence and by happenstance entangled betwixt love and war.

If we accepted dates as reported, as per calculations and suppositions, Lementine should have been six weeks pregnant after Germany captured her and took her into Bavaria **c.** July of 1916. Then, **Christmas Day**, 1916, they released her as part of a swap. Later, discharged from the academy and from the country, she birthed **Vilma Carolina** immediately upon reaching New York City, **c.** January of 1917.

For the next decade Lementine's and Vilma's whereabouts remained unknown. It was at the eve of the depression that they reappeared. The daughter enrolled as a 5ifth–grader at the **St. Louis IX Academy**. The mother labored as a dispatcher at the **Lux Haus Autos** warehouse.

A **Chronicle** essay that Lex fetched revealed the academy expelled **Vilma Carolina** for **pregnancy c.** 1933. The father wasn't named. No attempt was made to identify the guilty, if the guilty they were, save that they were among the warehouse's transients – **allegedly**. Then.... At midnight, sixteen years old and thirty weeks pregnant, she retreated to the **girl's room, said her prayers** – to quote a witness – and jumped out of the 3hird floor window.

That article's imagery was atypically even grotesquely **raw**. The editor's bent waxed explicitly where they inserted a black & white photograph. Tinted red by age, the photograph exposed the macabre visage: two men stood at the upper, right window; **Vilma Carolina** lay tarped at the street. The image's expression wasn't coy about its subject – yet – it struck us as strange that the tarp's contour failed to convey the victim's development.

Decades after the suicide – as documented many, **many** times over – when the night's quiet and still, she returns. **The Girl in The Window** returns. She's a shape, less a figure, more a suggestion. Frequent details include: running and shouting apparitions viscerally **felt** as much as **heard**, echoes of voices (of words like **get me out of this**, or, **I'm burning burning burning**), even, fires' crackles – alarms were tripped by the effect.

In addition to that reportage were signs common to **abductions** – delirium, hysteria, **fear** of ordinary, everyday objects, and lost / jumbled time & space. Compiled into Lex's dossier were tales that originated after the suicide and continued into the '40s and the '50s. Witnesses related their hearing cries, **cries like a baby's** or their feeling impressions **of something**, of something they couldn't identify, prowl the street where **Vilma Carolina** died.

Let it be noted that **c.** 1967 a man's body had been removed from the **girl's room** after a fire. The fire's cause wasn't understood but its damage was said to be extensive. The issue of the man's identity defied the police's effort. Straight into the midnight of our investigation its mystery persisted, filed as case 19B78C at the **John/Jane Doe National Database.**

By the end of the '70s, the warehouse hosted a sequence of mystics eager to sell a theory. Put to the test, however, all of them – who or what ever they purported to be – were set adrift. After Thadius A. Stevenson's expedition, as an act of desperation, the ownership **sealed** the whole, entire 3hird floor.

Sites to match the warehouse's reputation served as beacons, drawing and claiming those sensitive to the paranormal. Often, they are not well adjusted folk. We should have expected interlopers. We should have expected and acted accordingly. We failed and that fate impelled us to play it by ear.

As such we randomized our course – and got lost.

Jason & Paul – our twins and resident –**ists** (geo & bio) – admitted they were stumped. **We oughtn't be lost**, they insisted, **the streets are the streets.** Then they confessed of the eccentricity of the environment. **It's out of kilter.**

We got lost yet that realization of our stray came from elsewhere. Not from the streets – the streets **were** the streets. Not from with–out but from with–in. Unspoken parts of our brains had been triggered and their power to suggest alarmed us. Perhaps we veered into a whirl of **madness**? – a **disturbance** ethereal and gossamer! As we tread into **Little Berlin**, further and further aloft of the greater city of Denver, unaware of that progress due to the stalker sparking the scatter, it felt as if our chemistry **tipped**.

By itself the effect might have been dismissed as nerves. Except the effect wasn't by itself, **alone**. There was the warehouse. There was the neighborhood. There was the vagrant. Taken **together**, the paradoxes we faced jolted us into a shared, frayed experience.

In spite of midnight, the sky was brighter, the moon was fuller and larger than any of us recalled.

Then to our surprise the **Lux Haus Autos** loomed into view.

Above ground it sported three levels of windows. Below ground it revealed a cellar. At its front we noted how its doors were gated by roll–down / pull–down metal. Its sides were alleys enshadowed by its neighbors. Everywhere we gazed, its solid, real brick cladding conveyed a stern, European facade, typical of early 20th century design, incompatible to the taste of the gentrified.

We assumed the site had been converted into a tenancy – else – into a storefront. That **reclamation** failed to consume it felt welcome if odd. The establishment retained its industry's scars. The rough, brittle texture that gilded its masonry amplified the scowl of its grime. The glare of its gates matched the weathered, shattered pavement that encased its perimeter.

The **Crew** struggled to find a signal. Our mobiles linked to **satellites** not to **towers**. Given that midnight's wide open sky we grumbled, confused at the predicament. So it was peer–to–peer for us as a compromise although that drained batteries.

Relegated to watch–duty – always – I kept my eyes and ears alert even as that street splayed its emptiness. To our front and sides there was nothing, nothing – **save** a jagged grimace composed of warehouses by warehouses – their lights, their lights **extinguished**.

I sat at the curb to journal. Lex and the twins hustled to get their voices into their sets. We prodded the case: how it wove in and out of that era's events. I plunged, again, into my summation of Thadius A. Stevenson's 1974 report.

Vilma Carolina, The Girl in The Window, was sixteen years old and thirty weeks pregnant when she jumped to death. On paper her father was a French soldier and her mother was an American nurse. It was in Paris, **c.** 1913, that her mother met her father among classmates. Promptly, they turned into fiancés. Lementine and Auguste planned to marry then the war broke and wrecked the pair.

To stay together, they volunteered their services to the effort. Auguste was struck at the **Somme.** Lementine was captured then taken into Bavaria. The postscript of their doom was that arranged, good-will release Christmas Day, 1916, thirty weeks into term.

Lementine **changed.** She didn't speak of Auguste. She didn't recognize her colleagues or understand her duties. Students noted the extent to which her disposition altered. Especially how her manners assumed more Continental, less American characters. They wondered how she spoke French free of accent. **Rumors** circulated at the academy. Professionals – stressed by the calamity of the **Somme** – presumed the alteration was spurred by widowhood (although evidence of marriage had not been presented).

Amongst reporters the matter of her catch & release became fodder for gossip. They poked at the fringe of the mystery and their newsprint speculated a timeline. They concluded:

It started like any day started – like any early, late–July morning at an allied field hospital. A unit north of Geneva telegraphed their request for assistance. That alerted the staff to rouse the team: **she** and a pair of British nurses joined to a surgeon. They, the medics, got crammed into an ambulance manned by a trio of drivers. That trio wasn't known to the staff and spoke a dialect **vaguely** familiar to the surgeon **not** to the nurses. The drivers opted for a shortcut through a pass; the staff wasn't comfortable yet acquiesced to experience. Then – just as the sun cracked the sky – the ambulance raced into the front, never to be seen or heard again.

Except **Lementine,** its survivor, and she refused to clarify how they had been captured.

Weeks after her release then her discharge, Lementine returned to New York City where she birthed **Vilma Carolina.** Records of the era weren't available to conclude whether or not she contacted her wealthy, Bostonian family. Ostracism? Howsoever she got by, she traveled the interior of the US throughout the '20s. Wheresoever she stopped, though, she worked for a variety of German international firms – **engineering** firms – contracted by **Ford.** As such she floated about circles that catered to men later identified as exiled German mystics connected to the **Thules** and to Ludwig Straniak – a magician & rival to Alistair Cooke.

Note that after her daughter's suicide, Lementine relocated to Germany. Her last known address, to where she forwarded French and American veteran correspondences, amounted to a Bavarian post office box. Her last known picture – a snapshot labeled **Baghdad / 1937** – surfaced c. 1957 among the archives of a deceased **Thules** prophet. Stevenson **et al** assumed she survived the Second World War.

We were sober as we make it a point to be. While on-duty we cannot predict what, if anything, may or may not be unleashed at an investigation. As we sat and spoke of the case into our recorders, I felt the onset of a disquiet that my recitation only served to heighten. I felt that we got lost. Lost not in **space** but in **time**. We encroached into mysteries – ancient yet tangible – so unlike rustic ghostly legends and indifferent to physical and mental hazard.

It was as I contemplated everything that I **noticed**. I waited. Was it a trick? – a mischief of light and shadow? I waited – to give the situation the chance to settle. If, **if** it weren't the truth, my persistence ought to debunk the impression. I wanted to dismiss it as the excess of the imagination. As if, to stifle that agony we tumbled into, we wished to see anything to jump-start the heart. Try as I may, I couldn't stifle that shock I felt coming like a wave cresting suddenly, unexpectedly.

The **Crew** spotted my stir.

Look! I pointed to the warehouse – to its upper, right window.

A figure that didn't exist only a few breaths ago **appeared**. A figure shaped and featured like **a** girl – so we agreed – gazed at us as we gazed at it. **That** girl – she watched us – we couldn't believe it. We shuddered, petrified as we gawked at each other – but we wanted to see it? – and see it we did – **the** girl....

Vilma! we shouted – the twins added, as they were oft to: **don't jump.**

Lex stole a picture of it. They used a flash. We (else I) panicked. What if that flash alerted residents? But the image it captured! And the excitement it drew! Lex couldn't say if the girl **responded,** yet, I noted the journalist's eyes and the curl of the lip as if I caught their face mid-scream.

As the **Crew** reveled at the fracas, my gut insisted I withdraw. It was I who kept a watch. I switched my attention from above to below. That street we invaded felt darker then darker; a waft of fog settled onto its track. Only a single, distant lamp far at the center of the street fought through that miasma. My eyes swept side-to-side to warn of interlopers. **The stalker? The police?** The situation felt too chaotic to be tenable; our thrill was liable to trap us. For a while I heard the flow of traffic, the trickle of cars, cars – one by one – echoed at the distance as the neighborhood yawned into silence.

Wait! Lex shouted.

The Girl in The Window vanished.

At the curb, then, we gathered to assess how to proceed. Giddy by the shock of it, by the power of it, the zone was too hot to quit. We hadn't encountered a shape that perfect since our attempt at the Dominguezes' mines. We hadn't encountered a shape that reacted and interacted like the girl ... **ever.**

We talked, **crazed** 'til out of the bolt I said: **Scramble!**

My attention hadn't drifted away from the flow of traffic. I noted that a vehicle sped **closer** not **farther** to the street's north end. As its headlights betrayed its intents, we scattered. The site was desolate; there were no vehicles, no dumpsters, little of anything, anywhere to mask our encroachment. Across the warehouse, though, the alleys parting the buildings offered their cover so we rushed into the nearest, widest passage available.

The alley funneled into stairs that took us onto a level just under the street's view. The passage ambled past that further and deeper 'til it stopped at a yard. Seeking what I thought to be a better shot at cover, I eked away from the **Crew** and the stairs, to continue through the passage. The alley was tight; the buildings at my sides, however, didn't obstruct my sight of the sky. My eyes split their interest, partly to the world below, partly to the world above, as I shifted forward to the yard.

I noted a brilliant paradox of color that engulfed my stroll – from the onyx at my sides to the sky overhead. It wasn't a midnight sky or a shade of twilight. It wasn't midday either. Maybe it was a blur? – admixtures of extremes? Maybe it was my perception distorted by exhilaration?

My exploration stopped at a tall, narrow gate. **Locked,** it checked any advance into that yard. I stood, gripping the bars, peeling the chains as I tried and failed to pry the gate. Just an arm's length away the yard's overgrowth called even as it disturbed. The gloom of its trees appeared so gray to my eyes that it felt unreal.

The **Crew** hesitated and rejected the yard; they plead for my return so I retreated to settle by the stairs. We planked the steps, keeping our feet at the bottom and our chins over our hands at the top. We kept just under the street's level; our sights aimed to that crest where the street itself spread like a boundary. Cast by the shades of the buildings that entrapped us, we kept **still** to evade detection.

The vehicle entered the street and approached the warehouse – driving north to south. It idled at the center. We didn't hear anybody get off or on. We didn't see the spotlights probe the curbs. We waited and watched, raising and lowering ourselves to pry that horizon at the crest of the stairs. My eyes kept darting to the sky. Framed by onyx, the sky attained a mystic shade of blue and blossomed into a burst of stars, a smatter of cosmos.

Then – the vehicle fled.

For a spell we stayed by the stairs – 'til a breeze stiffened through the alley – 'til a ruffle of trees against trees creaked out of the yard. A dog barked at the distance. That neighborhood's slumber – undisturbed as it were – compelled us to resume the adventure.

We reconnected in front of the warehouse and pondered what to do.

Lex passed the photograph of the window & the girl. The flash had reflected off the glass so that ghost became a blob. As I feared, it wasn't an image suitable for our channel. I lamented that we didn't take the thermal.

Who's game to enter?

The crime had been at the tip of the tongue. Nobody wanted to air it **explicitly**. At the onset we suspected that the **Lux Haus Autos** warehouse had been converted into a tenancy – therefore – a breach of its interior had been rejected. As it was a **business** not a **residence**, the calculus **changed**. Emboldened, it didn't feel like intrusion anymore. That we weren't disturbing anyone's **domicile** altered the nature of it enough to be palpable.

I itched at the chance to sneak into that warehouse. Our resident –**ists** were eager to enter. Only Lex wanted to leave – we coaxed them to stay and they volunteered to be our eyes and ears outside the warehouse.

The front had been too guarded to admit entry. Rather, we shifted onto the side and ambled through a passage like a driveway. Jason & Paul (and I) led while Lex trailed. We aimed for the rear. Around us the alley plunged into an abyssal shade of onyx that blotted its architecture. All **details**, windows, doors, everything that to daylight would have been, could have been exposed melted into inky voids. Ahead, expanding and evolving step–by–step, sprouted an uncanny yonder.

We should have fled.

Was it aware of us?

Were we aware of it?

The alley terminated; we stood confounded at a segment of pavement betwixt the dark behind us and the light before us. Our vista exploded and we caught a perfect view of the sky that fragments only teased. Across the space & time of a ghastly azure the stars twinkled as if they were jewels encrusted onto velvet. Ambling from the zenith to realms deeper and deeper below, we noted how the appearance of Man degraded the purity of heaven. Until we gazed – and gasped – at the base, the lot framed by grinding, decaying tenements.

The lot had been paved like a street. At that midnight it yawned a vista desolate almost abandoned as it flaunted scars carved by use. It rolled forward, toward a railroad that spurred into warehouses. It widened like a grin, spreading side-to-side 'til at its extremes it tapered onto intersections. Every so often we caught glimpses of cars driving **by** not **into** the lot. Otherwise – nothing – nothing ....

Why did it upset me?

We weren't drunk. Yet stepping into that lot, everything felt disjointed, everything. All of it – and the sum of its parts – upset the mind. That strange sky. That strange city. The neighborhood's character. The inconsistent and awkward dimensions (the lot was wider than the street). The shapes of buildings (tenements in front of us) assumed a hostile character in spite of their familiarity.

Had we ventured into a world so removed, **so alien** that it followed altogether alternate realities?

We stopped to contemplate the absurdity of the situation only to realize it wasn't simply a quirk of that landscape. It was the air – its drone, its chill, its odor that bespoke of ages earlier than ours. It was the land. It was the sky. **Midnight!** The cityscape that entrapped us transmitted its unwelcome. We didn't belong there and it wasn't because of that which we intended to do. Our strangeness was far too fundamental.

Where is the past? – the future? Don't they exist as physical as everything? But isn't reality hysteria shared **or** imposed by the globe's self-awareness? And if so, if so – perhaps – were it not possible howsoever unlikely to slip into realms thus askew of the present?

At the rear of the warehouse we found Dutch-style doors framed by thin, long panels. We wondered, as we hesitated, **do we, do we**? Lex faced the tenements ahead. Jason & Paul scanned the lot side-to-side. For a while I stopped – then – I formed a mitt from a scarf to match my fist and I aimed my punch through the glass. No alarm buzzed. No stir replied. Not a whiff of commotion followed my break save that timbre of tiny little bits of screes scattered at the floor.

I reached into the maw careful to mind the teeth. I fumbled for the door's locks – its top-half yielded but its bottom-half defied my efforts. To free the entire door I would have had to shatter yet another panel and I wasn't so bent. Still – we weren't alerted to a reaction of any stripe. Lights hadn't flickered at the tenements. Cars hadn't stopped at the intersections. Even the air hadn't whispered its warnings to us.

Lex paced the lot, facing the tracks, the far, distant roads where they entangled into the neighborhood. They gazed to us every so often; their eyes reflected my trepidation. I forgot what I said to the journalist except to warn them off the tracks and its spurs.

Jason & Paul mounted the hurdle I left of the door.

I followed, awkwardly, rusty as it were.

Past it, we crammed into the warehouse. A fog of pitch cloaked its realm. We kept it so as a caution. We suppressed flashlights and ignored switches as electronics impeded the work. That cellar wasn't a maze and to traverse it didn't compel us to be cartographers.

Our entry led us into a chamber devoted to furnaces and breakers. Foyers stocked by coal split it away from a vast, gothic kitchen that merged to a cafeteria. At its rear that area converged onto a corridor. We trampled as it twisted us this way and that way 'til direction itself melted into the ether. We stopped every so often to gawk at its walls – its walls supported thick and heavy doors – beyond them they hinted at stairs (up, down), at passages (in or out), at vaults, else, at rooms reserved for the employed.

Forward.

Onward.

Ahead, the corridor stopped – **abruptly** – at the threshold of the office. We staggered past that doorway, eager if not giddy to be washed by light. The office **blazed** to light whose source could not be detected. Its windows were frosty. Its views were distorted. Midnight bled through them but it wasn't enough, **it wasn't enough** to account for that light.

My impression of the office was colored by what I mistook to be its size. Except that as I entered its volume my steady, calm eye flattened its dimensions into something, something **ordinary**. Its floor, tiled black & white, supported a matrix of desks arranged three–by–three. Its vault, accented red by-the-by, formed or emerged out of networks of pipes that had not been beset by the modesty of cover. Its walls sparkled amber, a deep yet vivid swipe of yellow.

Jason & Paul gasped, surprised. I asked why and they pointed at the desks. **Electronics?** The technology we detected amounted to: bulky telephones, bulky typewriters, bulky copiers. Had the proprietors opted for analog over digital? Had the **Lux Haus Autos** warehouse taken hipster mystique too, too far?

We spread and combed, careful not to leave prints.

I approached a bulletin and examined everything that had been pinned onto it. I chuckled as my eyes drew to newsprint. Of course. Everything made sense. Didn't it? **Didn't it?** Of course **that** would have to be there to complete the warehouse's trick of time & space.

It was a copy of that essay Lex fished out of microfilm. The article dated to 1967. Under that light, its type was illegible, though, its picture was superb. I recognized it, **immediately**. It was that, that '30s photograph. Amazingly, it hadn't aged, if it were true, it hadn't aged in spite of decade after decade of exposure. The imagery's power – focused and sharpened – struck so raw a chord I wasn't prepared. Details of that tarp and what it covered tantalized my understanding. Multiple outlines of shapes – the smallest at the front, the largest at the back – spurred a shiver that cascaded my spine.

I shrieked at Lex's signal – they squawked into my mobile.

It's getting weird, they said of the outside – they had forced a route from the back to the front of the warehouse via the lot.

At the curb, the reporter heard and saw trash quiver.

Trash? At the curb, Lex? I asked.

Jason & Paul grimaced – they didn't appear upset.

I replied: **Just stay frosty, Lex!**

They insisted that we flee.

Snickers tweaked out of the twins – and I wondered if it weren't part of a rouse.

Our mobiles de–linked.

Didn't we want to run? The site was hot, hot.... Too hot to leave.

We continued and located stairs to the 1irst floor.

Gazing at that flight, weren't we struck by how hostile the shape of it appeared to be? Light, dammed at its crest, oozed step–by–step to its root where swirls of colors wet our boots. Didn't we want to believe it was midnight, **midnight** flooding those stairs? We climbed, hammering foot over foot, breaking and shattering pools of lights collecting at its steps. We climbed and the whole, entire warehouse felt as if it were aware of us.

Upstairs, the layout disoriented us. We were not prepared for its enormity. Its **inner** capacity exceeded its **outer** dimension. We couldn't fathom if the optics were by design or by innovation. Until we noticed a feature that confusion rendered imperceptible. From outside we judged the warehouse stacked three floors over its cellar. From inside we realized its 1irst & 2econd floors had been merged into a single level approximately thirty feet tall. Its 3hird floor, if it existed, ought to be directly overhead.

We scrambled to find access for what may or may not have been left of that 3hird floor. We spread from area to area, sprinting past corners and nooks, fanning into aisles. The warehouse had been crated to its limit and that congestion frustrated our progress.

Attention to detail revealed a subtle yet distinct anomaly. It was a cable that dangled at a vault toward the warehouse's rear, left corner. That cable latched onto a rectangle four tiles wide by nine tiles long. That rectangle wasn't flush against the ceiling. Rather, it jutted by an inch so or so. Its tiles were painted a shade that almost, **almost** matched the ceiling. Its borders were choked by dust spread by air.

We wondered if the rectangle were freed by yanking the cable.

I piled crates into a heap that permitted my climbing and reaching the cable's end. Thus grasping and wrapping it to my palm, I applied my weight and it drooped a little, a little 'til it stuck. I posited that a mechanism other than that cable controlled the access. Jason & Paul insisted that the rectangle and the ceiling separated. So I tugged even as I feared the snap of the cable would have been the end of everything.

The cable **slacked** and we ran.

The rectangle **yawned** – its far–end pivoted as its near–end twisted and rocked. It tumbled away, **away** like a leaf parts a tree 'til it wrecked into crates. It left a void that resembled a maw – with teeth at its edges – with a tongue, **no**, a ladder slipping, stopping, slipping as it projected to the floor.

Silence muzzled the warehouse except where it broke to our laughter. We, standing at the foot, gawking at the head, examined the ladder to gauge its sturdiness. As we grasped its fame we startled. A vibration heretofore imperceptible transmitted from the ladder to the warehouse. Our bodies rumbled; in spite of its erstwhile real, physical intrusion, buoyed by levity, we dismissed it as more imagination, less reality.

Paul **not** Jason itched to be 1irst – the younger's commentary prepared the elder's.

My thoughts returned to Lex and their whereabouts.

I turned to the window that faced the street. **Trucks** parked at the curb. The street wasn't empty? But we hadn't felt their arrival. And, certainly, **certainly**, we hadn't loitered that warehouse unchecked for hours upon hours.

It was my turn to ascend.

Thirty feet should not have felt so high. I climbed, rather, I forced my feet to scale that ladder rung by rung. I didn't want to face **anywhere**. Was it its shake or my shake? As with everything that midnight, it wasn't a particular element this or that way but the totality of its alchemy that inspired dread. I didn't want to face **anything**. My eyes tracked the twins ahead – they encouraged my advance. Why didn't I retreat? Too late – wasn't it just **too late**? – and as I passed that last, meddlesome rung and as I jumped into a labyrinth, I fathomed the ordeal it would be to reverse course.

The 3hird exceeded the cellar's gothics and the merged 1irst's & 2econd's proportions. Excitement propelled us as we traversed a maze too vast to be yoked by that warehouse's perimeter. It wasn't a conundrum. Or, so we supposed. It wasn't an intent to mislead but to point if not to command our attention onto **its** goal.

As such, if such it were, we rambled into the center of the labyrinth. It had to be the atria. Corridors rayed out of it. Corridors from where **or** to where? We stepped into its midst – far enough to see that the atria had been forged by the union of a domed vault and a columned ring. We approached its only article – a seat like a throne – a skeleton of wood endowed a physique of metal and capped by a crown of feathers, a headdress whose brim displayed strikingly, alarmingly crisp swastikas beaded black and white, red and yellow.

We froze, afraid of it, of what its figure, its symbology implied. It was eerie yet visceral what that object – and its physical **emanation of fear** – awoke at the core of our biology. Wasn't there a sense – a sense neglected 'til withered and rotted – a sense suppressed by the conscious – ignored except if invoked **mystically?** Wasn't there something, **anything** – to save us – that across the abyss of time & space meekly insisted **we straddled thresholds unsecured for man.**

Determined to shatter its power, I recalled to the **Crew**, how tribes throughout the continent featured that symbol prominently into their art – thus – the regalia may have been authentic then repurposed by mystics and **Indianthusists** of ill-intent. Except that the swastikas that had been embroidered onto the brim of the headdress were formed of crescents bordered by circles. It had been too, too carefully constructed to be a mistake. **That** version of the swastika was the emblem of the **Thules**. The **Thules** or their sympathizers claimed that volume – that whole, entire warehouse had been their handiwork.

Layers of dusty, ashy debris caked surfaces throughout the atria. Everything had been kissed by fire. It got to our hands then to our eyes. We itched and labored to breathe.

We tread past that throne – as it shed the worst of the ash – toward a kink where that vault focused into a passage. Right at the brink of that passage, at its threshold, we tripped and shrieked. After a spell to collect our wits, we stopped and examined the floor. The atria we tried to escape served as a nexus for networks of cables. We couldn't say where they originated only that they radiated from the circumference to the center of the vault (behind that chair). Where they met, they braided and continued into that exit we stood by.

The sight of them – so imperfect, **so organic** – they resembled vessels. Vessels that transported current not blood. They throbbed and their resonance impelled surfaces to fuzz. **Alive?** If alive they were.... Couldn't they be? Weren't they simply arteries and veins of an immense organism?

The network's cables varied – varied by type and varied by age. It wasn't a **singular** but a **plural** effort that spanned decades. Perhaps it had been laid by those who investigated **The Girl in The Window**. Or by those who hexed the realm into the state we found it.

As if to defy the architecture's **evil**, we grasped and yanked at a wire. Just to hold it, it felt as if its vibration could have ripped my flesh to shreds. I tugged – and Jason & Paul assisted – 'til we heard a snap. It came from the atria – from the chair. Alerted, thus, we caught sight of a spark. A spark – a burst of light against dark, arcing from the nexus to the ground, splitting by twos, by fours, by eights, splitting more and more dimming into the void where it vanished.

My mobile **shook**.

It was Lex: **Why'd you cut that cable?**

Lex? Is that you? What's .... What's wrong?

I struggled to recognize the voice through that accent. The very, **very** start was lost to the ether. The bulk was saved into my recorder and transcribed as:

"Transmi ... we don't have ... battery's past pri ... won't ... a charge ... can't ... re ... I found you by accident! Listen to me, what we saw, **The Girl in The Window, it's not Vilma Carolina**. Stevenson spilt the details to me. Father wasn't French. Mother wasn't Ame .... They killed Lementine and switched her with a lady already impregnated by the **Thules**. Conception ... was timed to a **ritual. Vilma Carolina** was supposed to be the last of a sequence of **star-children** – a chain – a lineage – crusaders brought it into Europe from a tribe of heretic Babylonian Arabs. That sequence brought their cult toward its goal – star–children whose bodies would be compatible ... **shaped** for a **specific** entity. Remember Lee's pre/post inflation genesis conjecture? **Vilma Carolina's** baby was supposed to be the vessel for an entity of that epoch. The **Thules** instigated their channeling into her fetus the night of her death. It spurred changes ... **and she felt it**. Stevenson told me that 3hird floor was converted into an asylum to keep her isolated for the birth. But that creature metastasized – it beca ... listen to me ... the **consciousness** of that entity ... it didn't leave the warehouse **completely**. ... brations kept it sated ... it alters time and space. The **Thules** were about to impregnate somebody who would have been Vilma's cousin when ... war stated earlier ... they expected. Stevenson expanded the mechanism to bottle it ... you ... you listen to me ... you're breaking alre ... Jason 'n' Paul are ... are gone ... still a chance ... if you get away **right now**."

Static crackled.

I stood agape: was it Lex?

Jason & Paul continued into the exit ahead. I followed the twins right 'til its end. Our trek stopped in front of a door – a door whose frayed, azure frame stood encrusted and sealed by salt. A sign had been attached scarcely disturbed to the doorknob – its front read **Amy, LEAVE** – its back sprawled empty. Slats, above and below that doorknob, formed weak analogs of windows. We tried our flashlights. We tried our mobiles. We tried and failed to detect what, **what if anything**, waited beyond that door.

If not for that which we suspected, we could have – **certainly** – we would have ignored the door and fled the warehouse. We stopped to argue. We traced and mapped onto the ash of the floor our steps throughout that 3hird level. Hadn't we accomplished so much and damaged so much to retreat? Wasn't that doorway yet another drop into the ocean? Especially as we felt it had to be the entrance into the **girl's room**.

We assaulted the door. It resisted 'til our violence cracked its seal. Then our strike wreaked havoc. Then – it trembled – **it trembled**. We shrieked at its reaction. Its slats loosened, dropped. Its gaps weren't wide enough to let us reach through. We kicked and, **and** it caved. It caved into the chamber beyond the threshold and shattered at that spot where it hit the floor.

Vilma Carolina – it was her room – it was her **asylum**, if Lex (if Lex it was) was believed.

Alarmed by a surge of air that past as if through our bodies, we turned and scanned the area we fled only recently. Where was the passage? Where was the atria? The architecture lost its vastness as the realm settled into silence. Where did it go, **the magic**?

Under the threshold we struggled to accept what became of reality.

It was the very top, right of the warehouse. It was the girl's room. Pitched and so much so that flashlights did not penetrate that chamber. Jason & Paul rushed into it. I wouldn't. **I couldn't.** Frozen to where I stood, I hesitated.

The twins had vanished into that jet at a point only feet in front of my eyes. I heard them. Or was it that I felt them? Their boots pounded at floorboards. I couldn't see therefore I couldn't find them. And then – then the screaming…. I was engulfed by a whirlwind of voices like a train of conversations. As if a century's worth of dialog condensed into a bomb that burst at my ears. Its impression – wasn't it a scream? – **a howl** – declared its tumult in-to perhaps out-of existence?

It was a prank. Why – yes, yes – it **had to be** a prank! A joke instigated by Lex and brought into fruition by the twins. A 4ourth conspirator was the vagrant who chased us. A 5ifth conspirator was the girl who lured us. It had to be a joke for our channel's benefit.

I teetered betwixt running for the ladder or for the chamber. I kept to the threshold and its salty, chalky frame, putting out of my mind the end of that 1967 article.

To call their bluff, I pointed my flashlight into the chamber without regard to whether or not it was spotted by neighbors. I didn't find Jason / Paul. I didn't find anything ... **anybody**. I felt as if only that chamber and I existed. So I wondered, if I went to the window, **if I went to the window,** then, yelled – why – **that** had to do it. They'd have to stop me. They'd have to stop me – else – we'd get caught.

Jokes over y'all – I shouted, determined to end their tomfoolery.

My blood froze.

That tiny little girl's room didn't leave a spot to hide. Not a way in or out unless time itself were a doorway. For at the wall, at that spot where we saw the Girl, the Window **was bricked**!

★

Exiles

3–PM sirens called the shift's end.

Workers – men and women naked alike – hoisted pickers to shoulders then filed through corridors of what they reaped. Their bodies pooled into centers where **taskers** exchanged tools for uniforms. Children invaded the fields that adults evacuated; they carted its bounty to its prep at levels elsewhere. Overhead, panels spread aside and damp, sun–kissed air poured into the farm. Dew rained onto thick, verdant edibles and workers, too, by–the–by.

Conan split and wandered away from the chatter to the solitude only a shower provided. That spout's drip, warmer **not** cooler, washed a day's worth of dirt off his skin. Its splatter, spreading and melting into the air, animated fragrances of leaves – the whole entire farm **echoed** the wealth of that season's harvest.

Wasn't it easier? – **easier to tolerate**! – as opposed to the **meateries** of his youth and the reek that assaulted the nose. That was back way, **way back** when the **Old Authority** encouraged luxury. He shuddered at the zeal of the memory. **Why**? – why strike **like that**? – why return **like that**? – **fresh**, as if the years a lifetime spanned were dreamt like a fantasy.

"Not much left to do, just, cross the **i's** and dot the **t's**," cracked RamBam, a burly, Nordic figure, twenty odd years Conan's junior, who drifted into the showers. From askance the ear then the eye alerted to an intrusion – the shift arrived at the locker–room. **Solitude** burst at its seams. "Gonna work gravel?"

Jesus Miguel 'Conan' curled a lip; he thought and replied jointly: "Maybe?" Harvest stopped at summer. Conditions weren't right for farming from July to December. Due to that crisis, the **New Authority** extended jobs for either prep or mine work, cool, out–of–the–sun jobs, doled by age: preps for the child, mines for the adult. "Ah, Chavo, I'm gonna relax."

"Tried **that**," he laughed as children stormed into the locker–room, singing and dancing. "It's the worst, isn't it?" A glimpse of reality kept unstated formed simply to vanish yet its perception transmitted perfectly from younger to older man. "Who shouldn't I forgive that I **out–grew** prep–work?"

Engineers shaped the farm into a pyramid. That structure's design wasn't intended for **Earth** but for **mothership** use – **for migration**. As such, it would have been the tenth of twelve attached to the **Cali** – except – the **Cali** fled without it.... So they **repurposed** it.

The pyramid's apex stood 500 feet over the surface of the desert. Its upper 3hird encased the fields; they modified its frame to split as required to control the farm's light and water take. Its lower 3hird consisted of vast networks of chambers; they kept its climate anywhere from sixty-five to seventy-five degrees Fahrenheit – **wintry** – throughout the year. They devoted the rest to manufacture – to prep-work harvest and preserve it for years.

As remote and forgotten history attested, their commune had always been that region's center of commerce. Even after migration, after that sort of activity ceased to be relevant, they retained their importance as the largest, richest extant **Golden League** city. Other cities at the coast either starved or thirsted into the void. Their pyramids sustained them with efficiencies that required just a fraction of the space and the time of conventional farmland. More were planned then scrapped by the **New Authority** – its efforts to set birth and death rates might have been impeded if there was too, **too** much abundance to distribute.

The shift (and Conan) re-connected at the lobby in front of a booth that assumed their crew's **standard**. They cued to update their '**rations & allotments**' cards. Far ahead, lifts took workers to fields. Far behind, windows blotted the Sun's angry, red scowl. The lobby's glare hadn't been extinguished merely whittled – dimmer and dimmer – to copy the midnight of yesteryear and to that degree where a speck of lux hurt by contrast. Only at intervals – at booths, at elevators, at windows – were engineers impotent to thwart the eye's thirst for light.

Doors (to theaters) gridded the lobby. Colored stripes framed their entries and coded their contents – their **films**. Workers – from shifts coming or going – commingled as they patronized free of charge.

Children weren't admitted – a prohibition that failed to stop how they gamed those passages for whiffs of A/C. Every so often somebody walked in or out of a theater. They scrambled to reach its access. They raced to catch its door. If it didn't shut … they **scored** and celebrated by fanning it about. Kids called it '**rocking the breeze**'.

Teams, as it were, dueled at a doorway by Conan. Alerted to their activity, he paused and caught that theater's playback. A documentary came into focus, frame-by-frame, across the doors as they swayed. Its action erupted and startled the lobby. They saw a rocket project and slowly, slowly **torture** its trajectory through the sky. They heard a voice struggle to narrate against the violence of the display.

Or, could it be, that their unease was their reflection? – subjective **not** objective?

Films were **arbitrarily** resurrected for entertainment and were neither dubbed nor subbed. That wasn't entirely a lack of technology, rather, a lack of effort. The voice was tainted by accents centuries forsaken. Its articulating proved impossible to gauge. Its jargoning, too, would have been obscure to anybody vulgar of history.

For, the voice declared, that rocket was **America's** test of the engine to the stars. A machine built to defy its skeptics as it jumped from fiction to fact. If it worked to **NASA'S** specificity, the voice continued, it would be the breakthrough the world waited for motherships and for migrations yet to be.

Conan took every shift the **New Authority** allotted. But year after year the work took its toll. And at fifty he wondered how much was left to give. Retirement held firm at sixty–five in spite of promises to the contrary. Few ever reached sixty. By fifty–five they worried if they would be next. Not all who failed to retire did so **naturally**.

At the street, protected by his uniform, he pressed his visor to his eyes. Their amber lenses painted that world a unique spectrum of color. The Earth, as it spread from the western coast to the eastern range, reflected a barren, wasted buff. The air assumed an eerie shape, a ghostly form, as winds dispersed sands. The sky itself was fire. The Sun, haunting the Pacific, didn't sink as much as melt, like a puddle of crimson, trickling drop–by–drop, raging at its edges.

That eve the waterfront was desolate except for the patrol. Recently, their watch thickened and persisted right into midnight. They were a paranoid lot – not without cause, it should be noted. Their activity revived fears of raiders striking for revenge.

Theirs wasn't what the coast of California used to represent: an easy–going beach–front life. For a millennium their commune abutted valleys **not** oceans. It had been so when his family settled that area the final year of Mexican rule. Calamity gained it a new and different identity as an oasis, makeshiftly enlarged until it collided into a (swollen) Pacific.

He ambled south to north across a venue where industrial and residential zones mixed. The architecture wasn't pleasant even when the old city was the new city. Considered to be superfluous, it languished, abandoned. Coils of streets were stripped. Pavers weren't required. Vehicles weren't issued. People walked to and from wherever. Warehouses – many that had been converted into tenements – were either empty or getting darker and darker by the day as the requirement for shelter abated. Businesses continued if subdued although the government claimed it didn't interfere. Sports persisted as did markets and restaurants. '**Tabu Stops**', as they were known by, resurged to flaunt their ban.

At the perimeter of the **Soccerdrome** he found a crowd. Like much of the city, its structure had been ripped. Pickers, who may or may not have been sanctioned, reduced its body to its skeleton. The **New Authority** intervened to halt that trend, though, when they found a use for its arena.

A sphere of eight, immense monitors spun as it broadcasted yet another trial over the **Soccerdrome**.

The particulars involved five men and five women. Stripped to breechcloth, they stood profile, body-to-body, displayed from shoulder to foot. Their skins baked as a prosecutor, a woman clad by white, paced and spoke of the facts. Mostly – that they had been caught trying to escape the commune. By a rather logical if twisted feat of legalism, the **New Authority** interpreted that as an act of treason. A lawyer – a man clad by black – rebutted for the accused and gave voice to ideas that resonated below **not** above. That there were too few of them. That they ought not to kill each other so impulsively. **That what is sowed is reaped.**

The case went to the jury then to the verdict – unanimous, of course.

He caught the trial at its climax. That crowd dispersed after the evidence exhibited the guilt. The case was swift, like all of them, **like all of them** at the **Soccerdrome**. Only a crew of the morbid stayed to watch its end: complicity trapped its audience.

One of the guilty (**a sixteen year old man or woman**? he couldn't say) fought against the restraints. They yelled; the distance muffled the statement. As they tussled, they slipped, tumbled and – **perhaps** – for flutters of eyelids their face projected onto the crowd. The monitors swapped to a view of their judge – a stern if sexless visage.

After a very, very long pause the broadcast returned to gawk at the condemned. They stood atop a platform arranged by sex. Guards applied nooses. Lawyers, for and against, whispered then withdrew. Jurors filed after the advocates.

Everybody waited for the judge to issue the order.

The coverage had been perfected to a science. The camera didn't waver. Rather, it tracked them as they plunged. It panned down, down so that just the bottom halves **not** the top halves of their bodies would be shown. It was enough to convey the struggle of bodies plumping like fruit swelling as they ripened.

Hanging – the New Authority considered it efficient. Not **humane**, per say. Although that was more like a feature than a bug.

Rhonda flipped the monitor's channel; its view switched from hanging bodies to flying rockets; its program exhibited a documentary that soothed their eyes. Little of its content disturbed the **strangers** gathered at the salon. Except for parts of its narrative about **goldielocks zones** and **international cooperation.**

As its volume faded, its program exited their imagination. They resettled, diffusing about the salon, silencing, **gradually**, silencing. Events came to a stop; faces gazed faces; eyes and lips together appeared to communicate a sense of doom. Their subject had to be broached. Still, they were game to anything that refocused their attention. For a spell the wind became their wonder as it howled through the warehouse.

"Nobody tried to stop them," Professor Tom resumed their conversation. "The danger failed to register. All of us, weren't we upended by the raid?"

"Keh, I could have sworn it was **Lopez** who called it a **temporary** government. 'Til they got a new – **a new!** – mothership built," Engineer Alicia interjected.

The husband and wife pair clung to the vagaries of their (obsolete) professions.

"I remember that governor. Exiled to Vancouver?" Carlos Abel mused – a politician of the **Old Authority** and that warehouse's eldest. "He didn't accept how the **real** government escaped aboard the Cali."

An old, wizened woman, wheeled a cart into the chamber. Mugs steamed like smoke as she served coffee from seat to seat. They reserved that delicacy for their monthly **tribal** rendezvous.

"We knew, **that night**... Whatever may be out there, **out here**, we're alone," Carlos Abel sipped a drop of coffee.

"They owe us," Dr. West insisted.

"But," interjected Rhonda – the youngest of that tribe of strangers – "what's the proof Denver exists? Or that it's **better**?"

"Alicia?" Tom cued.

The engineer leaned into their circle as if to whisper: "**Radio**. Signals are coded. We can't say what that's about, either, or, just yet. Telemetry says they come from east of the Rockies. It's got to be Denver. It possesses sources powerful enough to reach us. Keh, the Golden League always thought it too valuable to recycle for motherships."

"I agree with the doctor," spake the old, wizened woman, "**they** owe **us**. We know the **monsters** itch to return. Look ... it's a matter of time. Weeks? Days? There's lots the **New Authority** keeps wrapped. Radio tells everything. Years ago Vancouver repelled a strike. The **monsters**, they retreated into Oregon. Built a base at the Pacific. Oh, we spy ... we watch, wait ... **sabotage**. We know what's coming. Aren't as many of us left. Sister Cities? We can't fool ourselves. I've been to Soma and to Yuma. They're five kay a pop. Vancouver can't help any neither. Too far."

"Alright, so, how are we getting to Denver?" prodded Rhonda; she hesitated then abstained from her coffee. She gauged her neighbors. Strangers, the lot of them, they shared a bus for what had to be the longest **and** the shortest five minute ride. If parallel worlds weren't the dreams of esoterics perhaps, **perhaps** they would be engaged not by dread but by amusement whilst accelerating to **Zeta Reticuli**.

A woman, a mechanic from Vegas who had been transferred to work at the **Cali**, explained their logic: "As I recall it, twenty kay were already aboard, yet another twenty kay waited for a ride. The way it was, we might have been working all night and day to transport the rest. Only a quarter made it by the time of the attack. The Cali panicked and launched. They left a lot behind. Lots of fuel. Lots of food. Vehicles. Weapons. Of course, pyramids. What a disaster.... All of that had been intended for the migration. Alicia and I were bused to the pad that morning. Lopez wanted to know what could be salvaged. Of course, the **New Authority** confiscated everything of value – military **not** civilian stuff. What's left of the convoy that reached the Cali, the last, **last** bus, it's mothballed at a hangar and it won't take us a day to fix it."

Professor Tom added: "For supplies, we've been hoarding and prepping for over a decade. That's enough food to reach Texas. That pad, you know, after they stripped it, they forgot it. It's not part of their radar. We know ... we tested the idea, Alicia and I. So, we hide a few days for the engineers put the bus together. Then – it's the mountains. The Golden League carved tunnels to connect what's left of the continent. If we find them, we're good, we're good for a long, long trip."

The Sun's light withdrew its vigor as it settled into a shade of umber.

Conan entered the salon through the loft's door. A massive, wooden edifice, Rhonda's parents ripped it from their farm and installed it so it spread side-to-side. He turned and waved, sorry for the disturbance. Tom and Alicia greeted him with their customary **Jesus**. Carlos Abel offered him a mug of coffee. But it was refused. And they watched the man retreat into the kitchen.

Windows, aimed at the Pacific, blazed at the fire of the sunset – 'twas late and they judged it wise to adjourn.

Tom and Alicia implored Rhonda: "Tomorrow. **Midnight**. Yes, it's a matter of hours. If you and Jesus want to be part of this, leave your door unlocked. Tomorrow. **Midnight**."

The strangers retreated into their lofts.

Rhonda sighed.

The documentary resumed as images of planets came in and out of focus. Astronomers cataloged millions upon millions of worlds.... Only a few had been named: **New Rus**, **New Quin**, **New USA**.

By the monitor, a passage connected the salon to the kitchen. A brisk walk exhausted its length – and it yawned into a strangely bright and intimate chamber. The kitchen retained a glossy, white decor. Its walls were painted abstract, floral patterns. Fake minutia like verdure and random sounds of flowing waters or calling birds were added to that diorama. All of it together completed a stylized illusion of nature. A nature that didn't exist beyond museums of documentaries.

They stripped their uniforms – naked, except at their breechcloths, they met with a tight if sloppy embrace.

Rhonda and Conan were a couple that opted not to wed **traditionally**. As per the law – as understood by Carlos Abel – even to cohabitate skirted a charge of a felony – theft of resources or so the argument could be arranged. They could have claimed they wed the eve of the raid. Who would have objected? The **Old Authority** took its archive aboard the **Cali**. Who **could have** objected?

"Nena, you wonna go? It's OK. **You gotta go**."

"Do I want to go through that? I don't know, Conan, I don't know."

Wasn't there comfort and aid to routine?

Conan raised the carton of groceries from his left hand to his right shoulder. The bodega stocked just a fraction of what he ordered. It would be rough.... Better to have anything than to have nothing.

At the waterfront, the tide lured waves onto roads. Drains caught and routed the waters into the generators for power. A little more, **more** – **an inch**? – and the city would have flooded. Already his feet soaked.

The Sun – distant yet immense – crept moment–by–moment into noon. Tendrils like flames writhed at its rim. Wisps like sparks ruptured.... It roasted the planets. All of that **shape** throbbed to a frequency that baffled astronomy. After its expanse perturbed Mercury's orbit and vaporized Venus's atmosphere, its rage jolted the Earth.

Professor Tom explained that the Sun's uptick of violence was spurred by Jupiter's perihelion. The giant, stormy world churned the Sun's surface. They weren't certain if the effect would be transient or permanent. Either way the Earth's doom continued as a matter of fact.

The Sun wasn't always so angry.

Everything changed after a world that had been rejected by **its star** – and left to hurtle through depths of space and time – smashed into **their star**. The injection of that material into its core altered its nucleochemistry and adjusted its equilibrium. The Sun expanded, as if its age had been accelerated – **that** crimson visage dominated the last, thousand years. If not for history's record, nobody **alive** would have known the days of a yellow star.

So winters became summers. That heat released a fury to reshape maps. Poles melted. Oceans swelled. Nations flailed then toppled. Life perished at the equator; survivors migrated to either northern or southern extremes, to where the climate wasn't already a desert.

People tried everything to mitigate their circumstances. A few nations formed marine **later** abyssal cities. The **Golden League**, a fragile network of former, US states, attempted to settle underground. Valleys, like theirs, were filled for that purpose. Their efforts failed. Eventually they all agreed: the way to survive **as a species** was to abandon the planet.

A mile into Conan's journey and the road mazed by the relics of the attackers.

Left to rot, the **New Authority** thought itself clever not to repair the damage, substantial as it was. So the raiders' fleet clogged their harbor while the Pacific's waves battered yet preserved its sinister character. The anchor of that fleet – the **Altair** – sometimes listed, sometimes capsized – sometimes speared further into the heart of the commune.

He recalled, as the mind was wont to do, the fright of the raid. Sirens shattered that eve a quarter of a century ago. Their fight spanned from dusk to dawn and fated twenty kay lives. Their strike kept the battle away from the mothership. But the **Cali** panicked and launched partially assembled and populated. And at that juncture, its rockets blasting, filling the sky brighter than the Sun, they knew they were alone, like a beast, **cornered**.

Not a single raider escaped.

A struggle for power unfolded at the midpoint of that attack. Factions, later to be known as **Old or New Authorities**, split apart when the **Cali** verged nearest to jeopardy. The **Old Authority** opted to run, to slip through danger. Everybody raged, **betrayed**. Nobody contradicted the reaction. The **New Authority** took advantage of the situation to secure its mandate.

Afterward, the government dissolved the order of society as it existed. Castes, upper to lower alike, were homogenized by erasing the city's enclaves and by forcing its residents to integrate. They suppressed the elites' freer, wilder excess then enforced the workers' puritanism. They regulated even scheduled pregnancies to stabilize the population. Children weren't guaranteed to live; too many, too soon were a waste of resources. Production itself transferred from private to public management to command efficiency. Farms were collectivized. Recycling (mining) was **invented**. It kept everyone employed and diverted from **reality**.

Rhonda hopped onto the rear as Conan straddled the front of the bike. The engine revved and they sped a hasty route through the city. **They were late!** – 'twas what they feared would have, **could have** happened.

At the outskirts, where the city dispersed into raw, unfinished gridwork, the **Authority** erected a hanger. Out of that factory, workers assembled their mothership piece by piece. Convoys transported engines and pyramids and everything of value onto the pad farther and deeper into the mountains.

Construction ceased and that night activity centered on migrating **not** engineering. Buses deployed without interruption to and from that hanger. For hours upon hours they transported passengers into the mothership, the **California**, which stood five miles taller than the range that encompassed it. It was the third of three – **and the last** of a mothership formation whose 1irst and 2econd components, the **Nevada** and the **Oregon** respectively, already orbited.

In spite of their dalliance, they arrived by sunset. It was dark, **eerily**, dark – the way nights were intended to be. He remembered vague, wintry trips as a youth, towed by his family, for jobs at Soma or at Yuma. The city's nightly patterns of lights were unchanged only masked by the Sun's fire that churned at the horizon right into midnight.

He didn't remember where he parked the bike. The lots were full, cramped – spaces after spaces were taken. He didn't remember where, **exactly**, where he parked just that he stopped and that she embarked. As air wasted a sort of panic settled into their awareness. Security appeared then pushed them into the hangar. **Where were they going**? – nobody explained anything.

It was a shock to enter the factory. He hadn't never, ever witnessed a sight that defined by advancement. The equipment slumbered yet their readouts continued to beat rhythms of their own, **as if alive**. Something about their climate proved impossible to gauge – although the fear they animated echoed dimmed, faded remembrances. Was it a scent? Something cool? Something warm? Maybe the color of the light? – their readouts were like stars. All of it? None of it? There was simply an energy about that atmosphere that altered his perception. A city of twenty kay fit into that hangar.... Every so often he prayed he only dreamed it.

Conan and Rhonda pressed into an abyss that served as a platform. The structure's ends were open. Transports, shaped like bullets, coiled from front to back end. At the back, a fresh supply waited. At the front, a ripe fleet weaved onto the ramp and rushed into the road – to entertain its passengers' last taste of Earth.

They were jostled by a crowd that crossed their path. Although, amidst chaos, their hands parted, their eyes continued to tether each other. She stopped to gaze at him from step to step. He didn't let her face or her green drab pack out of his sight.

While their guilt's weight lifted – as they didn't arrive late at the hangar – the thought of separation crushed his spirit and replaced his dread for regret. His steps came heavy as his world slipped away. She couldn't stop dragging him forward, onward. He couldn't let go of her grip. Security couldn't keep from pushing them toward the buses.

Rhonda approached the bus she had been appointed. Conan squeezed her shoulders, her hands. A cue formed. A tribe of strangers gathered and displayed tickets. She stared through watery violet eyes. He fought to speak yet cracked against the inertia of language. Their union inched, inched to its end.

In front of everyone, she stroked his braid and kissed his cheek – **was it?** – **was it?** – **goodbye?**

Then – then **the sirens** – **then....**

He found her where she sat transfixed, upset at the corner of the bed.

The chamber's dimensions rivaled the salon's. It wasn't as cluttered by furniture. Only a minimum was found – that which would be required of a bedroom. Its windows were modest, too, just so wide, just so tight, like eyes that could not look away. Orange and wood grain veneer dominated its construction – a trend that appeared hundreds of years ago and by persistence continued. They called it **documentary** as its style copied what the media preserved.

Conan combed his fingers, thick and rough, into Rhonda's curls. Her hair was feathery as a bird's fleece ought to be. Her skin was ruddy, tinted as if shaded to match his. It must have been her weekly dose of Sun.

Rhonda stared at a green drab pack. By accident that eve she found it and yanked it from the closet. It had been stored for a quarter of a century. For years and years, as the Earth swept its orbit, that pack hid – untouched, unpacked – **ashamed.** Or – was it watching and waiting – slumbering until that time it would be essential again?

She had been ticketed and scheduled to board the **Cali.** If they had gotten to that hangar sooner, perhaps, if a bus or a seat were available, perhaps, she would be free. But they ran later. And they did so by their choice to sate a whisper of passion. Such was the price to pay. What if they hadn't so mocked that dying world?

Standing while she sat, he cupped her hands into his hands and brought her arms onto his waist.

"You gotta go."

She tugged. He yielded – giving further and further into her embrace – until they resettled at the bed and lay side–by–side.

"What're you thinking?" she asked.

"How young and full of life you are."

"Liar!" she teased and brought his palm onto her belly. She eked a smile. "We conceived that night, you know, you know, **don't you**?"

"Rhonda – I knew it then, I knew it now."

Wasn't there a day they didn't relive that night? – and its consequences. While their experience of the attack diverged, they shared a common guilt, a **singular** guilt. They struggled to voice it for fear of the hurt the subject was certain to cause.

"My parents were right – I wasn't ready – **malnourished,** is what they said. Tina always got the better of everything. Always stronger.... Wasn't I frail, Conan? I wanted to be free. I forced it 'cause I wanted it. When they wouldn't let you come aboard, I got so angry, **I wanted you with me whatever the cost.** The doctors ... they did what they did the best with what they had. Stillborn. It wasn't only the stress of the raid. My body won't let me.... "

He snatched her into an eye–to–eye embrace.

She shivered in spite of the heat.

"Don't you believe it. None of it!" he gasped, wetting her lips with his kisses. "I'll make love to you 'til I die. **Nena!**"

Rhonda wanted off that planet since she was old enough to be told of its doom. Her family wasn't deemed elite so it wasn't granted a seat aboard the **Cali**. Most farmers weren't. Most anybody wasn't. Unless certain conditions were met....

The secret of **travel** waited centuries for discovery. Adventures, more error than trial, took them further and further **still** into the universe at large – firstly, to the edges of their system – lastly, to the worlds of their neighbors. Agriculture for travel was engineered from scratch. Entirely novel fields of exo–ethics and exo–civics jumped from theoretical to practical. They brought psychology into the mix as they progressed toward **migration**.

The development was for the rich **not** for the poor to afford. Leaders touted cooperation but a sham was a sham and everybody saw it. Rivalry – **and violence** – tainted the early years of the red star. Unrest spread as populations shifted from the tropics to the poles. Weaker nations faded. Stronger nations survived by embracing then advancing the state. Then, as humanity by conflict and by environment tumbled into a population under a million, society settled into a fragile state of equilibrium – neither peace nor war prevailed – only a particular often despondent sense of defeat permeated the world.

States that endured hoarded the **alchemy** of travel.

Yet what Man accomplished was crude. Wars prevented their opportunity to refine their experience beyond a few runs to nearby stars. Motherships were kludged together from scraps.... Inefficiency left room for merely a fraction to migrate. Requirements were strict by design to be scarce. Preferences were partially mental, partially physical – and wholly **reproductive**.

The **Authority** made it known that, if a woman aged fifteen to twenty–five were expectant by a certain window, they and **a relation** would be given entry. Immediately, her parents took stock of their employees and sought the fittest, healthiest male to impregnate their daughters. For that duty, Conan was paid generously. Tina, at twenty–five, had been granted weeks, days to conceive. Rhonda, at twenty, frail due to deficiency, was diagnosed **infertile**.

"You're such a perfect **man**." Rhonda kissed his lips and yanked his braids – a brazen act of intimacy he grew less resistant to as their time passed. "Why can't they see that? You belong with us. The way I am, you know, I may never, ever get pregnant anyhow. What'll it hurt, if we take just a moment, just a moment."

"Nena, y si te duele? y si te lastimo?" Conan blushed yet smiled to tears. "You got somewhere to go. **Forget me**. Forget me...."

A knock at the door stirred Conan.

Rhonda – she sat by the edge of the bed. She had watched for the midnight hour to come and go, as promised. She had waited for the ruckus to reverb throughout the warehouse. Knowing that knock itched to strike, she wasn't startled by its rap.

"Nena," he whispered under the cover of the blanket. "**Go**."

She sat, exposed. The night's dusky, swarthy aura oozed through the chamber's eye–like slits. Its light stroked her skin, her features, her details…. The affection it gave was like a lover's. For a stretch of a smile he was awed – and crazed by jealousy.

Rhonda curled like a cat by Conan.

They held onto each other as if a mistake would have upended the balance of life and death. That knock at the door had been their alarm. At its wake the strangers' plot advanced. Voices echoed but couldn't be grasped. The tribe beckoned – **them**? – **others**? – to escape. A cascade of activity surged as minutes lurched forward, onward into uncertainty.

Midnight became 1–AM then 2–AM – by 3–AM the warehouse resumed its slumber. Not a sign of life was felt in or out of that structure. Except for the patrols at the waterfront that, like the Sun's eerie, ghostly red, came day and night.

"What'll happen to us? Wasn't it a stupid idea? All of them, so, **so** many of them, leaving. Leaving this building empty like nobody'd notice."

"We don't have to stay. The Golden League dug tunnels throughout the valley. The city's full of 'em. We'll break into 'em and wander 'em eastward. **Unnoticed**. We'll make it to the hangar. I'm sure they'd leave us **something**. Maybe my bike? We'll ride it to the mountains and escape to where ever we want to go."

It was too late to sleep, too early to wake. What else was there to do but chitchat? They tattled of their pasts, their families. Their entry into adulthood consumed a lot of their intimacy. He suffered against a caste that tried to erase not simply the distinctions but the desires of sex. She lived at the middle of society; her family schemed to climb out of its state; her parents agonized about how to stud their daughters like animals.

"I wasn't surprised," he chuckled. "A lot of families wanted my stock. It wasn't just your parents. They all wanted it done like **how a bull is worked**. I gotta tell you, yeah, I wanted it done like **natural**." He shut his eyes and blushed. She stroked his braids that draped his cheeks. "It was different for us, **for us**, boys and girls weren't supposed to notice each other like that. And there I was, thinking what I was thinking was gonna happen. Yeah, what stuff, **what stuff** I thought I was. I did it into a cup in front of a doctor."

"Mom and Dad let us chose – and we wanted you. Didn't realize it would be like **that**. Conan, I'm sorry."

"Don't be. No. No.... It wasn't done right, it wasn't done like, like how a child should be brought into this world. It's a spirit that we're making together. Each of us has to be there, you know what I mean? It's silly. I wasn't that prime, I guess. Not by the government's standards. My kids will be workers, farmers. At least they will **not** be here. But – I – **appreciate** how it was done like **that** for Tina and the girls. Like **anonymous**," he laughed. "It was you.... **It was you** I loved. But you were this frail, frail little bird. And I was this brute too scared to hurt you that way."

"I knew that night you loved me. I felt it, all of it, everything, everything **you** felt for **me**. It was a thrill **because** I loved you too.... Remember, that herd my folks hired y'all to move, Tina and I, we'd sneak away and we'd watch. The way you rode that bike. The way your jeans squeezed your legs. I burned for **that – and you gave it to me**. You were this mountain of a man – and you didn't treat me like I'd break. How'd you notice me? How'd you **even** notice me?"

"The farmer's daughter, **believe it**, I noticed you!"

A courier arrived to deliver a disk; he asked about her neighbor's whereabouts by–the–by. It had been a month since any other tenant received their mail. Rhonda shrugged, bewildered – stumped about where they could be.

"The professor wanted to visit family elsewhere. Yuma? Soma? Elsewhere **south**. That's about it. The rest don't talk about their families."

"Well, ma'am, if they return, give 'em these cards. Their disks will be ready at the office."

The courier passed stacks of notices then resumed his route.

Conan stared at the horizon. A mile of coast, exposed by the tide, extended into the Pacific. The watch patrolled that waterfront. At the distance far, far away, ahead he noted the suggestion of a craft, as faint as a mirage. Its shape speared through the waves. Its appearance disturbed the guards.

Rhonda raced into the salon. Her grip failed as she rushed. Her vanished neighbor's abjured mail scattered at the floor. That disk, however, endured unperturbed its voyage straight from the door to the player.

"Hey, sis!" Tina came into view at the monitor – the intrusion drew Conan from the window. "It's a year already." It had been a year to Tina, a decade to Rhonda. "I miss you. Even Mom and Dad. Oh, if you find Conan, tell him everything's OK with Abraxas. Doctors are watching him like all of the babies, like all of the babies **born after we left**. Got to be sure they develop OK. Nobody's tried to raise kids this way. We're part of this **experiment**. Anyhow, they keep us busy and we've got lots and lots to do – like our farm."

She wept – older and younger sisters swapped. How long would it be for her next yearly update to arrive from the **Cali**? A year for Tina ... **what would it be for Rhonda**? The motherships were set to speed up for ten years, to coast for forty years, to speed down for ten years – a total of sixty of **their** years separated **Sol** from **Zeta Reticuli**. How many of **Earth's** years? thousands? **millions**?

"Remember how it was with us girls? I donno. At least Mom and Dad let us go outside. Outside, **here**, there's nothing, there's nothing **at all**. There's no **outside**. Just stars. Jordache and I climbed to the roof of the farm. It's full of that glass that's not glass. When the lights dim, they stop being a mirror, they let you stare into space. Stars, Rhonda, and shapes like you can't believe – and we're going into it.

"It'll take three generations to reach Zeta Reticuli. We, the Nevada and the Oregon, are fully docked. We're going to the same exact world they allotted us. A water planet bigger than Earth. They don't know much about it except its air eats a lot of yellow and circulates methane and cee oh two. That's what makes it home. They only gave us just enough fuel to reach it, you know, just enough fuel to reach it **and not an inch beyond that**.

"Ours, it's got to be the **worst** trip to boot. The rest of the North American motherships break at different stages to reach different homes. We won't, though, we'll be left alone.

"Aren't we fooling ourselves? Everything's crazy. We're going to all sorts of places. Not just us but the other motherships. We're spreading thin. We're never, ever going to see each other again."

As concocted by defunct, terrestrial powers, (as realized by a millennium of determination), the plan was to spread far and wide into the womb of the galaxy. Astronomy identified candidates for homes yet it couldn't predict what to expect upon arrival. Success wasn't guaranteed to anybody. Of the planets that had been allotted, nobody knew if they'd continue to be habitable or if they'd welcome the migration. Or if the life that may or may not already exist would be compatible to Earth's. If even **one** mothership took root, that would be enough to keep humanity extant.

"Told you it's been getting jittery. Nobody really thought it through. The toll it's taking. I think the loneliness started when the South American motherships parted ways a few weeks ago. They're headed to yet another arm of the galaxy and they couldn't stay with us. We'll never see them, never hear them again.... It's a question they ask a lot now. What'll become of us?"

After a break Tina returned – with a different uniform and a different setting.

"We passed a system that wasn't charted. It had a few planets. A moon that wandered in and out of the goldielocks. Jordache got word of a mutiny aboard the Jersey. It undocked from the York and the Penn and bailed for that system. Now the whole, entire operation's riled. It's like chaos. Our motherships' captains signed a pact to continue as they planned. Jordache's got a point, though, **their plan**, it's hundreds and hundreds of years old and put together by people who aren't around to rule anymore. Who's to say, if we find a better world, we ignore it?

"I tell you, sis, I'm going to live to see this through. It won't matter if I'm a hundred, I'm not going to die trapped here. I'm gonna walk real land again and breathe real air again."

The feed (and disk) ended. They stared and the monitor reflected their faces like an onyx mirror. Sunset flared into the salon – a fiery, scarlet blaze swept side-to-side. Winds howled and shook the warehouse. The structure replied with a bizarre, random melody of its own as the air piped into the vent.

Light dimmed – red swerved into black – stars burst into view **and sparkled**. It was the Sun – it heaved then drew back, back **into itself**. Then the light returned. Then the Earth rumbled. Their star ejected a shell of plasma. That summer it molted frequently yet **that** event felt different.

"Did **we** start this way? Billions of years ago.... Did we escape a dying star? Maybe we forgot where we came from but not **who** and not **what** we were. All those stories, those gods, weren't they about men and women? About **us** all along? Who do we have but each other at the end? Nena.... She'll make it. When they get home **that** will be their reality. **Earth**? – just a paradise they got kicked out of."

The Sun wasn't setting anymore.

After the **Cali's** exit, word spread that a mothership would be constructed to rescue the commune. By then, though, the continent had been stripped in order to form the fleets they had already launched. They depleted all the energy and all the mines the Earth offered until at last there was nothing left to give. Off-world resources proved too burdensome to exploit due to a profound lack of equipment and experience they suffered after migration. Years passed, decades came and went, and the window of opportunity to escape simply shut.

The atmosphere charged as the Earth itself was bathed red. They began to sleep by day and wake by night. Weather raged – winds battered mountains – waters flooded coasts. Generators teetered in and out of service. So, too, government failed to maintain order.

Rhonda and Conan retreated into the oasis of their abode – their bedroom. Shortages and threats forced them to cram it full of supplies. They shut and barred its doorway. They propped its heavy, wooden frame. Alone, they settled onto the bed, side-by-side. The heat couldn't be diverted. She shut her eyes and bit her lips. He resettled atop, protecting her body with his body.

Out of the waterfront they heard a riot – it wasn't a raid just a city at the end of its tether.

The Earth ... it trembled, it knew – somehow, someway, **it knew**. Each and every shudder brought chaos to its climax. Sound, too sharp, too deep to be from lungs throbbed into their skulls. Smoke erupted and splattered the windows but the fire came from above **not** below.

"Rhonda!"

The Sun was everywhere.

★

About the Author

Fruitjack

Who **is** this abomination?

Fruitjack's wandered through many fandoms, wearing almost as many names as faces. You may have known him as **Abraxas**, or as **Ren**, or as **Snovelor**, or – if you go way, way back – as **RD** of Thundercats infamy. It doesn't matter who or what that notorious crammer purports to be, if they're around, you know there's trouble ahead ... and behind.

Their origin story is far too convoluted and paradoxical for a couple of paragraphs to give it justice. They may or may not have burst out of an orifice; that or they've always lurked about the abyssal depths of time and space. Having come from elsewhere, no matter how you slice it, they remain for ever and ever outcast among mankind – doomed, as if doomed it were, to exist as a self-aware stream of text posted to the Internet.

Fools! Unbeknownst to the innocent and unsuspecting, Fruitjack pursued a triplet of degrees in physics, travelled extensively among people, and even lived a few all-too-brief years in Colorado. They have vowed to return again to the wild green yonder of that glorious state. Tremble. You have been warned! There have been other achievements and assertions but they are far too gruesome to catalog any further.

No longer pursuing the cheap thrills & spills of fanfiction, Fruitjack has devoted the years since the **Great Mayan Downer of 2012** – *are we dead yet?* – to original science-fiction and fantasy realism – or, as it is understood by you of mere flesh and blood, "horror".

www.ingramcontent.com/pod-product-compliance
Lightning Source LLC
Chambersburg PA
CBHW030516020726
47494CB00004B/1117